Elapid

Third of the Mick Grundy Thrillers
by

Alexander Francis

ARCUS VERBA™

Elapid

TM

Cover design by Alexander Francis

ISBN: 978-1-942420-13-2 print edition

ISBN: 978-1-942420-12-5 e-book

In Appreciation

Two sources make this series possible, and I would like to give appropriate credit where credit is due. First to Google for their wonderful search engine, their maps and their translators. I can't imagine a world without these necessary tools, and I sincerely hope we never lose these gifts to humankind.

The other very important tool is Wikipedia, the single greatest asset to human knowledge since the invention of the printing press. Congratulations to its founder for a brilliant piece of work. If you use this tool, as most people actually do at some point, please make a contribution. We all owe something, some more than others.

My editor is a prize. She is an amazing talent at finding my mistakes, oversights and occasional outright stupidity. What would I do without her? Her name is withheld at her request but I want all my readers to know that this work as well as my others are not done in isolation. It takes a team. So to her...a big kiss and a heartfelt thank you from me.

Alexander Francis

Table of Contents

Other Mick Grundy Thrillers

The body was still in the car, and Simon leaned in with Jonny's flashlight in one hand. Its passenger was partially upright, but his pants and underwear were down around his knees. The lower part of the face was missing with the upper teeth exposed like some kind of upside down white picket fence. Blood and tissue fragments mixed with glass shards were throughout the car.

The Lieutenant pulled back and stood up. "Damn," he said.

The shaking returned, and the shadow man stood there with his hands describing small arcs in the night air. The shadows from the fence played across his face as he fought his body's urge to faint. In the distance, a peacock's cry hung in the night air. There was a subtle motion from the other side of the fence, and a woman's silhouette appeared framed by yellow light cast from tall poles standing guard in the parking lot.

Read Excerpts from other novels by Alexander Francis

www.afnovels.com

Prologue

Western Iranian Desert

The rising sun sent a shaft of piercing yellow light across the arid world of the desert, impacting the pale sand, instantly raising its temperature, unofficially marking the start of another hot day in western Iran. The snake understood, by experience and by genetics, that a sheltered place, hidden in shadow, would be necessary to survive another day, and he started moving, slowly at first, but faster as he was urged along by the inexorable and rapid increase in heat from irradiated rock and sand. He slid silently along, gliding effortlessly over small furrows in the sand, seeming to understand where his erratic path would end. A close inspection would show that his scales were glossy, but his pale color hid his shape so perfectly that movement was the only way to detect his presence, and there was no predator close enough or brave enough to impede his progress. He abruptly stopped, raising his head from the sand, extending his tongue briefly, sensing for either predator or prey in his path. Once stopped, frozen like a photograph, he became nearly invisible, safe, remarkably dangerous, the lethality of his folded fangs always ready to inflict death or suffering on the small or the large with an unremorseful and lightning strike of his head. Perhaps by instinct or prior knowledge, he moved toward an abandoned shack, the only large object on the horizon except for slowly moving pumps scattered about in random order but of endless number, the array extending out of sight toward the distant mountains. There was a small crack at the base of the shack, just wide enough to admit a small mouse, or a cobra, and he silently disappeared from view, safe for the moment, hidden from both eyes and sunlight. When darkness again enveloped the world, and the sand cooled, he would emerge, exploring his domain, killing as he saw fit and doing it with the regal splendor of a timeless king of the dessert.

Chapter 1

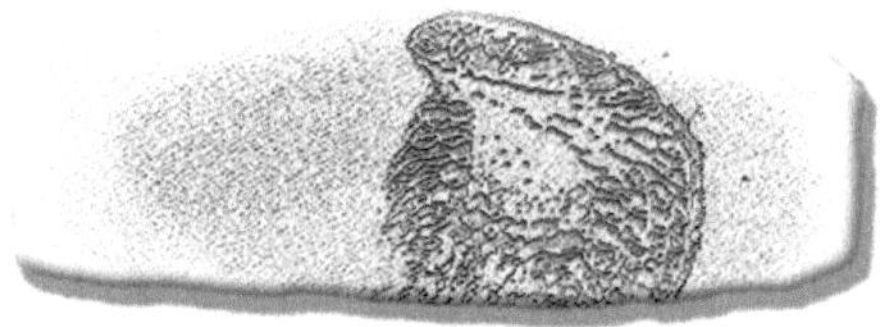

Target

Sunrise Beach County Park...Tacoma
1900 Hours

The last remaining rays of the sun were being consumed by the trees on Vashon Island, across the narrow channel of fast moving water, and evening was extending its big hand across the little park, the light fading by the minute. The deep sound of a motorcycle moving slowly wafted in little bites, riding on humid air, causing them to hunker down farther behind the rock.

"Think it's him?" the bearded one asked nervously. His eyes opened widely, exposing his anxiety. He fingered his weapon for the umpteenth time, clicking the safety on and off.

"Quit playing with that gun. You're more dangerous than he is, you cowardly dog. Of course it's him. He's right on time. Now stay out of sight until I tell you. You know his reputation...we will only get one chance at this, so when you shoot, make it count, because you will only get one shot," Quadura barked, slapping Ahmed's shoulder for emphasis. The sound drew closer and as the big engine slowed, it coughed out its rumble in irregular, erratic idling, the racing motor's complaint about its diminishing fuel. Quadura waited until the bike passed their position to sneak a look around the side of the boulder, peeking through the weeds. A black motorcycle, one without a trace of chrome, a matte black reflecting no light. There was something dangerous, but strangely compelling, about this machine. Quadura got the same feeling as when he had looked over a precipitous drop back in the mountains near his home. The danger tightened his insides but still he resisted wanting to look away, something inside making him ready to face the risks, stand up or jump off, getting death over with, sooner rather than later.

"Wait until I tell you, Ahmed," he whispered to his companion who was rapidly clicking his safety on and off, perspiring heavily in the cool air. "He will be most vulnerable when he removes his helmet." The motorcycle had stopped, its motor protesting with a roughness, a growl, impatient to leave. It was still running, its rider likely looking over the terrain, carefully assessing danger. Quadura recalled the briefing which emphasized how utterly lethal this particular target was. A killer with few equals, a man to be respected but mostly feared, an unpredictable opponent with a savage streak. The motor continued to turn over, growling, muttering, but still running. Quadura chanced another look, this time closer to the ground, harder to spot, his head touching the soil as he looked at the black riderless shadow only fifteen meters from their position. The rider is gone, Quadura's mind screamed, taking the only chance of success away from them. Now, they were the prey, and Mick Grundy had become the hunter.

"Ready?" Ahmed asked, his voice quiet but audible, followed by a nervous cough.

"Stupid!" Quadura whispered and struck Ahmed with his elbow. Both sets of eyes widened as they realized that there was no refuge if they left the shelter of the large rock. Nowhere to run. Even if they could get to the car, this fast motorcycle would easily overtake them. The whole plan now seemed shallow, childish, and improbable. Over lunch in the sun, the contact had droned on about how easy this hit would be and how important, how rewarding. Mick Grundy loved women and had never been known to harm one. It would be easy to bring him to this park to meet a lovely woman in distress. An out-of-the-way place for a rendezvous, sexual mischief, and to meet a paying customer who only wanted help taming a wayward husband. It was stupid, patently transparent, and Mick Grundy wasn't following the plan. If only they didn't have the rifle, they might pretend it was mere intellectual interest, not homicide, they wanted. Too late for that ploy. Quadura started to sweat, questioning why in the miserable unlucky universe did he have to agree to do this? Money wasn't enough, no matter how much, for such an assignment. At the briefing, he paid little attention to his target's background, because this hit was obviously so easy. Now the memory of what was said came storming back into his mind. Grundy was ex-Special Forces, ex or current CIA…they didn't know for sure…and then the most important item. He had a long string of killings behind him, some with various guns, though many using only a knife. A list only partially known, constantly denied, but assumed to be approaching one hundred. Or more. He was trained, ruthless, unremorseful, and, the worst, he would suffer no repercussions for any activity, no matter what he did. The CIA protected him, hovered over him like a cloud, acting father and mother to him. This was the singularly most dangerous man on the planet to be loose and stalking them, as he was likely already doing. Quadura resisted the urge to throw up, looking around as well as he could for any sign of movement.

"What are we supposed to do now?" Ahmed asked not too quietly, continuing to play nervously with the safety on his rifle.

"Plainly, we are about to die. We have executed a plan doomed to fail from its inception. Mick Grundy will kill us, and we have only ourselves to blame. We came looking for him only to find his shadow, and now we have run out of options."

Tacoma Marriott Courtyard Hotel

0130 Hours

The night clerk looked up in surprise to see a man standing in front of him. The lobby was deserted, as usual, at this time of night, and the man had made no noise during his approach. The clerk could perceive that the guest, if he was a guest, was angry and looked at him over his small round glasses with a pinched forehead. He wore an old-style grey fedora hat, pulled low, and his raincoat was buttoned at his neck.

"Sir? Can I be of assistance?"

"312. Checking out," the man said and slid two plastic door cards across the granite counter, waiting grimly for the clerk's response. Sammy scooped up the cards and bent over his computer terminal, furiously clicking at the keys and, in a moment, looked up.

"Mr. Gaust, Mr. Porter Gaust? Is this correct?" Sammy asked politely.

"Of course. I'll need my car brought around and hurry please."

"You were registered for another two days. Is there a problem with our facility?" Sammy asked.

"No. I just have to leave. You remember I said fast?" Porter Gaust said anxiously and started drumming his fingers on the black granite.

Sammy didn't respond but continued clicking on his keyboard.

Finally, the sound of a printer came on, making a little whirring sound, accompanied by small clicks. Sammy noticed that the counter top was moist from the man's hands when he slid the completed bill toward him.

"Sign here, please," Sammy said and pointed to the correct line with his pen, watching the man with objectivity as he hastily scribbled at the appointed spot. The man, calling himself Porter Gaust, was trying to disguise himself and was also attempting to hide his heavy German accent. Why is he in so much distress? Sammy wondered to himself. Shrugging, he punched the small red button which would summon the Bell Captain. "One moment, sir, and I'll have your car brought around. Do you have bags with you?"

"No. No bags. Where will the car be?"

"Just outside the front door. May I ask what happened to your bags?"

"No bags. When will the car be here?" The German accent was more evident now and so was the impatient anger.

"Sir, if you leave any belongings in the room, there will be a charge applied to your account…do you understand this?"

Without comment, Porter Gaust headed for the door with long strides, looking both ways from under the low brim of his hat, his head flicking back and forth in a birdlike way. After he went past the outside glass door, Sammy could see him on the sidewalk, pacing back and forth, continuing to look around for some possible lurking threat. Sammy knew that at this time of night it might take some time for the garage attendant to be summoned and find the appropriate car. After all, this wasn't Las Vegas where people came and went at all hours expecting full service no matter what time it happened to be. On a hunch, Sammy picked up the phone and hit three numbers in rapid succession. Brindle Davis was being paid to be the house detective, among his other duties.

He may as well earn his keep.

Three rings and the phone clicked off. Brindle had hung up. Sammy dialed again, pressing his lips together in anger. This time a voice croaked back at him. "Yeah?"

"This is Sammy. I need you to go up to 312 and check it out. Now, Brindle."

"What for?" Brindle croaked again. Sammy could almost hear him scratching himself and tried not to picture what part of the man's fat body was being scratched.

"Why now?" the voice croaked, more awake.

"Because I said so. Get up there right now, or there's going to be another report."

"Shit!" Brindle said and slammed the phone down.

During the conversation, Sammy had briefly looked away from the entrance. When he looked back, expecting to see Porter Gaust still pacing, he could see no movement. Interesting. The door frame flared, lit up by headlights as a car pulled to the curb. There was a moment of photographic stillness before the attendant got out and looked around, leaving the car running. Sammy could see him looking both ways up and down the sidewalk before coming around the car toward the entrance.

"Sammy!" he shouted, half in the door. "Didn't you just send for this car?" Sammy came around the desk and walked rapidly toward the entrance, grumbling to himself.

"He's right outside and in a hurry!" Sammy said, closing the distance.

"There's nobody out there," the attendant replied, shrugging and looking over his shoulder. They both went back outside and looked around. Herr Porter Gaust was no longer in sight.

Chapter 2

Reunion

Interstate 5, South of Seattle

Special Agent April Chauncy couldn't shake the feeling that she was being watched. She had used her FBI training, her best spycraft methods, to detect her pursuers but had no luck spotting them. It was probably a team, a very good one, that had her in their sights, and she suddenly felt the urge to press hard on the accelerator, to see what would shake loose. No, that would let them know that she was aware. They would just change tactics. On the other hand, she wondered why was she being targeted, if she was. It was possible that her imagination had been too keen, had imagined a threat where none existed. It had been like this for a week and still she had no positive visual clue to go on. Tails this good had to be well-trained and rehearsed as well as adequately funded. That's government level, ours or…well, some others, she reasoned. Why? She wasn't currently assigned to anything big at all, nothing really important had come across her desk in several weeks. No one at her own agency had any reason to suspect her, none at all. The FBI would have called her in and grilled her thoroughly, if they had the slightest reason. Other American agencies would not dare shadow a ranking FBI agent like her. It had to be foreign and that was why she was worried. Only the Russians were that good. Then she remembered Sasha, shooting her in the back, the daughter of a high ranking GRU official. And the shooting was a mistake, because Sasha's gun had no ammo. A reprisal would not be out of character for them. After all, they had been hunting Mick Grundy for years, constantly, never giving up, no matter how many of them he dispatched. Eventually, they would get him, and now probably her.

She spun the wheel hard, flooring the accelerator, and the lithe car leaped ahead, the hood coming up slightly as it accelerated for the approaching freeway exit. She crossed three lanes, braking aggressively to slow, then jerked left, stopping on the overpass to watch the traffic below for any blunders from those following. Nothing. The traffic flowed smoothly as before, and no cars changed position. She shrugged and lunged forward, taking the next left to re-enter the freeway going north. Either she had imagined the whole thing, or they were much better than her. She tried to put it out of her mind and focus on her day-to-day life. But she couldn't. It was still there, nagging at her, pulling her attention to the rearview mirror. She was being tracked, she could feel it in her bones.

April was born attractive, and not just a little bit. She remembered past derisive comments from both men and women about her looks. "Plastic," they frequently remarked. "So perfect as to look artificial" was another. They joked, occasionally cruelly and to her face, about her being a robot, "because nothing living could look so good." It toughened her, hardened her about it. She was aware of the good and bad of looking like she did. The bad was the attention, unwanted attention, especially from undesirable men of all kinds. The good was the intimidating effect her kind of beauty had on people. It threw them off, made them feel inferior in some way, giving her an edge. The other was the surprise of her competence, her toughness. No one ever expected a fabulous beauty to be physically and mentally tough, and that is why she had advanced so quickly in her career. April was not only smart, she could have any man she wanted, any man, but she wanted only one and that one was the exception to the rule. Mick Grundy had avoided her for six months, not even a postcard. In a way, she understood his motives. He was protecting her like he always did, letting her avoid the stresses and risks of constant pursuit and the hellholes that he had to live in to escape death. It was because he loved her, she knew, because they would use her to get at him, even kill her if it would draw him out. She still thought about him nearly every day and for sure every lonely night. Mick was the only man she would ever really love, and he was the one she could never have. What a wretched world this is.

She stopped in her driveway, adjusting her makeup in the rearview mirror but actually watching for any movement in the house across the street, but as usual, seeing nothing out of the ordinary. The car, in fact both cars, had been swept repeatedly by the FBI at her request. The technicians were starting to think that she was paranoid, but at least she knew that was not the way she was being tailed. Her house had been swept also and was reported as bug free. Still, she didn't believe it and was always careful about conversations while there. She couldn't live this way much longer and was considering a transfer to Washington, just to break the cycle she was in. She had been working the Seattle office before Mick Grundy came in to her life, but she was still here now because of him. She suspected that he continued to haunt the Tacoma area, but after repeated searches proved futile, she gave up. He didn't want to be found, especially by her. She was positive that he was still around, because corpses with his trademark killing method still turned up at odd times. Usually a .45 slug to the head but almost as often, a slit throat, at times both. And then there were some who had clearly been interrogated with a sharp knife before dying. Tracing the body's past history usually led to dead ends, because they were agents or spies whose pasts had been invented.

Chapter 2

April opened the garage door and moved the car inside, checking her Beretta before getting out, just in case. She went into the same search method each time, varying the pattern, just in case. It made resting possible, to know, really know, that no one was inside waiting for her, and there wasn't, at least today. She came up to the bedroom and removed her work clothing, pausing to look at herself in the mirror. The same thought struck her this time as it did each time, and she pulled the mirror away from the wall and inspected behind it, just in case. After a relaxing sigh, she took the rest of her clothing off and headed to the shower for a long hot soak.

The water was hot, just at the point that she could take no more, and this was the way she liked it. As she hung, letting the hot water flow over her neck and back, she thought things through. No, she couldn't go on like this much longer. The stress was mounting to a point that she knew would result in personality changes or poor performance at work. Something, some noise, made her stop and listen, quickly shutting down the water and standing still with the drips from her own body making soft noises against the floor. Nothing but her hyper-anxious state again. She got out and toweled off, standing in front of the full length mirror, the overhead spotlight casting deep and flattering shadows, yet rimming her with the translucency of life. Yes, her body was perfect, full breasts with perfect nipples, tight waist, flawless skin and ideal body weight. A vision of womanhood which would arouse any man living, and she knew it. Some men had told her so. They swore that they would leave their wives or girlfriends, change their jobs, give her anything. She had heard it all, at one time or another. But she had slept with only one man. She had given herself to just one and wanted to do it again over and over forever. This man was the one she loved, desired, fantasized about constantly, until his image was part of her own brain. She didn't even own one photo of him. No one did. All the images which had ever been taken had been destroyed by the relentless CIA, and for good reason. There were only a few people who really knew what Mick looked like. Most had seen him as a shadow, just before they died. Others who had seen him didn't really know whom they were looking at. Except for April Chauncy. She knew every scar and blemish, ever muscular bulge, every hair on his body, because she had owned him briefly, oh so briefly. April felt the tears well up again, the choking sensation of suppressed grief. The denial of her physical and mental happiness. Here she stood, naked, the perfect, passionate, sexual woman, yearning for a man who was likely only forty miles away, the only mate she would accept in life. She threw herself on her bed, drawing the covers around her and folded up in the fetal position, sobbing herself to sleep as she did so often.

The room was dark, black in fact. The only light was from the dial of the small bedside digital clock. April realized that she was listening; that was why she had awakened, it was to listen. Something her sleeping brain detected had given the signal for her to awaken and listen. She slowly slid her hand under her pillow and grasped the handle of her extra pistol, a heavy, chrome plated .357 revolver, given to her by her once proud father. Again it was her imagination, her anxiety, that had falsely awakened her. Or perhaps it was her hunger, because she had gone to bed again without supper. She lay there, still curled up, holding on to the cold handgun and feeling foolish. This was no life for a young woman. She had to change, to move away and try to start over, to forget Mick. Somewhere, someplace, was a man who could make her happy, make her forget. She was thinking of what this man would look like, what position or profession he should have, when she felt the heat of a hand just before it clasped over her face and mouth. The man's other hand went for the wrist of her gun hand. The man was strong, a grip of steel, and had rough, thick hands. A face came close to hers and whispered in her ear, very quietly, very briefly.

"It's me. Don't move and don't speak. You are being watched, and there is a listening device in your house." The voice from Hell. It was Mick Grundy. His hand came away from her mouth, and his lips found hers, and they pressed their faces together in silent passion. "No words," he reminded her with a whisper close in her ear. "I have clothing for you. Take everything off, everything. It may be bugged. We are going to leave here tonight. Take absolutely nothing with you from this house." She nodded that she understood, and his hands came away from her.

She felt the jumpsuit fall beside her, and she stood up, making little noise. Mick had moved away from her and was invisible, even his breathing was undetectable, a phantom likely dressed in black. April quickly pulled on the jumpsuit and zipped it up. A pair of shoes was pressed into her chest, and she quickly pulled them on. Mick's lips found her ear again, whispering, "Hook your hand on my belt and follow me. Make no noise." He led her to the other bedroom and to the window, which was standing open. He took her arm and directed her hand to a rope which had been tied off and hung out the window. He indicated that she should go first, and she eased out the window and slowly descended the rope. Mick silently followed. Once outside, there was scant light making them nearly invisible as they crouched low, heading for the rear fence, finding the opening Mick had made earlier. It was low, dog-sized, and required effort to transit. Mick led her across two other yards and several fences to a small alley where they stood erect for the first time since leaving her house.

"Ever ridden on a motorcycle?" he asked.

"Not something I'm interested in," she answered.

"First time then. All you have to do is hold on to my waist. Tightly, very tightly. Don't let your leg touch the hot pipes. Don't look around. Just hold on. We are only going about ten miles." He handed her a helmet and helped fasten her strap, then swung his leg over the black machine, offering her his hand for assistance. She swung on and pressed against his back, and the motor started instantly. The violent lurch forward caught her by surprise. Nothing she ever experienced had accelerated so rapidly, not even the large jets she used so frequently. Then there were the corners as the bike slammed suddenly into them, leaning so far that she knew it was going to crash, the pavement seemingly close enough to touch, the machine moving faster and faster, so fast that she shut her eyes and pressed and held on ever harder. April had her man, separated only by millimeters of clothing. Her arms held him in a love embrace again, this time from the other side. He was hers once more, and she was never going to turn him loose again.

Chapter 2

Chapter 3

The Haven

Back Roads North of Tacoma

The motorcycle cut through the black night like a saber, impossible to follow, drifting effortlessly down deserted roads, blue flames licking out of the exhaust as if they were the outlet of the furnaces of Hades, the shriek of the engine echoing from the trees. For April, the ride was furious, exhilarating, exciting, and by the time the machine slowed, making a gradual sweeping turn into their destination, she was starting to relax and enjoy her position behind Mick. She knew his history with motorcycles. It was a long love affair with fast machines, refined on racetracks in Europe. Mick had raced professionally for a short time, and this fact alone was enough for her to trust him tonight, but she also knew that he would never let anything happen to her while he was present. She started seeing boats on stands undergoing repairs, and she was beginning to smell the sea. Mick slowed the motorcycle, nearly inching along, carefully traversing a long narrow dock with dark water on either side. April increased her grip and turned her head so that she couldn't see the water. At last, the motor shut off, revealing the stillness of the night and the sounds of small waves coming from the bay. They had arrived, but where? She dismounted, took off her helmet and looked around. They were in a large boatyard, and in the distance, across the water toward the south, she could see the twinkling lights of Tacoma. In front of them floated a dilapidated barge, rocking slightly in shallow waves.

"Home sweet home, April. Welcome to my abode." He put his arm over her shoulder and kissed her on the cheek.

"No wonder we could never find you. This is where you have been living?"

"Only recently; I move around a lot, never too long in one place. A trick I learned by experience."

April bent down and tried to peep into the darkness toward the barge. It was long and low, the deck partially covered by scraps of lumber. It looked abandoned, unusable, and she expected to see hoards of rats milling around, beckoning her aboard with their pink noses. Mick laughed, took her hand and helped her walk the narrow gangway. Once aboard, Mick pulled the heavy plank in, leaving no way to exit or board the craft. They went down a dark hatchway onto a nearly vertical staircase, Mick locking the hatch behind them. He flipped an electrical switch, illuminating a neat, clean and well-equipped kitchen. "Bedrooms are to the left, lounge is to the right," he said. April walked around, intrigued by the vast difference from the outside to the inside.

"How did you come by this wonderful boat, Mick?"

"It was a drug dealer's hideaway. He doesn't need it anymore."

"You mean he won't come by and claim it while we are here?"

"Never." She understood. It was a hidden prize, unknown to even the locals, and its owner was undoubtedly fleeing or dead. A perfect place to hide for a few days. In the light, she finally saw Mick's face and was taken aback. She recognized the same hard face with its deep set grey eyes, the small depressed scar on his cheek and also the longer one on his neck, but he had a moderate length beard and longer blond hair that curled against his collar. His familiar, crisp, military appearance was gone, replaced with something more scruffy. Even his body language was more casual, more at ease with himself. This image was in conflict with the one she had carried in her head for the past several months, the one she conjured up in her dreams and in her hopes.

"My, you could stand some grooming, Mick. Have you been too busy to shave?"

"I hope you're kidding, April. I was about to tell you how utterly beautiful you are, but I think I'll hold off for now."

"Come to me, little boy," she said and wiggled her finger at him provocatively. They embraced fiercely, pulling each other in, kissing anything and everything, scarcely taking a break for a breath. She murmured, "How much I needed that. I thought I would never see you again." She quickly returned to kissing him, unable to fill her needs or slake the passion which had built up over time.

"Oh, I've seen a lot of you, though. I've been tracking you for two months. I know everything you do, whom you see and what you say to them. Some hotshot FBI you turned out to be. You never saw me once!"

"So that was your presence I felt. I knew that I was being followed!"

"No, dear, you never felt my presence. You had a tail, a very complicated, sophisticated tail. I followed them also."

April looked shocked. "Who are they?"

"I'm not positive, but they are Americans working for an American agency; otherwise, I would have taken them out. You also have bugs in both cars and in your home as well as several tracking devices."

April pushed away from him, incredulous. "But my cars and home were swept. They assured me that I was clean!"

"The ones who assured you are the ones who planted and installed the devices. You gave them the golden opportunity," Mick said.

"My...our...own people bugged me!" she exclaimed. "Why?"

she demanded.

"In my opinion, they were looking for me. They knew that we had been close. It was the only way they had left to find me. And in one way, they were right. I was as near to you as I could get."

"But, Mick, aren't you still protected by Ron Zeskie and the CIA, not to mention Army Special Forces?" she asked, and started nervously pacing the kitchen.

"Ron keeps in touch. Listen, April, where have you been? This administration has chosen a different path than we expected. There have been some strange appointments, and the entire character of the government has changed, and not for the better. There are still a lot of earnest hardworking men and women in the agencies, but there are now some zealots who have a hidden agenda. But I don't want to go into it right now. We are safe here for the time being, and Zeskie is going to meet us in a couple of days and explain what we must do and why. Meanwhile, you and I have some catching up to do, remember?"

April turned toward him, both her recent agony and present stress recognizable on her face. "How could I forget? You, of all people, know that I'm not seeing anyone. I cry myself to sleep almost every night, because I miss you, but no longer. You are mine, mine, mine." She stopped, hesitating briefly, taking a deep breath. Her tense face smoothed and became flawless again. "But first you have to feed me, because I am about to starve. Any food around here?"

The Barge, Hylebos Waterway

0621 Hours

April opened her eyes a tiny crack, at first confused as to where she was, and peered at the elaborate ceiling with squinted eyes, remembering. She felt the warmth of Mick's shoulder against hers, his hip against hers. This was the most wonderful morning in years…perhaps ever. She didn't have to get up, had no calls to make, and there was no way for anyone to contact her. And she had Mick right beside her. He said that they had at least two days before Ron Zeskie got back from Germany, and until then, they could focus on enjoying each other and nothing else. The cupboards were well-stocked, and there was every possible expensive electronic gear installed for entertainment. There wasn't any reason to leave the boat, none at all. She had Mick, and he had her, and that was all that mattered anyhow. As far as she was concerned, she would be happy to continue this life forever, just as it is right now. In fact, she had a sense of foreboding about the meeting with Zeskie. He was going to send them on a mission, Mick had hinted as much. Missions are always heavy with danger and risk. April didn't want risk or danger any longer. She wanted nothing that could risk losing Mick now that they were back together. It was a dark cloud on the horizon, and if you thought about it or watched, it would grow larger as it moved toward you, finally becoming more important than anything else. She wanted to run away, go to a paradise someplace away from the civilized world. Two people alone cannot change anything, they just get used up trying.

"Rest well?" Mick asked, his head turned away from her. He reached over and stroked the smooth skin of her thigh, and she turned toward him and drew closer.

"Best sleep I can remember. You?"

"I never sleep well. Too many things have happened to me that I can't forget. I'm happy, though. Having a woman in my arms who loves me…" He didn't finish but instead rolled over to face her, kissing her gently on her eyelids and nose. "I love you, April."

"It's the first time you ever said that, Mick."

"I've been afraid to admit it, much less say it. You know the reason." April did know the reason. Mick had never fully explained, but Zeskie did, one day in Germany. Mick's wife had been killed by terrorists on their first day of marriage. She and he had one night together, only one. They were trying to kill Mick…to keep him from discovering a spy, and didn't care who else they killed. Mick had severe injuries from the bomb, barely surviving himself. When he recovered, he was a different man, one whose single purpose in life was revenge. And he had it and continues to have it. Revenge has become a way of life, the only one he knows. Zeskie told her that Mick dreams about his wife frequently, about the moment of her death and how he was unable to save her. The dream punishes him remorselessly, because he can never resolve it in his mind. Guilt mixed with lost love will always be there. His biggest fear is losing any woman that he would come to love. It would kill him if it happened again, so he has always chosen to live without a lover…until now. Her tears welled up without expecting them, shortly gushing out as if a small dam had broken.

"Tears? Aren't you happy? Something I can do?" he asked, stroking her hair tenderly.

"No, these are happy tears. Tears that have been saving themselves for the right man and you are him." Mick drew her closer, and they were skin to skin from nose to toes, their legs and arms intertwined, their lips pressing against the other, feeling the warmth and the pulse of their lover becoming part of their own body.

"Mick. I have to ask you a question," she said in his ear.

"No need. I know the question, but I don't know the answer."

"I do. Want to hear the answer?"

Mick shook his head "no". "Your answer is to run away and hide from the world. Remember that I've been trying to do that for years. It doesn't work like that. They find you eventually."

"We should go farther away, much farther," she suggested in a small voice.

"Our side is also looking for us, so there is really no place to hide, at least for very long. We have to fight back, because there is nothing else we can do. I was never going to contact you, April. You are too precious to me to lose, so I have just been looking out for you and keeping in the shadows, until you became the target, and I had no choice except to get you away."

"So are we outlaws? Neither one of us has been anything but loyal to America. We've broken no laws," April said.

"You've broken no laws, at least," Mick laughed. "I am the one they want, and the only reason possible is that someone fears what I will do, someone highly placed in our government and privy to its secrets. What this person or persons is most afraid of is that I will be asked to act, that I will be set in motion by some authority or some deed. And what they fear has come true. I have been forced to take action, and I will. There is no worse evil than being traitor to your own people. Now for your part in this. Whatever risks I take, the last thing I want is for you to be in danger. You and I will work together, but you will stay out of harm's way. There is no negotiation about it. I still remember Berlin when you nearly got killed trying to help me. You aren't going to repeat that mistake again, are you?"

"Just like you, Mick, I'll do what I have to do. My only want is that nothing happens to you. That means that we both have to stay safe, doesn't it?"

"You are as impossible as you are lovely. If I didn't believe in God, I would, after being with you. It would take God to design something as perfect as you, and here, lowly imperfect me, has you in my arms. Thank you, God."

"Mick, can you just clear up something for me?"

"I'm waiting."

"What do we use for transportation? We can't ride around in the daylight on your motorcycle."

Chapter 3

"We are going to meet Zeskie at the Fish Market in Seattle in two days. You will drive the car left by the drug dealer. It's out in the lot covered by a big green tarp. I'm riding my bike, because I have more mobility and more options. Anything else?"

"Can we kiss and make up?"

Chapter 4

A Very Public Secret Meeting

Corner of Pike Street and Pike Place, Seattle
1100 hours

April Chauncy walked out to the curb, looking both ways again, the fifth time. She was anxious, as Zeskie anticipated, but he also expected more self-control from a Special Agent of the FBI. He watched as she fussed with her long brown hair in the reflection of the plate glass window behind them. Looking at her, the casual, almost sloppy, way she was dressed, no one would expect that she was a tough, experienced agent, one that had killed in the line of duty and one who had narrow escapes with death on more than one occasion. She was a marvelous creation of beauty, this April Chauncy, he thought. So remarkable, in fact, that she might have been a glamorous big star in some other life. Today, she was more like an attractive tourist, only getting the occasional glances from passing men, because her loose, faded sweatshirt over her torn jeans successfully hid her female form so well, her long pony tail giving her a decidedly youthful appearance. Zeskie looked down at his own attire and shook his head in amusement. His knobby knees were showing under his light orange Bermuda shorts, short bristling hairs, standing at proper military attention, arose from the otherwise bare skin of his white knees. He laughed again, catching the reflection of his image from the dirty plate glass behind them. A slightly portly man in a baseball cap wearing jogging shoes. Who would possibly believe that he was

Chapter 4

Ron Zeskie, European Station Chief, CIA? The real tourists, on their various missions to soak in the sights of the famous fish market, passed by without a glance. It was a good way to hide, designed to obscure the important meeting taking place this morning. The last place you expect to find anything is usually right in front of your nose. Each time the door to the market opened, there was a whiff of complex aroma enveloping him, a mixture of fresh bread, fish and shellfish, raw and cooked, swirling with the fragrance of flowers, and accompanied by the cacophony of sound arising from a busy working market.

Mick Grundy was the important one, the necessary ingredient to the mix of professionals assembling incognito this morning, and he was late. Zeskie had worked with Mick many times before, most recently on a mission to Germany. They had hoped, especially Mick had hoped, that Russian assassination teams would stop trying to kill him after what he had done for their Mother Russia, but yet another team had been waiting outside the American Embassy in Berlin even after the Russian Ambassador had personally assured him that he was no longer to be pursued. Once back in the U.S., Mick had gone back into hiding but was constantly hunted, forcing him to always remain alert to threats, moving from place to place, occasionally resorting to killing in self-defense. What a life, Zeskie thought sadly. The beautiful woman pacing the sidewalk had gone with Mick to Germany but had also been denied her happiness when they returned. Mick had refused to put her in danger by staying together, even though they had fallen in love during their mission. April hadn't seen Mick previously for at least six months, or even heard from him.

April turned, pointedly looking at Zeskie, alerting him to something. Her head swiveled back to the street, and he followed her gaze up the steep incline of Pike Street, flowing with tourists from the big hotels several blocks away. It took him a moment to realize what she had seen. A bright, single headlight was working its way down the hill, and from this distance, it seemed to be emanating from a little dark ink spot. Zeskie put his hand up to shield his eyes from glare, while the motorcycle drifted as if being slowly let to earth by an invisible parachute, the air vibrating with the deep rumble of a racing engine as it came closer, the rider cloaked in dull black leather, masked behind a reflectionless black helmet. Mick Grundy was on his way.

At that moment, someone tapped Zeskie on the shoulder, and he turned his attention away from the street. An older, shabby woman was extending her hand toward him, smiling blandly. Zeskie hesitantly deposited some cash in her hand, reading the number written on her palm, and watched as she disappeared back into the squirming living mass snaking in tangled random patterns inside the market. He waited until April turned back toward him and, using his hand, discretely flashed the number fourteen, then disappeared inside the chaos of the market.

Trying to act casual, April strolled down the sidewalk toward the only available parking place suitable for a motorcycle. Several other large bikes were there, bristling with chrome and black leather, lined up in a uniform row. At first, April's focus was on Mick's bike as it made its way through traffic, gradually growing closer. An unexpected shout made her aware of her more immediate surroundings.

"Hi, babe!" a gruff voice called out. "You lost?" The man was standing amid a small group who were similarly dressed in leather jackets and jeans. April glanced at him briefly and turned her focus back to the street. He was bearded, an irregular and matted tangle of dark hair hung limply below his chin and neck, his gut overhanging his wide belt.

"Hey! I'm talking to you!" the man yelled and started ambling toward her. She could hear the others amusement at this impending confrontation.

"Get lost, jerk," she said, otherwise continuing to ignore him. The sound of Mick's approaching bike grew louder as the shadow of the big biker came toward her.

"You! Don't you want a ride, babe?" he laughed in a guttural way. "We got a group here which will make your dreams come true!" He was nearly beside her, and her mind was whirling with her choices. She was undercover today and didn't want to either show her badge or use force against this fat thug. Mick's bike came to rest just in front of them, and he shut it off, pausing to take in both April and the bikers, the dark visor giving the impression of a fearsome insect inspecting them as though they were a source of food. The fat biker glanced up just as Mick swung off and started unstrapping his helmet, and they met eyes. Mick's face, its depressed scar on his right cheek and the longer scar on his neck, competed with his hard grey eyes, forging an intimidating visage. But when he spoke, the effect was deeply chilling, the voice from Hell, right out of the gritty special effects of Hollywood, a voice hinting of violence, likely to erupt in any given second.

"Problems?" he asked, moving with deliberate, methodical slowness, his eyes fixed on the fat biker, a jungle cat approaching its unsuspecting prey, the fury of an impending attack masked by the lack of bellowed threat.

"You'd be well-advised to start running," April said to the biker.

"You guys!" the biker shouted to his fellows, waving them forward with his thick hand. Mick stopped, just off the sidewalk, calmly looking at the biker and his approaching men.

"This isn't going to be your day, my friend. You and your men are to get on your machines and leave while you are able," Mick said. His eyes and his voice made the biker hesitate; he was losing his confidence rapidly but didn't want to show fear in front of his fellows, the prey finally alerted by the crouch and tensed muscles of a fearsome predator about to spring.

"So, you are going to make us leave?" the man asked and spit on the sidewalk for emphasis, his bravado ringing hollow.

"Tell you what. I'm going to break one of your arms to help you decide. Then, if you want more, you can speak up or just leave," Mick said, slowly moving forward, tightening his grip on his helmet strap, his eyes locked on his target.

"You ain't no match for six tough guys. Just…" the comment remained unfinished, because, at that moment, his front teeth impacted Mick's helmet which had been swung upward with enough force to lift the man off the pavement. He reflexly grasped his face, but before he fell backward, another, even more forceful, swing of the helmet impacted his arm just below the shoulder resulting in a loud "crack" as the humerus bone split, sending him to the hard sidewalk in a helpless pile. Stepping onto the sidewalk, Mick dropped his helmet and started moving toward the other bikers.

"Any more brave men among you?" Mick asked, continuing to advance toward them. The group collectively hesitated as the first victim writhed in agony behind Mick. Their arrogance had faded, none willing to test the stranger further. They backed up, still huddled together like sheep facing a wolf.

"Now get your fat asses out of here before I lose my temper," he growled. "And take that trash behind me with you. Ten seconds."

"Hi, beautiful," Mick said in his breathless way, his eyes turning soft and caring. He put his arm around April's waist and gently pulled her close.

"You are a human tornado, Mick. We were supposed to keep this meeting secret," April said. Behind them was the sound of several motorcycles being started at once. Without glancing back,

Chapter 4

Mick picked up his helmet, and arm-in-arm, they headed toward the market door.

"Them or me, just like the all the others." He wanted to kiss her, to pick her up and spin her around in his arms, but this public setting was not the right place. They continued to walk slowly, blending in as love-struck tourists while they approached room 14. The smell of seafood was intensified by the sight of a whole salmon being tossed over the heads of the appreciative crowd who whooped each time it happened.

"Did you miss me at all, Mick, all those months?" April said in his ear, pulling closer until their hips rubbed together as they walked.

"I thought about you day and night, you know that."

Chapter 5

The Action Plan

Room 14 Pike Street Market

Ron Zeskie stood as Mick and April came in. "Well, if it isn't Mick Grundy! Welcome and thanks for coming." He stuck out his hand for a shake, but Mick embraced him for a manly hug.

"Good to see you again, Zeskie. Forgive me if I don't kiss you on both cheeks," Mick said and shook his hand with a smile. He looked around the room, taking in every corner, even scanning the ceiling. It was seedy, dirty, with only one entrance and no windows. An excellent choice. A flimsy wooden table was in the center with mismatched wooden chairs lined up on both sides. Mick surmised that the room was often used for card games, the private, high-stakes kind. Since room 14 had been chosen by Zeskie himself or by one of his agents, there was no possibility of listening devices or video hardware hidden in the cracks. They would be able to have a private meeting, at least this time.

Zeskie pulled his messenger bag to the table and snapped the locks open. "This is the first time we have been together since the Berlin mission, isn't it?" Zeskie observed. They all paused for a moment, remembering the whirlwind of events of the last mission. Success, but at the cost of many lives. "We are meeting in secret, because there are persons in our government who have acquired power but have foreign allegiances. If we work inside the system, there will be eyes watching us with hostile intent. Some are just obeying orders, some are filled with a sort of religious rapture, some with antiquated leftist ideology. We can't trust the agencies of the U.S. Government with any assurance. Individuals in the various sectors are different, some can be fully trusted, and we are an example. You pick and choose your friends very carefully in this environment." He paused to clear his throat and his thoughts.

"For the last decade, Iran has sought to acquire nuclear weapons, and they are close, very close. Simultaneously, they are developing delivery systems. All primitive by our standards, but still destructive on a vast scale. The potential is to cause a nuclear exchange. No…that's incorrect. The end result will be a nuclear exchange, and one that will kill millions, perhaps most of them Iranian. Versions of those nuclear weapons will eventually be acquired by the same groups who currently favor suicide bombing. Not one of them will hesitate to incinerate millions of innocents. Not only will the Mid East go up in radioactive ash but also parts of Europe, Russia and, most regrettably, our own country. You would think that common sense would prevail, but logic and reason are not part of religion, certainly not part of that version of Islam. In a world using wisdom and logic, a kind of a rage would take hold of its leaders and the enemies of humanity would be put to the torch themselves before they manage to set the world on fire. The unthinkable appears inevitable. What events some of us see as preventable are being carelessly ignored by the majority. The next World War is right around the corner." Zeskie leaned forward, momentarily losing his focus, the horrible specter of nuclear war filling his vision.

After a moment, he continued, "But I don't think its completely hopeless. People like us concentrate on doing one little thing at a time. We do the doable, the possible. It's all we can hope to achieve, but it will make a difference, perhaps enough to turn this ship aside."

"I agree, Ron," April said. "Let's concentrate on unwinding their networks first, and in doing that, we will find out who their supporters are in Washington."

Mick had been silently listening but now spoke, his gravely voice commanding attention. "Zeskie, do you have sources who can identify where the Iranian networks are concentrated?"

"I can do better than that, Mick," Zeskie said. "The entire network filters through one particular cell and largely one individual operating near Berlin. He is a radical cleric who has the ear of Ali Khamenei, the Supreme Leader of Iran, and speaks with his voice. He runs the network for the rest of Europe and also instructs the agents they have managed to place in our government."

"Has the CIA identified the Americans involved?" April asked.

"There are suspects, of course, but these people are political appointees, protected fully by the current administration. As such, they are out of our reach. Unfortunately or perhaps fortunately, we are not given to political assassination in the U.S. We can only act within the law," Zeskie observed.

"Not all of us feel that way," Mick said.

"I can't support any of that, Mick. While in the U.S., you have to use lethal force only in self-defense or for the protection of others. Of course, what you do abroad and which does not involve American citizens…well, I just don't want to hear about it."

"A hypothetical, Zeskie, just for guidance. What do we do when, and if, we discover the identity of those Americans who are actively helping Iran obtain the bomb?" Mick asked.

"Expect them to vigorously deny any involvement. They, their supporters, and the liberal press will claim that they are only helping to avoid bringing the U.S. into another war. Or that they are trying to avoid a larger religious war with Islam, and they will accuse the accuser…us… of crimes and hate mongering."

"Can't we just tell the American people the truth? Expose these traitors for what they are?" Mick asked.

"Mick, most of the public are tired of foreign wars. They don't want to hear about it even if the liberal press would print it, which they won't." Zeskie discretely tapped Mick on the leg and, when they met eyes, winked at him. Zeskie obviously already had a solution in mind, one that he couldn't share with April.

"Now, about recent events in Tacoma, which have a link to the present matter. Special Agent Chauncy, what does the FBI know about it?" Zeskie asked.

"We got a call recently from a local hotel in Tacoma. A guest disappeared suddenly in the early morning hours, leaving luggage in his room and his car parked in front of the hotel. Strange enough in itself, but it was what was in his room that was interesting." She looked again at Mick before continuing. He didn't return her glance, in fact he didn't move at all, or even breathe as far as she could tell.

"The room was in disarray, with luggage half-packed and clothing scattered as if the guest had left in a panic. In his rush to exit, he left behind a small bag containing a stack of passports issued by several countries, all using differing names, but using the same photograph. There were several empty envelopes in the trash, but chemical testing confirmed that they had contained cash money, U.S. currency, in fact, a large amount of it. We don't know if he took a passport with him, but if he did, we know the photograph he was likely using. We have distributed this image to all exit points around the country but so far he has not tried to leave. There were also several magazines of rifle ammo found, and all are loaded with explosive ordinance manufactured outside of the U.S."

"Ron?" she asked, looking at him. "Can you take it from

here?"

"Sure, Special Agent Chauncy," he said, and sat up to the table, pawing inside his briefcase. After finding the appropriate folder, he again reclined in his chair. "The individual you have been seeking was traced by the CIA and the NSA. We were able to backtrack his travels for some time, and we also have received good cooperation from Interpol. His real name was Henrich Jatoul. He was born in Syria, Alawis mother, German father. A summer romance for the father, who left before the child's birth. Jatoul was raised in Syria but moved to Germany in his youth. He was most certainly recruited by the current Syrian government for espionage early in his life. We believe that he was a devout Muslim of the Shia sect. I need not remind you that in our current environment, Iran dominates the activity of Shia worldwide. Iran is protected by Russia, so there is also that link. Jatoul traveled frequently to Lebanon and also within Europe. He was fluent in Arabic, German and obviously spoke accented-English.

"May I interrupt you for a moment?" April asked, holding up her forefinger. Zeskie put his papers down and waited. "Two things, Ron. You refer to this Jatoul using was. My other issue is more to the point. What was he doing in Tacoma?"

"I'll answer the second part first," Zeskie said. "He was here to hire a killing. The cash, the ordinance, you see. Someone very important, given the preparation. The ammo was likely carried into the country using a diplomatic pouch. Jatoul was arranging a hit. Notice I still used was. The FBI can stop searching for him, because we know that he is no longer a problem. When the remains of his body will be found is the only uncertainty."

"Who was his target?" she asked, then thought better of her question. "Then why, what was the motive?" she wondered.

"To stop what this conference will accomplish before it even met, April. They don't want us to act. It's that simple."

"Should I ask what happened to the hit man or men?" she asked quietly.

"No, April," Zeskie responded. "And that completes the circle, doesn't it? The reason for this conference is to uncover a resource the Iranians have buried somewhere in our State Department or even higher. It's obvious that not only do their people know about our suspicions but also whom we would call on to find their source. That confirms our worst fears that an agent or agents are well-placed, high in our government circles, powerful and well-connected. This isn't going to be easy." Zeskie tossed his pen on the table and rocked back in his chair, putting his hands behind his neck.

"I don't get it," April said. "How was this man Jatoul connected to the Iranian quest for nuclear weapons?"

"Jatoul's wife is the daughter of the cleric in Berlin I mentioned. Jatoul was the messenger and money man for his father-in-law," Zeskie explained.

"Jatoul's death is bound to make them all happy, don't you think?" April asked with sarcasm.

"Even more than you can imagine. I have reason to believe that Jatoul's body has been consumed by pigs, a fact which will some day be discovered. To a devout Muslim, the idea is unthinkable, even unutterable. A rather fitting end, I would say, but his people, especially, won't like it," Zeskie added. Mick never looked their way and seemed unconcerned and uninterested by the entire conversation.

"*El intikam*," Zeskie said. "It means vendetta in Arabic. You can be sure that everyone connected with Jatoul will be after his killer. They won't discover for sure who it was, but they will assume, and the result will be the same."

"What's next, Zeskie?" Mick said, impatiently, while frowning, obviously wanting to change the subject.

"You and Special Agent Chauncy will be working together again starting now. You will travel to Paris as common tourists and make your own way to Berlin. I will return directly to my posting in Berlin, passing timely instructions and information directly to you as soon I can. Trust no one; let no one know who you are and what you are doing in Berlin. Your first orders are to gather data on this cleric and his friends so that we might put together an action plan. Surveillance, my friends. No bloodshed…yet."

"Will I be able to contact my German family?" Mick asked, looking at Zeskie.

"Not in the open, at least. It won't take the Iranians long to start looking for you, and your old Russian friends might even help them do it. By the way, how's your Arabic?"

"Not bad," Mick said.

"Farsi?" Zeskie asked.

"None."

"If that's all, Ron, Mick and I have some more catching up to do," April said, trying not to appear overly anxious to leave.

"He's all yours," Zeskie laughed. "Mick, I will personally see that your precious motorcycle is placed in storage and the paperwork, including passports, travel documents, and money, will be delivered to you in a couple of days. Until then, you two go to this hotel," he offered Mick a sealed envelope. "There you will find money and other things I left for you. Don't return to the barge again, just in case."

"You know about the barge?" Mick said with surprise.

"I keep up, dear boy," he said, then added, "anything else?"

"My helmet, too, Zeskie," Mick said and placed the beat up helmet on the table. A portion of a human tooth was still imbedded in the plastic.

"Not a chance, Mick. We'll have to buy you a new one when you get home.

Chapter 5

Chapter 6

Paris

Orly Airport

They were arm-in-arm, walking casually, whispering and smiling to each other as they walked down the movable ramp leading away from the big jet. Both were very well-dressed, even for Paris. A casual, romantic trip to "*La Ville-Lumière*" for two people who could easily afford the high life, shopping the Avenue des Champs-Elysées and dining in the best Parisian restaurants. A rendezvous in public. The woman wore a pale silk chemise decorated with small red embroidered flourishes. Tasteful, yet extravagant. Around her neck swung a highly reflective diamond, tethered by a slim gold chain. An otherwise innocent male, tempted to *jeter un coup d'œil furtif*, would have his eyes seared by her deep and exposed cleavage. The woman was stunningly beautiful, regal in bearing, turning every male head whom she passed. Her escort, not meant to be hidden himself, was dressed with discretion, his dark blue pinstripe suit was accented with a contrasting yellow silk bow tie above a crimson vest just peeking from behind the double-breasted jacket. His shoes were of immaculate polish and matched the rather expensive-looking leather case carried in the crook of his arm. They chatted alternately in British-accented English, switching frequently to flawless French. The true continental couple who had arrived for *apassionnante visite*, no price too high.

On the way to the international customs gate, Mick readied

their passports and gave her a last lingering look. She was ready and her visual impact alone would overwhelm the officials guarding the entrance to France.

"*Bienvenue en France. Passeports, s'il vous plaît,*" the man said. He smiled wanly but his eyes were searching and cautious. He held the passports one at a time, looking them in the eyes, hoping for some sign of weakness or duplicity. April smiled innocently, but her provocative being had the desired effect. The man could simply not concentrate with her standing in front of him. Looking into her eyes brought visions of another existence, one that didn't include bureaucratic delays for anything she wanted. And she wanted into France. Who was this mere official to deny her anything in the world she would desire?

"*La France espère que votre séjour soit longue et agréable, monsieur, mademoiselle,*" he said, tipping his hat. He rushed to stamp their passports, even holding the exit gate open for their entrance into France.

"That was easy, just like you said," April remarked with a giggle, taking Mick's offered arm, and they walked slowly away not pretending to be in love as any observer would gladly confirm. Outside, waiting at the curb, a long black car displayed a sign in the rear window, "Heddings," its driver looking nervously around, waiting on his passengers.

Mick nodded to the driver and stood by while he opened the rear door and smiled graciously as they got in. "*Rue du Mont Thabor…Renaissance, s'il vous plaît,*" Mick instructed in perfect, unaccented French.

"*Vos bagages, monsieur?*" the chauffeur inquired, looking puzzled that such a pair would have no luggage.

"*Il a été envoyé à l'hôtel, le chauffeur,*" Mick said sharply. The driver shrugged in gallic style and tipped his cap.

"How are your German skills, April?" Mick asked as the big

car elegantly floated into Paris.

"Not nearly at your level, but more than the last time we were there," she said.

"You've been working at it then?"

"I hoped to be able to converse with your relatives in their native language some day," she said, adding, "Even though, as I remember, they all speak excellent English." Mick looked thoughtfully at her as he understood the implications of her efforts.

"They all like you, April. They would be very happy to see you as another member of their family some day."

April Chauncy melted a little from his words and sagged into his shoulder, letting the smooth ride and the beautiful images of France passing by lull her into a sense of contentment, even if it was temporary, a dream about a dream. "I love you," she said.

"I love you, also," Mick responded.

The gracious desk clerk at the Renaissance saw at one glance that these two needed special consideration. There was confidence radiating from the well-appointed gentleman, but also something else. A man not to be trifled with, a hint of aggression, a man who would be quick to anger should he be not accommodated. And the lady! *Mon Dieu*! Easily the most magnificent trophy in Paris! "*Pouvons-nous vous aider avec vos bagages*, monsieur?" he said peering over the counter at the missing luggage.

"If you look at your records, my good man, you will find that our baggage and our clothing awaits us in our room. Is this not so?" Mick said disdainfully.

The clerk quickly and without argument looked at his computer screen, then slapped his face in surprise. "Indeed it's true! Forgive me *monsieur, mademoiselle*." He rang the bell summoning the busboy, who appeared as if by magic.

Once the tip had been paid and the door closed, leaving them finally alone, their eyes were for each other only, and they embraced tenderly as if this kiss was the first kiss and the last kiss, and they would soon separate forever.

When they finally parted, April asked, "Want to take your makeup off now?" She playfully pulled on his artificial nose.

"Yes, I can't wait. It makes me feel as if I have been transformed into a puppet, and some person behind me is pulling my strings. And my eyes are burning from the contacts."

"I'm glad Zeskie warned us that you were on the pickup list. The plan worked! We were never given a second look today."

Mick was quiet, busily pulling the artificial flesh off of his face and leaning into the mirror. "You can't be sure about that. If they are smart, they would let us pass, then follow us to uncover everybody connected and sweep the whole bunch up when they were ready."

"Sure. That's official policy, but I don't think they spotted us. You were very careful to never look toward the hidden cameras. In your disguise, I wouldn't have recognized you myself."

"The smart thing to do is to leave this place in a few minutes, just in case you're wrong. Make sure to wipe down everything you touched."

"What about our luggage?" she asked, looking over at the matched leather set by the door.

Mick pulled out a pair of latex gloves and tossed them to her. "The small one has the stuff we'll need. The others are empty. Take your clothes off and put them in the plastic bag you'll find in there. You'll also find handguns for each of us, new passports and credit cards, courtesy of the ever resourceful Zeskie. Better hurry."

"Don't I get to see Paris and live the high life even for only a couple of days?"

"Later," Mick said, knowing there would never be a later. He was used to life on the run, never just taking in the sights or pausing to entertain and court a lovely woman. He sighed. That was the reason he tried so hard to keep April out of his crummy life. He loved her and wanted better for her than he could ever offer. Now, as ever, it was a simple choice. Survive or die. Being with her increased the chances of failure, of detection, or of exposing weakness, for both of them. He was no longer able to think just for himself, to run when necessary and hide in any available snake hole. Then there was the killing and torture. April wouldn't tolerate his methods of obtaining information when it was critical. She wouldn't agree with doing what he had become notorious for...efficiently and ruthlessly dispatching his enemies with no concern for law or morality. He hoped that when they got to Germany, he could park her safely with Triska and then do what was necessary to accomplish the mission, on his own, without her supervision, but mostly, without her witnessing his brutality.

Chapter 6

Chapter 7

The Connection

In the distance, the hills crept by silently and slowly as the train hurtled toward southern Germany, but closer to the track, the signs and tunnels made a hiss, reflecting energy from spinning steel wheels back into the cars. The train was modern and smooth, and there was a rocking sensation to the ride, a very comforting one. For Mick, it recreated the last time he had ridden a train with a woman that he loved. A bomb meant for him and his wife was skillfully left in the seat just in front of them, ending her life in a split second and changing his forever.

April nestled against his arm, happy and at ease, but Mick watched. He watched every motion, assessed every face, surveyed every package. Surprised once, but never again. It made the ride to Stuttgart torture, every clicking kilometer of it.

"Achtung Passagiere, kommt dieser Zug in Stuttgart in zehn Minuten." came over the loudspeakers, and the mostly German passengers started rustling their belongings. The ever efficient Germans. Punctual and exacting to the last detail. The train noticeably slowed, and Mick watched the familiar city slide slowly into view.

April roused and stretched, her forearm grazing his face, intentionally he felt, her fragrance arousing him as her slender arm returned to the comfort of his side. "Where are we?" she murmured sleepily, yawning at the last word, then smiling at the sound she made.

"Pulling into Stuttgart. Remember who you are on your new

passport?"

"I'm Paula Schmitt. Born in London and married to a handsome German investment banker called Paulus, that's you. We are here to visit relatives and will return to Berlin in a few days. I speak German with a British accent, by the way very difficult for me to do, and I am frivolous and flirtatious. Want to see?"

"Perfect. By the way, you are just as becoming in casual clothing, actually better, more approachable."

"And you in your corduroy jacket. Very nice. You look very good with dark hair, and we trimmed it to the right length." April fingered his hair playfully, pulling a lock over his ear and giggling. "Are we going straight to your grandmother's apartment?"

"I haven't actually told her that we are coming. She's an old Cold War spy, you know. She's very crafty and always knows more about everything than you would expect. You can't just call her on the phone. We have a method worked out for contact."

"Such as?"

"She wouldn't like it if I told anyone, even you."

"You don't have to explain Triska to me, Mick. I remember being mind-searched by her during casual conversation. What about your two brothers: Kurt and Peter?

"Triska and I have a bond. She is like both the grandmother and mother that I never had but always wanted. We are not related by blood, but I am closer to her than I can describe for you. She comes first."

The train's communication screens flashed that Stuttgart was the next stop and instructed the passengers to remain seated. There was a rush of air somewhere under the train as it slowed more forcefully, pushing the passengers forward in their seats. A last jerk to full stop was accompanied by an instant opening of the doors, allowing the platform noise to enter and mingle with the hushed voices of the passengers lining up to exit. Mick placed his hand on

April's thigh, a signal to wait for a moment. He wanted plenty of room to maneuver and a nearly empty car before getting up. A habit which had stood the test of time.

"Do you think we have time to buy a few things, Mick, like more clothing, or personal items?"

"Be patient, dear. One thing at a time. We don't want a lot of stuff to drag around just yet. Luggage is burdensome, it can slow us down."

"Yes, Mick. I know how you work. You can live with insects in a hole in the ground for weeks. You ignore how you look; in fact, you cultivate that look because it frightens everyone. But…I am a woman about to meet her…" she stopped suddenly in mid-sentence.

"Your future in-laws. And you want to look nice?"

"Yes. Is there anything wrong with that?"

"Not at all. To my eyes, you look wonderful as you are. I don't know what you need, but I can't imagine any clothing making you look better."

"Well, I can. We are going to shop for clothing before I see Triska. I have to look good to feel good." Mick sighed but kept it internal. He remembered the old contact method they had worked out. A certain little bistro, a specific and slightly unusual food order and a tip of a certain amount, no more, no less. The trigger would be pulled and Triska would be summoned. She would do the rest. It was virtually foolproof.

"Could we at least go to a nice place and eat a filling German lunch before shopping?" he asked.

April looked at him for any sign of duplicity. She knew that he always managed to have his way with things and could make events look random while actually controlling them minutely. "Are you up to your tricks again?" she asked, eyebrows raised.

"No, just hungry," he smiled innocently back at her. The

crowd was thinning, and they rose from their seats. Mick was right about traveling light, but April had hated tossing the beautiful ivory shift in the trash. She felt lovely in it, and it caused everyone to look her way with either lust or admiration. She wondered if any stores in Stuttgart stocked similar French garments. They arrived at the platform, and Mick leaned against a post studying the crowd as they passed on their collective way to something important. "We need a car," he suddenly announced, pulling her toward the car rental area.

The small blonde agent looked up to see Mick standing in front of her. "*Kann ich helfen?*" she politely inquired. Mick looked past her to the parking lot, then back to the overhead sign listing the cars and their prices.

"Porsche? We would like to rent one, please." He hesitated briefly then spoke again, "Forgive me. *Wir möchten eines zu mieten, bitte.*"

"No problem, sir, I speak English. You would like to rent a Porsche? We have two. Yellow or Red?"

"Red. Red is faster, is it not?" he joked.

"I am informed that it is, sir. For how many days, sir?"

"May we return the car in Berlin?"

"There will be an extra charge, sir."

"Of course. Then for two weeks," he said. The girl looked at him to be sure he wasn't kidding. An enormous price for a rental car, not unheard of but rare. They quickly consummated the deal and sped away in a tight but very fast sports car.

"I like this little car. Very much like a motorcycle in some ways," Mick observed while turning the corners hard, allowing the car a slight drift and making the tires squeal. April was holding on and wishing he had wanted a big slow luxury model.

"Where are we going, Mick? We've already passed several

restaurants. Are you going someplace special?" April knew she was being deceived. Mick had no intention of shopping at the moment.

"There is a little place I remember. Quiet, nice, good German food. It's on *Urbanstraße*, not far."

"The contact for Triska is there I assume?" she said, trying to sound innocent. Mick glanced at her, his brow knitted and irritated, but didn't answer. April knew that she had judged him correctly. The sign of *Bistro i-Pünktle* was just ahead when he pulled to the curb. "Do you just call her from here or does another person?" she persisted, irritated herself by his deception. Mick snorted but got out and came around to open her door for her. April started up again while struggling to get out of the low car. "Maybe its a sequence of words, like a chant. Are you going to start chanting when we sit down? If you do, it's going to be so irritating. Embarrassing, too."

Mick stopped and looked at her with exasperation. He grasped her lightly on her shoulders and lowered his head. "April, do you want me to break a promise to Triska by telling you something I promised not to ever reveal?"

April felt suddenly sorry for the predicament she put him through. "No, Mick. I promise I won't ask again. Forgive me?"

"Of course, dear. Now, let's get something to eat and have no more talk about this subject."

He seemed friendly enough, just coarse and fat. But he smiled broadly when he stood there waiting for their order. "*Ihre Bestellung bitte.*"

"*Sauerbraten und Kartoffeln, bitte,*" April said. They both looked toward Mick who seemed hesitant to place his order. The waiter stood, pencil in hand, patiently waiting.

"*Sauerkraut und Eis, Schokolade.* Dank," Mick said without looking up from his menu. April and the fat waiter raised their eyebrows looking at Mick in surprise.

"*Sind Sie sicher, zu Ihrer Bestellung, mein Freund?*" he asked, tapping his pencil against his notepad.

"*Natürlich bin ich sicher,*" Mick said. The waiter shrugged and wrote it down, giving Mick a backward look as he left.

"Did you just order sauerkraut with chocolate ice cream?" April asked in a whisper.

"Yes, April."

"Is that the message?" she asked, cupping her hand to her mouth, her eyes wide with excitement.

"I thought you were done with that," he said.

"Yes, but it's so funny!"

In a few moments, the waiter came with the food. He put April's down carefully, smiling at her. He was even more courteous with Mick and placed the silverware neatly beside the plate, being careful to make the implements parallel with each other, nodding agreeably at him and smiling back at him before disappearing into the kitchen.

"Wow!" April commented. "Order weird food and become a celebrity. Who would know?" she chuckled, wiping her eyes with her napkin. "Are you really going to eat that thing?" she sputtered, laughing out loud and attracting attention from the other patrons.

"Do you remember that everybody in the world is hunting for us and would love to shoot us on sight? Is it a good idea to call attention to us on our first day here?" Mick hissed under his breath. She could tell that he was angry, and with anyone but her, he would become dangerous. Instead, he started laughing himself at the silliness of the whole thing. They put their heads together and rolled with laughter until they cried.

Mick finally got control of himself and straightened up. He took a big scoop of sauerkraut and chocolate ice cream and put it in his mouth, munching seriously. "Actually, it's edible, especially if you are as hungry as I am." They both broke down in laughter again, and some of the other patrons joined in. Mick picked up the check and looked it over. He reached into his wallet and counted out euros and carefully added change on top. A ten euro tip was laid to the side. April watched with interest but without comment. On cue, the waiter came by and scooped up the money, giving Mick a long look and a wink, then left, heading again for the kitchen.

"I wouldn't have missed this for the world," April said. She leaned back in her chair and covered her mouth with her hand. Her laughing eyes danced around the room.

"Calm down, April. This is very serious, you'll see," Mick said.

"The only thing left is for Santa to come down the chimney. I mean this is more like a Marx brothers movie all the time," she sniggered. Just as she finished speaking, there was a loud screech of tires outside of the bistro. Two sets of tires slid to a stop, shortly followed by car doors slamming. They looked at each other and both felt for their weapons as their smiles faded rapidly. All normal restaurant noise stopped abruptly as the door to the bistro swung open and two soldiers came in. Both were dressed in light grey uniforms with red berets, and both were muscular and confident. They studied the room and its patrons carefully before heading directly toward Mick and April.

"Most of my life, I have been the hunter. Being the hunted is not as much fun," April said quietly. "What are we going to do, Mick?" He didn't answer, but he was tense, coiled, his eyes hard and fixed on the approaching solders. They saw it also and moved closer but with less arrogance and more caution. Two more soldiers appeared, blocking the entrance. Another car skidded to a stop outside the cafe. Mick could kill all four of them, easily in fact, but outside the bistro was a big unknown. He decided to take a different approach and visibly relaxed, smiling at them.

The closest one strained his neck to see into Mick's dish. "*So sind Sie derjenige, der diese ekelhafte Essen bestellt?*" he said, an artificial smile on his lips. Mick chose to ignore the obvious and remained still, occasionally glancing toward the door which was still blocked by two large men.

"*Sie beide sind, mit uns zu kommen,*" [You both are to come with us] the soldier commanded, this time not smiling. Both men stood away from the table but with their hands on the grips of their holstered pistols. Mick nodded to April, and they stood slowly and made no threatening gestures. The first soldier's shoulder insignia had three diamonds…*Hauptmann* rank. He motioned with his head toward the door, his former smile replaced by tight lips. April got up first, followed by Mick, who took his time, his eyes testing the young Captain's willingness to escalate. The door was held open for them by the two other soldiers who moved back slightly. Another black car pulled slowly to the curb and sat there for a moment watching the little parade of seven soldiers around Mick and April. Mick had a good look at his potential opponents, sizing them up one at a time, his brain working rapidly, figuring angles and targets.

The new car's door opened suddenly, and a German officer's head appeared above the roof. "*Ihr Männer! Ziehen Sie sich sofort!*" [You men! Back off immediately!] he shouted. His men looked puzzled and awkwardly looked back at their commander who had suddenly appeared. They started moving away from Mick and April, leaving them in the center of a growing circle. Several cars on the busy street slowed to watch.

The officer came around the car and adjusted his cap. This one wore three diamonds in gold with braid…*Generalleutnant.* He appeared especially fit and the way he moved and held his head, he was accustomed, and entitled, to considerable respect from men under his command. Mick swiveled to meet this new and game changing threat. Violence was now nearly out of the question. The officer signaled to the *Hauptmann* to come forward.

"*Zwei Probleme Kapitän. Die erste ist, dass alle sieben von Ihnen waren zu sterben. Das zweite ist, dass dieser Mann ist mein Bruder. Wenn er nicht vollständig töten, dann würde ich den Job für ihn beendet haben.*" [Two problems, Captain. The first is that all seven of you were about to die. The second is that this man is my brother. If he didn't completely kill you, then I would have finished the job for him.] The young officer lost his color and looked back at Mick again, this time seeing him with different eyes.

"*Sie können unsere Männer zu nehmen und zu verlassen, Hauptman,*" the senior officer said. The young Captain gave a vigorous and snappy salute and waved his men toward the waiting cars, looking back at Mick before he left, trying to understand how this one man was capable of taking out seven armed soldiers.

"In trouble again, my brother?" Peter Koffman asked, taking his cap off, showing his bushy hair, slightly but handsomely streaked with grey.

"Only if it is a crime in Germany to eat sauerkraut with chocolate ice cream," Mick said.

"It's a grave crime and against everything we Germans were taught since birth," Peter said. They moved together, arms extended, and embraced, rocking back and forth as if they were in the clench of a lover.

"It's so good to see you again, Brother," Mick said. "And your timing was excellent."

"You're welcome! And I recognize this Venus beside you! Who could possibly forget the face which could launch a thousand ships, a face which could only be possible in dreams. If she didn't belong to my only brother, then I would be jealous indeed." He made a flourish of bowing at the waist toward her and took her hand and kissed it softly, letting her fingers slide through his.

"Greetings, April," he said. "Welcome to Germany." He gave her a sideways, disapproving look, "Don't tell me that you also ate that mess?"

"Peter, you never change! You have once again swept this little backward American girl right off her feet!"

"Don't give me that line!" he said, exploding with a laugh. "You are soft and lovely on the outside, but I know that inside, you are made of hard stone. I remember all too well! Say, why aren't you two married yet? Have you had a lover's spat?" His smile faded just a little when he looked at her face. *"Hoppla!"* he exclaimed. "That was a raw nerve, wasn't it?" The ever ebullient Peter threw his arms over both their shoulders, looking at them with pride. "I don't believe that either of you have eaten, at least not properly. Will you allow me to show you one of our better places?"

"One question first," April said, looking back and forth at them. "Mick, I didn't fully understand what was about to happen before Peter showed up. Were you about to take on all those men?"

Mick silently looked at her, trying to formulate an answer she could comprehend when Peter spoke first. "Of course not, April! My brother isn't a violent man, not at all, no matter what you have heard. He relies on his training as we all do. Mick is an experienced soldier and a man who has been driven against a wall many times, but he's not truly dangerous." Over her head, Peter gave Mick a quick wink. Thank God he had gotten there quickly.

Chapter 8

Großmutter Triska

Restaurant Wielandshöhe

You finally made General, I see," Mick observed, inspecting Peter's tailored uniform carefully.

"Yes, second in command in this area. My own office and secretary! Life has been good to me, but no more about me. Tell me about yourself, I haven't heard from you in over a year," Peter said, pursing his lips after testing the wine and rolling his eyes in the best tradition of a connoisseur, afterward patting his lips with his linen. He was giving Mick his full attention, nodding understanding to his every word and smiling encouragement at both of them. April sat back and observed carefully, something she was well-trained to do. There was something overdone about Peter Koffman's graciousness. She began to feel that some of his slick salesmanship, his fatherly attention, was going just a little too far. She wondered what Mick was thinking. There was no clue in his face or his manner, but Mick was the true master of disguise, even to his lover and his family. He could become anything anyone wanted, from the most distinguished debonair gentleman to the creature of your worst fears. He could operate in any of the cities of Europe, speaking native languages without accent and being nearly impossible to detect. His half brother Peter was always a big puppy, full of life, well-educated and obviously very physically fit. He was though, by comparison to his brother, inexperienced in combat, and April could not imagine Peter being the feared and relentless killer that Mick had become. Peter was hard to figure. Becoming a general in the *Bundeswehr* was no small thing, and Peter obviously had the bearing and demeanor of a powerful man, but…there was something a little too cultured, too refined, too continental about him. It bothered her, nagged at her, but she could not bring her feelings into focus. Likely, Peter had learned to do what Mick could do, just in a different way. An intelligent man who could appear to be one thing, but underneath something entirely different. A wolf dressed up like a grandmother, waiting on you to make a mistake.

"Oh, my world is different than yours, Peter. It would be hard to describe it to you. But I am so happy to see your success, your high rank and the adulation of everyone who sees that uniform."

"Where are you living in America?" Peter asked, looking back and forth between them. "Are you two living together?"

"No, Peter. April and I have just resumed our relationship. We have been too busy to be together until recently," Mick answered. Peter's eyes didn't believe the story, April could tell, but he just nodded and smiled blandly, hanging on every word.

"Mick, my brother, there is something I need to tell both of you," Peter said, speaking in a low conspiratorial voice. "You both are on the wanted lists. Your FBI has posted your names on Interpol. April's photo, of course, doesn't do her justice, but nevertheless, it is a good likeness. Your photo, however, seems to be missing."

"Yes, Peter. We are aware," Mick said.

"So, may I ask, did you come to Stuttgart to hide?"

"Are you not willing to help us hide, Peter?" Mick bluntly asked.

"It puts me in a difficult position, you know. I am expected to obey the laws, the BND would expect a senior officer to do no less."

"As it puts me in a difficult position. I know that you consider me a German, like yourself, and as such you will give me extra consideration, and I am sure that a man in your position is sensitive to the political drama taking place in the U.S. at the moment. We are a divided nation, more so than at any time since our Civil War. You can be sure that April and I have support from certain people of influence and that we are here at their behest. Is that enough explanation for you, Peter?"

"You misunderstand, Brother! I will not allow anything to happen to you while you are in our homeland. However, with respect to my position, we are forced to use discretion. We have to form a plan, if you will."

"I am looking forward to discussing this with Triska first, Peter," Mick said. He glanced briefly at April's face, giving nothing away in his.

"She is not related to either one of us, Mick. Why does she hold such importance for you? As far as I am concerned she is rather out of date. She continues to haunt the BND offices because the older ones still look up to her, but frankly, I would prefer to have her retired, as she should have done long ago."

"Triska is the grandmother of my wife, and frankly, I still love and care for her. In my experience, her knowledge does count for something, and she has a vast number of contacts. Never underestimate her, Peter."

"As you say, Brother." There was a stiff moment and the hint of friction hung in the air.

April took this pause as an opportunity to speak up. "I thought Triska was going to be alerted, Mick. Did something go wrong?"

"What about it, Peter?" Mick asked.

"We made Triska surrender her contacts and her methods long ago. The process was still in place, and I suppose that the Duty Officer felt he had nabbed an old Stasi operative. Luckily, I heard about it in time to rescue you."

"Rescue your men, you mean," April corrected.

"Possibly," Peter observed.

"Can you call Triska and ask her if we can come by?" Mick said.

Peter's face had a hint of consternation pass over it, but he quickly recovered. "By all means!" he said and dug for his phone. In a moment he dialed, and Mick and April could hear it ringing. At the seventh ring, there was a click then silence. Peter rolled his eyes and sighed. *"Grüße Triska, ich habe eine Nachricht für Sie von einem Ihrer sehr entfernten Verwandten. Könnten Sie zurückrufen? Danke."* He hung up but laid the phone beside his plate, tapping his fingers against the polished wood. Fifteen seconds later the phone softly buzzed, and Peter handed it to Mick without comment.

"I can tell you that sauerkraut and chocolate ice cream is not a good combination," Mick said into the phone. There was silence on the other end, then the phone started cracking with her voice. "Yes, it's me, and I have April with me. Remember her?" Mick said, smiling broadly. "Are you home?"… "Half an hour all right?"… "Yes, I love you also. See you soon." Mick clicked off and handed Peter the phone.

"Are you coming also, Peter?" he asked.

"I think not. Triska and I have our differences. May I give you a ride over there?"

"Not necessary, but thank you, Peter."

Peter tapped his fork against his empty wine glass, summoning the waitress. She must have been waiting, because she promptly appeared and came to his side, laying her hand delicately on his shoulder. The girl smiling so sincerely at Peter was very young and pretty in a buxom way. She wore a more traditional dress which was tight at the waist but pleated in the bust area, amplifying and calling attention to what was evidently already ample. And it didn't fail to attract Peter's notice as he wasn't shy about looking her over and patting her hand, thanking her profusely for her attention and good service and rewarding her with both a smile and a generous tip. His eyes lingered over her form as she moved away from the table.

"Before I forget, my brother, here is my private number in case you have to talk with me." He passed Mick a small card with the number embossed with raised letters. "And may I have yours?" he asked, ever polite.

"At the moment, Peter, we are traveling without one. As soon as we acquire a number, I'll call you," Mick said earnestly.

"And one last item that I am burning to discuss with you," Peter said. He seemed to scan Mick's face for information before proceeding. "About the DNA tests we ran the last time you were here."

"Stop right there, Peter. At this time, I don't want to know anything about it. Someday, perhaps, I will be ready but not now."

"I see," Peter said and looked disappointed. There was another lengthy pause in the conversation which signaled the end of the reunion of long separated brothers. "Well, if you both are full and can manage your own transportation, then I must be off. I look forward to seeing you both again, and please remember to invite me to your wedding should that happy event ever occur." Peter rose from his chair and shook their hands with sincerity. He nodded to the pert waitress on his way out.

"I couldn't tell who was lying more, he or you," April said.

"It wasn't me. I didn't tell him any facts, but neither did I lie. This was a big disappointment for me and one I never expected. He's changed a lot in one year, and I don't understand it. He said that he would protect me, you remember. There was nothing said about protecting you."

"I noticed. What does it mean?" April asked.

"He seems impressed with himself. I don't remember him that way before. It saddens me greatly."

"What was he talking about when he mentioned the DNA?" April asked.

Mick drew a big breath and let it out slowly. "My history, my origins. We know that Peter and I are half brothers and shared the same mother. My father is the unknown. I was told that my father was a Russian KGB agent who rose high in their intelligence circles. The man lied about everything and probably that also. I didn't kill him, but I was responsible for his death and watched him die. If he was actually my father, I would not want to know. The *Bundesnachrichtendienst* has his DNA and mine. Peter knows the relationship.

"And if he wasn't?" April asked.

"I don't want Peter to tell me, especially right now," Mick stated.

"I take it that you didn't even want Peter to know what car we are driving?"

"True, but I especially didn't want him to know what name I am using. Not yet. Not until Triska tells me that it's all right."

They parked in the alley behind Triska's apartment where Mick always parked. It was a strange sensation, taking another woman to that place where he and Anna had been so many times. Replacing Anna was a crime against the love that he still carried for her. That love had never dimmed and just now, walking where she walked, holding the door that she had come through, and soon to see the couch that they had sat in kissing and holding hands, brought her back to him as if she was still there, waiting for him somewhere. He remembered the fragrance she used and the pleasant smell of her leather jacket, the thrill he got when he put his hand around her small waist. His rational mind knew that she was gone, and he could only see her again in his dreams. If only he didn't have to watch her die every night for the rest of his life, and forever not be able to change it.

They stood in front of the doorway at the end of the long hall. Mick drew himself up and tapped three times. April could guess what he was thinking. Was Triska the same or was she going to act like Peter? And how would she feel about April standing there in place of her beloved Anna? April also felt tense. She was about to invade a sacred relationship and had no idea what was to happen when she did.

The door swung slowly open, and in the light stood a short older woman, somewhat stooped and frail but with burning intelligence pouring from her face. Triska. "Well, it's about time. I've been looking forward to this for a very long while." With one bony hand she clasped April's hand and with the other she pulled Mick's head down and kissed him on both cheeks, tears streaming down her cheeks.

Chapter 8

Chapter 9

Painful Separation

They sat together on the small couch, Triska in the center, holding both of their hands and looking tenderly back and forth at them with her faded blue eyes. "I knew that someday you would come back to me, Mick Grundy. And you, lovely April, how marvelous you look. There is scarcely a woman in Europe who could compete with you." Triska just sat there in complete happiness, holding on to them, feeling whole and fulfilled. After a long quiet moment, she collected herself, and her eyes took on their old look.

"This isn't just a visit from my long lost grandson, is it?" she asked.

"Yes and no," Mick admitted.

"I saw your names come across two days ago at the BND. You both are wanted and considered dangerous. I knew then that you were probably headed my way. Want to tell me about it?"

"Of course, and I'm sure you already know the answer. Our government is corrupt. Someone back there is afraid of what we might do. As a German, you realize how America has pulled back recently. How it has caved in to tyrants and shrunk its military. We are in rapid decline, and there are obviously some Americans who would like to see Iran achieve dominance in the oil rich Middle East. April and I could be a thorn which could pop the whole balloon."

"Why are you here?" Triska asked. It was a simple and obvious question, but its simplicity hid its gravity. Mick simply did not know the full extent of why they were there nor what the mission was going to be, nor did he want to articulate his needs, especially after he realized that Triska was in declining health.

"I wanted to see you first, because, as yet, only you and Peter know we are here. Later, it might be hard to get back here."

"That's not the entire reason. Tell me the rest." Ever the perceptive old spy, she cut to the heart of the matter. She patiently waited while Mick thought of a way to tell her something which would create an instant problem. He wanted to ask her to take April under her wing and keep her out of danger while he went to Berlin. April was going to explode, and he needed Triska's help to convince her to stay in Stuttgart and out of danger.

"We had lunch with Peter," Mick said, changing the subject for now.

"Oh? And you found him changed, didn't you?"

"I was counting on his help. Now, I'm not sure I can trust him."

"Peter is hungry for another promotion. Turning you in would do it. His own half brother could be the proof of his dedication to the BND. A notorious killer, sought by Interpol and the FBI, not to mention the Russians. A feather. I'm not sure that Peter knows himself what he will do. He is probably considering the options right now. It would be wise to stay away from him presently until he makes up his mind. My opinion, for whatever it's worth, is that Peter will make the right decision eventually, after he has time to think it through. Until then, don't confide in him or trust him too far."

"That's what I had already decided. Unfortunately, I may need the help of the *Bundesnachrichtendienst* to accomplish anything. Ron Zeskie of the CIA is directing this show, and he is in Berlin at the moment, but other than him, we have no support over here."

"Peter wants me to stay home and die, and he probably told

you that. I have few friends left over there at the Stuttgart office, but I have many more in Berlin, including the Director. There is also another resource I have been cultivating for years, and this is the time, my last chance, to use it."

"I was hoping to get you to help me, you crafty old spy," Mick laughed. Triska looked at April, then back at Mick, sizing them up.

"The last time I saw you two, you made me think that you were about to get married and live happily ever after. I still wonder why that didn't happen, because I can see that you both are still in love. It's a bad thing to see the love of your life in danger. They never allowed such a pairing for a covert mission in the old days. There are increased risks for both of you and not only just the chance of losing one another. The main risk is that your judgment is impaired, and the other side will use one of you to get at the other. It's not a good thing for you to work together." Mick could tell that Triska was reading his mind, and she was already working on a solution.

"Here's what I think," Triska started. "April's photo has been distributed widely, and she is so remarkable looking that she will be noticed, it's only a matter of time. You, Mick, are a shadow, a ghost, who can go anywhere at any time. They all fear you and for good reason. I think I know what Zeskie has in mind, and it's best you should work alone in Berlin. No one can tell that you are an American, because you really aren't one. You were born German, speak German and think like a German. You are invisible while you are here. April, dear, you are a liability for Mick. He loves you, but you will hold him back and put him at risk. You have to stay here with your Triska for now. I plan on becoming your *Großmutter* some day and having your children sit on my knee, but to do that, we have to keep you both alive."

All at once, April understood Mick's plan. He knew this would happen, knew that Triska would pick up on it and make it her own cause. She realized that she couldn't fight both of them, and tears started clouding her eyes before she could regain control of her emotions. She sagged into Triska while holding her hands over her face, hiding the tears which started flowing in earnest. Triska patted her leg affectionately and kissed the top of her head. "I understand, my dear, more that you will ever know. You and he would die for each other, but I can't allow that to happen, can I? There's my great grandchildren to consider, you understand."

April recovered a bit and sat up, looking at Mick with reddened eyes and puffy lips. "You planned this all along, didn't you? You never were going to let me help, were you?" Mick didn't answer or want to. April comprehended for the first time that Mick had worked it all out long before that night in her house when he had covered her mouth. He was always protecting her and always would and nothing she could say or do would change that. The emotions of anger, rage, fear, and finally acceptance swept through her head. There was absolutely no option for her right now. Alone, she would be swept up by the efficient German police in a short time. She stood out because of her accent but especially because of her singular beauty. She was going to have to comply regardless if she liked it or not. She also had no doubt that the ever scheming Zeskie always knew what was going to happen when they got to Stuttgart.

"Would you think this out for a moment and tell me what will happen to me if you get killed in Berlin? How would I feel? What would I do?" she asked in a throaty voice.

"You won't get over it, but you will be alive, and that will make me happy, even if I'm dead. As for the rest, once I'm out of the picture, they won't want you any longer. You will just go home and resume the life you have been living for the past six months."

"And if you are killed, I will always wonder if I could have prevented it," April said, more harshly than she intended. She remembered that Mick dreamed this very same dream every night, always wishing that he could have done something to prevent Anna from being killed. April could be headed for the same fate.

"This isn't going to be so bad, April. There is a lot we can do to help Mick from here, and there is a lot I am going to teach you while I have you captive. Then there's the shopping. I can't wait to take you shopping for clothes. A girl like you looks good in anything, I know, but the right thing can be heavenly. Do you have enough money to leave some with her, Mick?" Triska asked.

Mick opened the small satchel he carried under his arm and pulled out a small packet. He took out a stack of plastic cards three inches high and laid them carefully on the table and placed a thick stack of Euros beside it. Three more passports came out of the bag, and he placed them with the stack of money. "There are thirty credit cards here in various names and banks. You can buy nearly anything, except a car, with each one. Use it for no more than ten days, then discard it and use another one. Zeskie assures me that it will take a month for any of the cards to raise alarms, and by then we'll be gone. The three passports will let you travel without worry, but your face is a different matter. Your fingerprints and possibly your DNA are all on record, so you must be very careful."

"And just what are you going to do?" April asked. She sniffed and tried to clear her eyes.

"I am going to find a fast motorcycle and connect with Zeskie. Beyond that, I don't know anything." He slid a small black phone toward her. "Zeskie's gift. Only use it to contact me or Zeskie. You can expect that the CIA will listen to and record everything being said on it."

"Do you have one?"

"Yes, just like it."

"You told Peter that you didn't have a phone."

"Yes. I lied."

There was a long moment of silence when all that had been said was being absorbed by the three sitting on the couch, feeling apart from each other with their separate problems.

"Triska," Mick said. "What was the other resource you mentioned?"

"It's a long shot, Mick, dear. In the old days, I cultivated contacts in East Germany with the Stasi and other Eastern Europeans working for the other side, the communists. We did each other favors at times, even though we were in a Cold War. I still know some of them. They are all currently out of the trade but still have certain gifts and contacts which may be useful to you. All of them want to make up for past sins, so to speak, and want to deliver a blow for Western Democracy, if they can. Of all people, they don't want a return to the Soviet system or to be dominated by Islam. They will help you if you ask in the right way, and I can vouch for them. Unfortunately, they are mostly old now, like me, but in their day…well, I suppose that they were more like you than you could know."

"Just how do I contact them?" Mick asked. "Don't mention a word about sauerkraut and ice cream, please."

Triska laughed. "No, that was one of the silly ones, and it was unique. I have a long list, and I'll share a few names with you. You'll have to memorize it, because I don't want any of them rounded up by any agency. We've kept our secrets a long time, and it would be better to forget all those atrocities committed by both sides."

"When are you leaving, Mick?" April asked, not wanting to hear his answer.

"Tomorrow. I want to get this over with and return to you and Triska as soon as possible." The answer brought another round of tears, and she collapsed into Triska's shoulder again.

"There, there, dear April," Triska said, caressing April's head.

"We'll have each other, and we can make our own plans. You'll see."

"Triska? May April and I take you out for dinner tonight?" Mick asked. "You remember that little spot we used to go to together and practice our foreign language skills on each other?"

"Italian, wasn't it?" I think I recall which one. Of course, Mick, April and I would love to eat out tonight. By the way, April, what languages do you speak?"

"Very good French, thanks to college, and some German."

"Wonderful! Two weeks of immersion with me, and you will become fluent in German. By the way, your intended here is the only person I have ever met who can outdo me in language skills."

"Yes, I've seen him in action previously. Not many people can do what he can. He's like a savant."

"You two will use my extra bedroom tonight. Make as much noise as you please, because it won't bother me a bit. Breakfast at six."

Mick was awakened by the soft tinkle of cooking utensils and the sound of running water. Old Triska was up and already preparing breakfast while trying to make as little noise as possible. Mick had the strong urge to get up and help her, but the sensation of April's nude form against him dampened any such notion. Carefully, lightly, he put his hand on her hip just to feel the soft smooth skin, trying to burn it into his mind, just in case… She was a wondrous thing, so full of emotion, joy and life and so very beautiful that she was breathtaking no matter how many times he saw her. But she wasn't just a good-looking girl, she was a woman of substance, of duty, and wouldn't run from a tough situation no more than he would. Lying there, he recalled how she had killed her two captors, Russian thugs who had held her prisoner trying to force him to do their bidding. She was as brutal as he was, Mick thought, just as tough and resourceful, only better looking. Her ravishing appearance was a useful tool for her, because it charmed the men and disarmed the women. In a way, she was a chameleon, just like him, because people only saw the shiny surface overlooking the panther lurking beneath her skin. He knew that she could contribute greatly to this mission, perhaps even playing a critical role. But, there was no use thinking that way, because he wasn't about to put her in harm's way. This one just can't be taken away from him.

"You feel good back there," she croaked with her sweet morning voice. Her arm came around and patted him on his bare bottom. "Nice ass," she said.

"Yours also," Mick agreed.

"Is that noise from Triska already up?" she asked, twisting around to face him.

"Old but still energetic. You'll see."

"Please, please, Mick. Don't make me stay here. I want to be with you. You don't have to worry about me." Her nose touched his, and her face was close enough to be out of focus for him. She was trying her feminine skills on him, the powerful persuasion of her presence.

"I'm the first one to admit how capable you are. That's not it."

"I know, Mick. You don't want to see me harmed. I get it. But how do you suppose I feel about you being harmed? Can't you see it from my point of view?"

Mick knew that April was right. Plus, down deep, he wanted to keep her by his side. Separation was hard for him also. "Tell you what, April. You stay here and learn from Triska. She has a lot of knowledge she can pass on to you. I'll go up to Berlin and check things out, just look things over for now. If there is any way for you to help, I'll send for you. I promise I will."

"No you won't. I don't believe that promise, not for a second." Her lips formed a delightful pout.

"You heard Triska say that you are the one who can't hide. That means that even here you have to be alert and careful. We're not sure about Peter, and we are also not positive that one of those agencies hunting us hasn't managed to track us down. Don't let them take you, because they will use you to get me and it'll work. Trust Triska. She has a sixth sense about things. Once I'm away from here on a motorcycle, there's no possible way for them to get me, and I'll have Zeskie protecting me also. I'll likely be safer than you, so quit worrying about me."

April watched his eyes, going back and forth between them, thinking it through. She moved closer and found his lips, pressing hard against him. "For the first time, I see your point," she said. "We might as well get up and see if we can help her."

Chapter 9

Chapter 10

A Fast Trip to Munich

Mick looked them both over for the last time, his eyes betraying the agony it was causing him to separate from them. They were the two people, of all the people on the earth, that he cared about the most. In fact, they were all he had left to care about and riding off with them standing on the curb watching him, love in their eyes, was nearly the hardest thing he had ever done. He started the motorcycle and sat there for a moment with an aching heart before finally flipping his shield down and rolling away.

"He hated to leave," Triska observed. She placed her arm around April's waist, and April's arm found her shoulder. They stood still, holding on to each other, until the bike turned the last corner and was gone.

"Yes, he did. The thought that we might never see him again…" April couldn't finish her statement and instead wiped her eyes.

"We're talking about Mick, you know," Triska said and patted her hand. "He's going to be fine. That's the way we have to think for now. He promised to keep in touch, and he always keeps his word. Now we girls get to go shopping, and I happen to know the best places, and you happen to have no limit on your cards! And there's lunch!"

"After all my work and my fine record, they put my name and photo out as they would a common criminal. I'm angry about it. I have to hide from my own people, and I've never done anything remotely against the law. So…if I'm spending the people's money today…well, they owe it to me, don't they?" April said as they walked back to the car.

"It clears any guilt from your mind. I remember feeling the same way at times. Besides, you need clothing just to do your job, and the better you look, the better you will perform. Don't you feel that way also?" Triska encouraged. They started walking back toward the little red Porsche, arm-in-arm, both starting to feel better about things.

The morning was a whirlwind of shopping, and the resultant bags started to fill the little car's trunk and backseat as they made the rounds of the best clothing stores in Stuttgart. Triska insisted on speaking only in German and encouraged April to eliminate English as much as possible, and as the day wore on, it became easier for her to think in German. They ended up on *Kronprinzstraße* and made a quick decision to eat at the *Maredo* just across the street.

"Well, my dear," Triska said and raised her wine glass in a toast. "Here's to the most fun shopping I have had in a long while!"

"But, you didn't let me buy anything for you," April complained.

"At my age, no clothing would make me more appealing, I'm afraid. But I'm happy that we made good selections for you." Triska was looking out the window, across the street to the shopping area they had just come from. She smiled at April and paused for a moment. Something made April uneasy. There was an issue, a cloud, which had entered the room. Her sixth sense was activated, and she looked at Triska with more interest.

"Triska? Is there something bothering you?" April asked, careful to continue to return her smile.

"You don't need to look, in fact, don't look. I'll describe it for you. There is a man across the street with a camera. He was there when we passed, and he is still there. Occasionally, he looks across the street toward this restaurant. He is somewhat fat, ill-kempt and has a brimmed hat, brown slacks. A working man, he is not loitering."

April smiled and drank from her wine glass as her eyes turned toward the suspect. He was looking back and leaning against a wall, partly in shadow. "Yes, I see what you mean," she said. "That was quick. You suppose he is working with Peter?"

"No. He's not BND, something else. I haven't seen others, so he might be alone," Triska said casually, ignoring the man for a moment.

"Not very professional, I would say. Want to guess as to his origins?" April asked.

"He's probably German but that doesn't tell you who hired him."

"What do you suppose Mick would do right now?" April wondered.

"Mick would capture the man and torture him, at the very least, but we aren't Mick," Triska said.

"What do you want to do?" April asked, deferring to Triska's superior experience.

"Understand that if Peter's people are watching, we can't get away from them. Your CIA is the same, but this doesn't smell like either one to me." Triska continued dining while thinking out loud. "You're probably not going to like my suggestion." She looked at April with her faded eyes which were harder and colder than April had seen before.

"Don't tell me that you would like to shoot the man?"

"Sure, but that would only let the other side know that we were aware of them. Normally, I would call the BND and have the man picked up for interrogation. Our problem is that you are on their wanted list so that option is not available. We have to run, and soon, before he confirms to his superiors what he has found. If that happened, we would have a problem, a big one. You've been taught some driving skills by the FBI, I assume?"

"Yes, I've had a couple of courses."

"Fine. As it turns out, that little car Mick rented was a good choice. Comfortable with it?"

"I've not driven it enough to know yet, but it seems perfect for high speed work."

"Here's what I want to do. Let's get in the car as if we were heading home. After a couple of blocks, pick up the speed, and we'll find out if they are playing tag. If they are, you should use your driving skills to leave them. After we're sure they aren't behind us, we are going to head toward Munich. Once on the Autobahn, you can drive as fast as you feel comfortable."

"What are we going to do in Munich?" April asked, her pupils widening.

"That's the part you aren't going to like. I'll tell you on the way, if we get that far," said Triska.

After they were seated and buckled in, April started the car, and they both looked around, trying to spot any interested party. "You might as well start moving, April, and I'll keep watch," Triska said. The little car lurched forward as April settled in, trying to get a feel for what she was about to do. "Turn left up ahead, and we'll head north," Triska ordered. After several blocks, Triska made a "tisk, tisk" sound and nodded to herself. "Got him. Black Mercedes, two cars back. Ahead, take a hard right, no signal, and speed up." April complied, studying her rearview mirror intently. "No…he's still there," Triska noted. "This time we'll be turning left. I'll tell you when. Then takeoff like you mean it," Triska said, her eyes not leaving the mirror.

The left turn was executed suddenly, and the little car sharply accelerated as did April's pulse. "Left!" Triska commanded, and there was a squeal of tires as the car dug into the turn. "Left again!" she bellowed, still watching her mirror. "Our pursuer isn't an amateur," she noted without emotion. April realized that they were attracting attention by moving much faster than the other traffic, and occasionally, they garnered angry horns or hard stares. If a traffic policeman stopped them, she was bound to be arrested. "Next right, take it hard," Triska commanded, and the car complied, shaking its tail loose momentarily before gaining traction and speed.

"Take this next roundabout, April. We will head toward the Robinson Barracks and see what they are going to do." The road sign read *Roter Stich,* and in the distance, April saw the American Flag hovering above several buildings.

"Where are we, Triska?" she wondered.

"This is a U.S. Army base on our right. I'm trying to see if they will follow us in here. If they do, then they are from your country. If not…no, they dropped back. I don't see any sign of them behind us." April slowed the car to avoid attention from the authorities, and they glided by the base, headed north.

"We may have lost our tail temporarily," Triska said. They continued north toward highway 10-27 which headed back south, toward Munich. After turning onto the large divided highway, April felt more comfortable, and they settled in for a long drive.

"How long is the trip to Munich?" April asked.

"Roughly one and a half hours. Depends on how fast you want to drive. When we turn onto the Autobahn you can, and should, drive as fast as is safe. They won't be expecting us to head south, so I think we can both relax for the time being."

"Now, can you tell me why we are going to Munich?"

There was a long silence as the car wove in and out of traffic, headed west and south, as the city of Stuttgart started to fade into scattered buildings. Finally, Triska said, "Mick married a girl named Anna, you know this part of his history, don't you?"

"He never really talks about it but, putting the pieces together, I know that she was killed by a bomb blast the day after their wedding. Other than that, I don't really know anything."

"She was a college student, and they met in a biergarten where she worked part-time. Her parents live in Munich, my son and his wife."

"No, I didn't know that. Your son? Are you close?"

"Alfred. In a formal way. We don't see each other much. He was raised by his father after the divorce. You see my career…well, it got in the way of our marriage. I was assigned to East Germany frequently when Alfred was young. We talk…that's about it. I never liked his wife. But my granddaughter, Anna, and I were very close. I loved that girl so much. After she died, Mick and I were drawn together, because we were all that was left for each other. Until you came into our lives, that is."

"You never said how all that is connected to this trip." April nudged.

"We are going to see them."

"Wait a minute, Triska!" April exclaimed and gave her a quick look. "How do they feel about Mick?"

"They have disowned him since Anna was killed. They haven't seen him since the wedding day."

"How do you expect they will feel about meeting his girlfriend? I'll be kicked out on my ear."

"Possibly, you will. Then again, they were wrong about Mick. It wasn't his fault that Anna died. The fault was with the CIA and the BND who were supposed to protect them. The killer was an old Stasi operative still under the employment of the KGB, or its nominal replacement. We…the BND…finally caught up to her last year."

"So you want them to accept me, because they were wrong about Mick?"

"Yes."

"I won't know what to say to them. 'Hi! I'm Mick's latest girlfriend and Anna's replacement! Can I be your new daughter?' Do you think that would work?"

"Don't be silly. Of course not. We have to take this a small step at a time."

"Why are we going there at all?" April said with some exasperation.

"For several reasons, but the first is that it will be a perfect place for you to hide. Even Peter wouldn't look for you there."

"And the rest?"

"It's about time this entire issue get resolved. It's breaking the family apart, and I won't stand for it another minute. They've even alienated poor Kurt, their only son. Kurt and Mick worked closely with the BND on some things, and Mick saved his life on one occasion."

"And, of course, there's Triska, who would like to make amends with the past. Am I close?" April asked.

"I have a lot to make up for, and there's little time left."

Chapter 10

Chapter 11

The In-Laws

It's just ahead, dear, on the left, three houses up," Triska said. "Don't act nervous, and let me do the talking," she advised. April parked at the curb, and they sat for a moment looking at the home. It was in the northwestern area of Munich on *Auenbruggerstraße*. A modest but orderly home on a small lot, undistinguished from its neighbors, with a well-groomed yard and a small two-car garage. If April squinted, she could almost make herself believe that they were in a suburb of any American city. Things looked familiar, ordinary, even welcoming, to her.

"What are their names again?" April asked.

"The last name is Michner, Alfred and Stella. You might want to call them '*herr*' and '*frau*' though, especially at first. Just be polite and follow my lead. Ready?"

"No, but here goes," she said as she opened the door and stretched from the long ride in a small cramped car. She followed Triska, looming above her like a trailing giant and feeling self-conscious about herself. Triska smiled, took a deep breath, and knocked on the door.

Momentarily, the door partially opened and a slightly portly man appeared. He was wearing a long sleeved white dress shirt over dark slacks, and he looked over his half-glasses at them, his head tilting from Triska to April, trying to comprehend who was standing on his stoop.

"Well, son, aren't you going to invite us inside?" Triska asked. Alfred snatched the door fully open with surprise showing on his face.

"*Mutter? Kann das sein?*"

"Of course it's me, Alfred. Who else do you know looks like your mother?"

"Please. Come in!" he said, and stood away from the door looking at them both as they came past him.

"And who is this, *Mutter?*" he said looking April over from head to toe.

"This is FBI Special Agent April Chauncy, *mein Junge*. April, this is my son Alfred." They shook hands politely but formally, looking at each other in a suspicious manner.

"*Mein gott, Mutter! Das FBI!* Am I being investigated?" Alfred exclaimed.

"No, no, Herr Michner," April said and laughed. "This is just a normal visit."

"April is a close friend, Alfred. I thought she should meet my son and his wife."

"Pleased to meet you, Fräulein. You may call me Alfred," he quickly said. "You seem too *begehrenswert*…attractive to be FBI."

"So I have been told," April admitted.

Alfred held up his finger and turned toward the back of the house. "*Mutti,Mutti*," he called. "Forgive me, Mother, but I also call Stella, *Mutti*, most of the time." He looked flustered, a bit confused as to what he should do with his guests.

"Alfred, the least you can do is to pretend to kiss your mother," Triska scolded.

"Please forgive, Mutter," he said and bent to kiss her on both cheeks. There was some rustling from the back room, and the door opened admitting a large but elegantly attired woman. She wore her hair partially braided and carefully sprayed in place. The golden hue of it attempting a youthful look that the rest of her made unconvincing. She quickly saw that two women had intruded on her home, one was the small but devious Triska, the other was glamorous enough to intimidate most women, even herself. She smiled politely, waiting to be introduced.

"Ah, Stella," Triska said with apparent heartfelt emotion. "You are looking so healthy and youthful. How do you manage it?"

Instead of an answer, Stella continued to appraise April, the greater threat to her dominance.

"Hello, *Frau* Michner," April said. "My name is April Chauncy. Please call me April." She extended her hand for a shake, and it was politely, but reservedly, taken by Frau Michner.

"Welcome, April. What brings you both to Munich?" Frau Michner asked.

"Catching up with family, Stella," Triska said and smiled in a non-threatening way.

"And you, April?" she asked.

"I'm with Triska. We are close friends," April said.

"*Fräulein Chauncy ist FBI,*" Alfred whispered at Stella, nodding toward April, which caused his wife to appraise April more carefully.

"*Bitte treten Sie ein und setzen Sie sich. Mama, Schnaps für unsere Gäste,*" Alfred said and waved them into the sitting room while Stella was left to pour the Schnapps.

"How very nice to see you again, Mother. What is the occasion?" Alfred said. He fussed with his pipe while waiting for her response.

Triska always had her own agenda, so Alfred wasn't all that surprised by her next blunt question. "Have you seen Kurt of late?" Alfred turned and looked toward her somewhat sharply, obviously a sensitive subject, and one he felt was not of her concern.

"What is that to you?" Stella asked from behind them.

"I just wondered if you will ever forgive any of us for doing our duty to the *Vaterland.* You remember whom I mean. The ones who put themselves at risk so that their countrymen may live and work in peace."

"Like the same ones who were not there to save our Anna? The ones who promised to be there for her and were not when she needed them?" Stella said, this time moving to the center of the room, her size dominating the group.

"Yes, I know that you are bitter about losing her. I lost her also. There has to be a day that the living are no longer punished about the past, forgiven, so that we can all move past mistakes and events that can't be changed," Triska said.

"*Mutter*, four years is not long enough to forget Anna," Alfred said.

"Of course not, Alfred. You should never forget Anna. None of us will, especially her husband of one day. He lives with her memory in a way that none of us can. He, above all of us, cannot forgive himself for her death but still you hate him for something that was not his fault. And poor Kurt. After you discovered that he was in the BND like his *Großmutter*, you couldn't forgive him either, then blamed me for your loss of both children."

"Is this why you are here, Triska? To castigate us in front of a stranger?" Stella asked.

"No, Stella, dear. I am here to make amends and to restore the family to what it should have been. You two are discarding a lot of happiness, and I am here to change that."

"We can forgive you, *Mutter*, even Kurt, never Mick," Alfred said.

"I'm going to tell you a secret, Alfred, something few people know, and I want you to think about it before responding," Triska said sternly, fixing them in her pale eyes. "Mick Grundy singlehandedly took out an entire nest of terrorist bombers. He killed every one of them by himself, and each one of them was about to blow up German citizens. He saved thousands of German lives that night, and he never got a single word of credit about it. On another night, he saved Kurt's life and was nearly killed himself while doing it. If you don't believe me, ask Kurt about it. The German people owe him a lot…more than we can ever repay, but instead, you know what we do? We hunt him like a dog and force him to hide like one. I'm ashamed of both of you the most, because he loved your daughter, Anna, more than you did yourselves. Anna chose him, loved him, and would have stayed with him her entire life. What do you think Anna would have wanted you to do? I'll tell you. She would want you to respect and love the man that she loved."

Alfred looked stunned and looked off into space while his eyes glistened over. He put down his pipe and wiped at his eyes with his sleeve. Stella never wavered from her position in the center of the room but looked as though she felt foolish standing there with nothing left to say. Triska had taken the fight out of them with one savage blow, striking right to the heart of the matter that had come between all of them since Anna passed away.

"We didn't know, *Mutter*," Alfred said as he rose from his chair. He crossed the room with his arms extended toward his small, frail but tough mother, and they hugged in silence. Alfred stood and turned toward April. "Sorry that you have to hear about our family tragedy, *Fräulein*. You shouldn't be a party to this."

"Oh, but she should, Alfred," Triska said. Alfred had moved to stand with his wife, embracing then facing Triska and April waiting on the next blow.

"April works with Mick. They were in Berlin several months ago working together and working in unison with the BND and the CIA. She is an experienced agent and well-respected by everyone, especially Mick Grundy. We discovered by luck that Mick was born in Germany by a German mother and is a half brother to Peter Koffman. He is in Berlin right now working on a problem about

Iranian terrorists. He will undoubtedly be placing his own life on the line for America and for Germany, and when it is over, live or die, he will get no credit or even mention of it from any of us."

That was the final straw, and Alfred leaned against his wife openly crying, sobbing against her shoulder, holding on to her for support.

"What can we do, Triska, to make this right?" Stella asked, wiping at her own tears.

"I need to know that I can trust you both before saying anything else," Triska answered.

"Of course, you can trust us, *Mutter*," Alfred said. "What is it that we must do?"

"I need you to let us stay with you for a few days. We can all get to know each other during that time. That's all I want."

"*Sicherlich, Mutter.* We are proud to have you both stay here," they both chimed.

"One last thing, *meine Kinder*. You can tell no one, not a single person, that we are here."

Chapter 12

Rendezvous in Berlin

The road sign read *Kurfürstenstr.* Mick slowed the motorcycle, lifting his dark visor, and looked around before pulling to the curb. This was the place he wanted. As usual, Zeskie had picked a rendezvous in a completely unlikely spot. This time it was a gay bar on an out-of-the-way street south of the center of Berlin. He could hear pulsating loud music reaching the street, and two slender men in loose clothing loitering around the entrance were watching him with interest. He sat for a moment, hoping that Zeskie would show up on the street and save him from entering the bar. Six minutes after, his watch said. Zeskie was always on time, always. Mick sighed and began to remove his helmet with one hand as the other shut off his machine. A male couple slowly passed him, looking him over studiously. They lingered at the doorway to the bar for a moment, looking back his way. One last look around assured Mick that Zeskie must already be inside, and he slowly made his way to the door.

"Suchen Sie für eine Aktion, hübscher Junge?" someone said. Mick turned to look at one of the young men hovering near the entrance. He had a lock of hair brushed over one eye and was wearing lipstick.

"Treffen einen Freund," Mick said and reached for the handle of the door, trying to avoid eye contact with the two men.

"Sein Name ist Ron?" one asked.

"Kennen Sie ihn?" Mick said, looking at them with more interest.

"Zweiter Stock, Zimmer 6. Er wartet dort auf Sie." the man said and

Chapter 12

winked at him knowingly.

Mick winked back and pushed the door open. A wave of noise, a mixture of laughter, conversation, and thumping music, washed over him while he attempted to see into the dark room. He moved to one side, holding his helmet under his arm, and leaned into the wall while his eyes adjusted. Above the bar there was a long line of pictures of men engaged in various sexual activities, some photographs, some drawings. The corners of the room were sparsely lit by single candles, leaving deep shadows where movement could only be assumed, not seen. It was the kind of environment that Mick feared the most, where an assailant could hide in plain view and where the normal laws of the jungle, detection by motion, smell or noise, was masked by human chaos and where his trained reflexes were of little use. There were at least three groups of men and also scattered couples spread out in the room, and some of their eyes were fixed on the newcomer, waiting for his next move. Mick pressed his back firmly against the wall, reassuring himself that his pistol was still there. Eventually, he could discern two doors, one leading to the toilets, the other to the stairs on the far side of the room. With a last look around, he started moving toward the door to the stairs, feeling many eyes following him.

The staircase was black with the only light source coming from the end of a long hall upstairs. Mick felt his way along, trying to keep his footing off center to minimize squeaks from the loose treads. Room six, he recalled the man saying as he tried to read markings on the brown doors after coming to floor level. The room numbers were either long gone or had never been applied. He counted doors from the forward part of the hall, the one overlooking the street, stopping in front of the sixth. He tapped lightly and stood to one side of the door, almost expecting it to erupt with holes and splinters from gunfire.

"Come," the voice inside said. Mick turned the knob and pushed, the other hand on the grip of his pistol. Ron Zeskie was sitting on the bed, open briefcase beside him.

"You mean you still haven't taken your clothes off?" Mick said and continued into the room.

"Later," he said, not smiling. "You are a little late. I was worried that you were afraid to come in."

"In truth, I was. Could you have, perhaps, met with me at a luxury hotel?"

"This place is as safe as you can get. Those men downstairs have been bribed and coddled by us, and they keep a watch out for strangers. Did you feel it?"

"They were watching me for certain. For what purpose, I wasn't sure." Mick said.

"Where is April?" Zeskie asked, eyebrows raised.

"I left her in Stuttgart with Triska, just like we planned. You know that."

"April isn't in Stuttgart. Did she phone you?" Zeskie asked.

Mick sat down heavily, looking ahead in thought. "Can your people check out the Stuttgart BND? Peter Hoffman was acting a little strange. This could be his doing."

"That's how I know April and Triska are missing. Peter called me. He doesn't know a thing and is concerned about them."

"How secure are our phones?" Mick asked.

"Good, as far as detection outside of the CIA. All calls are recorded, monitored, transcribed and submitted for review. I have supervisory status and decide what goes to Washington. But…"

"But, you are not one hundred percent sure that there isn't some back door channel? Right?" Mick guessed.

"Right. Sure, not positive."

"I would be worried except Triska is in charge. She is very capable, and she has had a lifetime of hiding from her adversaries.

Her only liability is that she is with a strikingly attractive woman."

"Don't worry about April Chauncy. She can hide behind her beauty. It's like being hypnotized by a lethal cobra. The victim can't see the strike coming until it's too late," Zeskie said.

Mick looked at Zeskie for a moment before asking, "How did you come to that conclusion?" He wanted to ask if they had ever had a relationship, April and Zeskie. His tone said it for him.

"Don't even think that," Zeskie laughed. "I read her file, and I met her before you did. When she looks right at a man, he stops thinking straight. Doesn't she do that to even you?"

"Sometimes. Certainly when she wants to," Mick admitted.

"You know which of your people we can trust?" Mick asked, changing the subject.

"Running an organization like this is done by loyalty. There is a feeling of working for your country, for its way of life. Then there is fear. No one ever knows everything or why certain things are done, whom to fully trust or who is watching. People under me will do exactly what I say and will ask no questions. Largely, the CIA works outside the States, and only the Director is supervised by the politicians at home. At this moment in American history, our Director is a loyal patron of the President and his appointees. We can expect that he will do their bidding. Out in the field, we only report to our superiors, and they report to theirs. You never go above your superior. In Europe, I am the top man. I have the final say of what goes to the Director."

"And still you won't fully trust them, will you?" Mick asked.

"I can use them and not trust them. It's enough."

"What about the BND? Are they a resource for us?"

"They have their own agenda. At times, our activities support each other, other times, not at all. We have to go with some caution there. It will be a need to know only situation."

"Ready to fill me in on what you expect me to do?" Mick

asked.

"There is a *hoseiniyeh*, or Islamic center, just south of Berlin Tegel airport. It is privately funded, that much we know, and has an Imam as director. Most hoseiniyeh are staffed by Mullah's and are used for education and gatherings. This one is Shia Islam and has gathered a larger than expected following. Most of the Islamic followers in Germany are of Turkish origin, and most of them are Sunni. We will choose to ignore them for the present. Tegel airport has five flights a day to and from Tehran, and the center I mentioned is only eight kilometers from the airport. There is heavy traffic between the two. The Germans have also been watching but have legal restrictions on investigation into religious activities just like we do at home. Both agencies believe that the local Imam is directed by Iran and is the principle link between Tehran and key people in the U.S."

"Just shoot him," Mick suggested.

"We might do that someday, but we want to find out a few things first. What is the reason or the mechanism by which he controls his puppets in Washington? Is it religious indoctrination, money or just blackmail? And, who, exactly, are they, and how does the link work? We need to know these things first before any containment plan is conceived."

"And my own government is hunting me to prevent me from helping," Mick observed.

"Exactly. Someone is afraid of your methods, your lack of respect for protocol and law. Your methods are the ones our enemies use themselves so they know how effective you can be."

"I'm willing to get involved, but I can't see how I can help in any way. I don't speak the language, don't know anything about Islam, plus I don't even have the protection of my own country," Mick said.

"You know people who know people," Zeskie said quietly.

"I know some from the BND, as you do. Is that what you meant?"

"No. People from the other side, our former and present enemies."

"Can't you just say what you mean, Zeskie? Why all this hinting around. Get to the point."

"Dammit, Mick. You are not that dense!" Zeskie said sharply.

Mick couldn't place what Zeskie was inferring. He had no friends with the Russians, that was for sure. There wasn't anyone else…except…Triska! She knew people, he had memorized the list she gave him. Those were from the other side, at least at one time, and they still might have many contacts from the old days.

"I have to ask, Zeskie. How did you know about Triska and her contacts?"

"Remember the CIA? We also go way back."

"So you knew that I would go see Triska, leave April with her, and she would give me some contacts from her days in East Germany?"

"How am I doing so far?" Zeskie chuckled.

"Couldn't you just ask Triska yourself?"

"She would never disclose names of individuals that we have been searching for years to find. Never. She would only disclose those to a family member that she trusted. And that's you."

"Didn't your people develop their own contacts? Why are these different?"

"Ours were double agents. The list you memorized were the real thing. They never turned, and the KGB had no reason to suspect them, because they were actually loyal. Our old contacts have largely been wiped out over the years, but this bunch were and are survivors. They would help Triska, because she often helped them, and they know people on the other side who are themselves well-connected. It's the other side of the spider web.

And you… you are unique, Mick. You speak many foreign languages like a native, and you can blend in to any environment."

"As I understand your plan, Zeskie, you want me to make friends with former and current Soviet era espionage agents and enlist their help to help bring down an Iranian-American network."

"Yes."

"Why would they do that? Why would they help me, an enemy of Russia, go against the current alignment of Russia's interests in the Mid East?"

"They, above all people, understand that the current Russian policy of assisting Iran will backfire, and it will cause eventual foment in the Muslim satellite countries of the former Soviet Union. The current Russian policy is about short-term gains against the West, ignoring the long-term consequences. Triska's friends might help us, but we need a mechanism to enlist their aid and that would be you."

"What exactly do you expect this bunch of elderly spies to do for our cause?" Mick said, somewhat sarcastically.

"We'll have to wait and see, won't we?" Zeskie returned.

"What do you want me to do next?"

Without answering in words, Zeskie retrieved a thick brown envelope from his briefcase and tossed it beside Mick. Mick opened it, also without comment, and spilled its contents on the bed. New identities, cash in three currencies as well as new identification badges spilled out.

"It's a variety of goodies for you, Mick. Some might be useful, especially if you have to cross borders or hide for some reason. I saved the best for last," he said and tossed another envelope on the bed beside the clutter. This one contained two passkeys, the kind that upscale hotels use, which are otherwise unmarked. A small slip of paper identified the locations. "I thought you deserved to sleep in a clean bed for awhile, as long as it lasts. Move back and forth between these two locations, and as time goes by, we will have others lined up for you."

"Thanks, I think," Mick said. "Now give me the rest of it."

"There are no orders, no plan. Contact Triska's people and go from there. Oh, one last thing," Zeskie said and pulled out a fobbed key. "Here is a nice car for you. Leave the bike in the garage where you pick up the car. It will be safe there, when and if you need it."

"I don't like cars. Too easy to follow and track," Mick said, ignoring the car key.

"A motorcycle is also limiting. You can't easily wear a suit while riding. You need both, I'm afraid." Reluctantly, Mick put the car key in his pocket. As usual, Zeskie had a good point. It would increase his range of options.

"Now are you going to take off your clothes?" Mick asked seriously.

"If I did, April would have my skin. No, thanks, but I appreciate the offer," Zeskie said and offered his hand for a shake.

Chapter 13

Grotten...An Old Spy

Mick pulled up in front of the shabby hotel and looked around before dismounting from his motorcycle. Even for Berlin, this entire block was seedy. Parts of East Berlin never had risen to equal the West, and it was evident in the peeling paint and broken windows seen up and down the narrow street. Paper and litter lined the gutter making the demarcation with the broken sidewalk difficult to differentiate. There was always the sensation of being watched in these areas, not by police or spies, but by desperate, disadvantaged souls who had few choices except to live my any means possible.

The lobby was dark, dirty and smelly as well as small. Two plastic chairs were by the only evident source of illumination, the narrow window looking out at the street. No one seemed to be behind the counter, in fact, there was no one in sight. Mick rang the bell and waited. A distant mechanical noise made him look over at the small elevator, and through the glass doors, he could see movement as the elevator descended, slowly coming into view. When the door opened a large-boned, fat woman emerged, tugging an old sweater into place, her unusually red-tinted hair stuck out at odd angles. She took another drag of her cigarette and looked Mick up and down before briefly disappearing to emerge behind the counter. She gazed at Mick with cold, pitiless eyes, waiting to hear why he was visiting this decaying place at the end of the world.

"Ich brauche, um eine Nachricht für Grotten verlassen... Sagen Sie ihm, dass sein Zug ist endlich gekommen." [I need to leave a message... for

Grotten. Tell him that his train has come at last.] Mick's voice had the usual impact, and the woman shuddered visibly as he spoke, his voice seeming to come from an otherworld creature, one which was slimy, poisonous, croaking at her from a deep dark cave, the creature which always hid under your bed or in your closet.

She put her hand to her mouth, and her eyes widened. This was a phrase that she hadn't heard in many years, but one that she had locked in memory, the same memory which recalled the march of boots toward her door in the middle of the night. A memory associated with fear and violent, secret death. Her eyes quickly searched the room as she stepped away from the counter. She had learned to fear the deliverer as well as the recipient of such messages.

"*Ich werde liefern Ihre Nachricht. Er wird wissen wollen, wie wir Sie erreichen,*" [I will deliver your message. He will want to know how to contact you,] she said, her voice cracked from fear as well as a lifetime of cigarettes and rivers of Vodka.

"*Ich werde zurückkehren. Wie lange noch?*" [I will return. How long?]

"*Morgen. Kannst du morgen wieder?*" [Tomorrow. Can you return tomorrow?]

Mick nodded agreement then decided to add a last comment, this time in Russian. This woman was left over from the time when Russians were in charge, requiring their German lackeys to do most of the dirty work of spying. He wanted to see if she recalled the old relationship.

"*Rasskazhite Grotten, chto staryy drug, malen'kaya zhenshchina, nazval.*" [Tell Grotten that an old friend, a small woman, has called.]

"*Konechno, ser.*" The woman understood and answered in Russian. Their eyes met, and hers were subservient, fearing to look at him yet fearing to look away, lest she appear guilty of something.

Mick rode away, his motorcycle in a hurry to depart from the hidden forest of eyes watching from dark corners. After a few blocks of sudden acceleration and hard turns, he relaxed and moved in line with the traffic, watching in his rear-view mirrors for any sign of a tail but spotting none. For the next two hours he rode like this, periodic bursts of speed followed by frantic turns, nearly at the limit of adhesion of the tires, until he was certain that there could be no possible followers, then he slowed to escape notice, blending into the normal city traffic, obeying all laws. The little garage arranged by Zeskie and his team was in a quiet residential neighborhood, a place few would ever notice, even the locals. On the third pass, he hit the button in his pocket, and the garage door opened, admitting his motorcycle, and immediately started closing behind him.

A grey Mercedes sat waiting for him, impressive yet invisible in Berlin traffic amid thousands of similar cars. Mick took off his leathers and carefully hung them above his parked motorcycle. He put on clothing from one of the leather suitcases, selecting a casual but expensive outfit that would demand respect in any posh hotel in Berlin. His enemies would likely search alleys for him, overlooking the more ostentatious world he was about to enter. The old theory of hiding in plain view had always been proven correct. He picked up the second, matching suitcase and placed it in the trunk of the Mercedes. Mick took a moment to study his reflection and adjust his bow tie. He would be French, demanding, presidential in bearing. A film director meeting with his writers, scouting locations for his latest movie.

He drove up to the entrance of the Ritz-Carlton and was immediately greeted by two lively attendants, both crisply dressed in tight grey uniforms. He gave each a ten euro tip to park his car, explaining that he was already registered, but allowing one of them to retrieve his single piece of luggage from the trunk. He carried his overcoat across his arm and walked straight to the elevator bank followed by the young man who carried his luggage.

"*Niveau dix*," he said to the operator.

Mick departed his room early the next morning, walking north on the broad avenue *Ebertstrasse*, toward the old Reichstag building, passing the Holocaust museum. He was dressed in a loose, faded sweater over jeans, this time just another working citizen of Berlin on his way to work. He passed a parked cab, its driver enjoying a quick breakfast until Mick tapped on the window.

"*Prenzlauer Berg?*" Mick asked, waiting for the driver's response. The man shrugged, but started the car, clearly not really wanting to go to that sector of Berlin but also willing to collect a fare. Things hadn't changed that much since the Wall came down. East was still East.

"*Sie haben ein Geschäft in Prenzlauer Berg?*" the cabbie asked, appraising Mick from his rear-view mirror. It was an area of Berlin avoided by most who knew about the frequent reports of violence and muggings near there.

"*Nur kurz, Sie können mich danach wieder hier zu fahren,*" Mick assured him, got in and waved him to start the short journey. It was a light traffic day, and the trip was accomplished quickly. Mick directed the cab to the curb in front of the old hotel and patted the driver's shoulder before exiting. The street was deserted, as before, but Mick stood for a moment giving the area a careful inspection before moving beyond the cab. The watchers were still out there, many of them, but they had no faces.

This time, the woman was already behind the counter, waiting for him. Mick nodded an acknowledgement, and after unhurriedly surveying the room, approached the desk and waited, his eyes leveled at hers. She had seen his type many times before. The muscular, hardened spies from both sides whose cold eyes showed their willingness to kill for the slightest provocation. Men, such as the one who stood there now, were always glad to crush the helpless like an insect, never being troubled by their actions and never punished later for any crime. In her youth, she was attracted to this kind of man, the danger, the roughness, part of the mystery of romance. She had survived because of her healthy body, her gleaming smile, all long gone now. All she had left was her fear.

"Er sagte zu den Namen der Frau zu fragen, dem alten Freund," [He said to ask the name of the woman, the old friend,] the woman repeated. There was a hint of tremble in her hands as she waited for his response. She seemed to anticipate his big hands pulling her across the counter at any moment.

"Triska," Mick said.

That was the word she was waiting for, the only word which would work. *"Er wird mit Ihnen zu treffen. Wo und wann?"* [He will meet with you. Where and when?] Without words, Mick slid a small paper across the counter, and with a last hard look at her face, turned and strolled out toward the waiting cab. She picked it up, her hand shaking so much that she had to use both to read it.

"Bundestagskantine, в полдень сегодня. Спросите Герман." His note was written in Russian. She recognized at least one part…the location. It was to be in the old Reichstag building, in the canteen. The rest was gibberish. She watched the cab speed away and then went to the door to make sure the man was gone.

"Gib mir die Nachricht," a raspy voice said as a speckled hand reached around her and snatched it from her hand, causing her to jump, startled, because she didn't know he was present. She turned to face him, his bald head tilted toward his note before looking up to meet her eyes with his. Gruber Dorff still frightened her, even after all these years around him. He reeked of cheap Schnapps and cheaper cigarettes, and his worn black suit was flecked with food and dust. Still, there was something dreadful about his intensity. The lines of his face were drawn in dark charcoal, and his tight,

purplish lips made his expression frozen, reflecting the effort of his life of subterfuge and hiding. After the Stasi dissolved, he had no place to go, no further demand for his only skill, and no pension. He lived some of his days around the old hotel but was gone occasionally for weeks before silently reappearing as if nothing had changed. Margo never knew Dorff's origins. He seemed to be part Russian, part East German, at home in both worlds, at rest in neither. They had been lovers, briefly, but long ago, and she was happy when he moved on. She was always afraid that he would tell her too much one night, then realize his mistake.

"*Sie haben gesagt, dieser Mann sprach zu dir in der russischen auf den ersten Besuch. Hatte er einen Akzent?*" [You said this man spoke to you in Russian on the first visit. Did he have an accent?]

"*Nein,*" she answered.

"*Ist er Russe oder Deutscher?*"

She shrugged, "*Wie Sie. Beide oder auch nicht. Wer kann das wissen?*" [Like you. Both or either. Who can know?] Her answer troubled Dorff. He looked back at the paper again trying to glean the mystery of it. The man knows Triska, knew the password and where to find him, but speaks and writes fluent Russian. It didn't make any sense. Long ago, he and Triska had come to an agreement. They were on opposites sides of the Cold War, but each had respect for the other and, sometimes, that helped information flow across the Wall when they wanted it to. She had spared him as he had done for her…more than once. After East Germany fell to the West, Triska had withheld his name from her superiors. There was a debt incurred, and it appeared that it was coming due. He recalled that Triska frequently became Russian when her mission called for it. She was impossibly perfect, and the Russians bought her act down to the last curtain, never suspecting. Now this man. Was he Russian? The KGB's successors finally becoming aware of his and Triska's secret relationship? Or was he

German, simply fluent in Russian, another one of Triska's legion of spies? The man knew about him, where he could be found, and likely, where he lived. Dorff had to keep the meeting or run and hide again. There were no longer many places left to hide and no money left to hide with.

Chapter 13

Chapter 14

Out Of The Cold

The Reichstag, Berlin

The hard marble floor reflected sounds of his footsteps off polished walls and ceilings, adding a hollow rumble to the ambient noise. Looking around, Dorff could almost make himself hear echoes of Nazi troops stomping up and down these same halls. He was nervous, unusual for him, and this massive building, the former center of the Nazi Empire, lent an air of importance to his meeting. Not that the building nor its history cared a bit about an individual's insignificant problems. This granite and marble structure stood as a symbol of an entire nation, their achievements as well as their follies, and Dorff was but an intruding insect whose dust would soon blow away, leaving not a trace of his existence. Dorff shrugged. He had been in worse places, more dangerous circumstances, before. There was a time that people feared him…little, short, old Dorff. He laughed at the thought now. Everything about him was old, his clothing, his mannerisms, even his friends, the few that remained. Whatever Triska's man wanted from him, he couldn't imagine. Yes, Triska, he recalled, a smile forming on his old lips. What a tightly wound little beauty she had been back in the day. Those blue eyes! They could look into your soul, but you could never read her thoughts at all. She was what you wanted her to be, or more exactly, what she wanted you to want. Dorff recalled her small waist and her curvy hips and the way she would gracefully look toward him with hair that partially covered her face, making her eyes and lips all his mind could focus on. He was always happy to see her, even though, down deep, he suspected that she worked for the West. There was a mystery about her making him want to believe that she was actually on his side, only pretending to work for the other side. He wanted to believe her, trust her. Part of it was simple male lust for a pretty little package, one too expensive, too exotic, for his level of pay. A daydream…a very dangerous dream. Then again, she had saved his life once and his career another time. He owed her, and he always paid his debts. If only he could see her again, in the flesh. He sighed to himself as he turned the corner and saw the sign for the canteen ahead.

Dorff stopped at the canteen entry, blocking traffic, but methodically scanning the patrons and staff, looking at faces, but more importantly, eyes. One pair of deep set eyes had locked on his. There was no doubt that the owner was the man he was scheduled to meet. The man was already seated, his back to the wall, his coat unzipped making his weapon quickly available. The eyes were of a killer, a remorseless but intelligent and resourceful killer. Dorff had known many such men and was, at one time, one himself. This one was young, fit, hard. As he closed the distance, pulled along by the eyes, he felt danger radiating from the man, an explosive force, out of sight for most, but not Dorff. The man had deep scars, one on the face, one on the neck, and a bigger one emanating from his soul.

Dorff stood beside the table, looking at Mick, wondering if he should have run instead. "Grotten," he said, giving his code name as a way of recognition. At first, the man made no response other than to look him up and down as if appraising a horse that was for sale.

"Speak English?" Mick asked.

"Yes," Dorff admitted.

"Then sit. You have found me," Mick said, indicating the chair opposite him with a nod.

"You know Triska?" Dorff asked, not really wanting to relax his caution yet.

"Triska is my grandmother. Sit. You are Dorff, are you not?" Mick inquired.

"Yes," Dorff nodded and pulled the chair out. The location was excellent and provided an unrestricted view of the entry door while having an exit in easy reach. The man was well-trained, whoever he was. "What is your name?" Dorff asked bluntly.

"You may call me Mick." The name seemed familiar to Dorff. He searched his memory, allowing his eyes to drift toward the ceiling, thinking. This was a name he recalled. There was much talk of a Mick, but he couldn't remember the context or the last name. Dorff sat down and, by force of training, studied his opponent carefully.

"What do you want of me," Dorff asked, his eyes searching for Mick's weapon, tracing the various bulges of Mick's clothing, trying to associate various shapes. He correctly guessed that Mick carried his weapon at the rear of his waist and wondered what caliber he would carry.

"I want to see if you want employment, what you think of working with me on a mission I have in mind."

"You know anything about me?" Dorff asked.

"*Stasi?*" Mick asked, knowing the answer. Dorff blinked. The answer was yes. He had been Stasi…in fact, a lifetime of working for the infamous East German intelligence agency. The same agency that spied not only on Americans but also their own East Germans, the agency that had several soccer arena-sized record warehouses of collected data on nearly every East German. He had been Stasi, but he was no longer proud of it.

"Once. What do think an old man can do for you?" Dorff

asked.

"You have any contacts with anyone still working?"

"There are some of us left. The ones I know now call themselves Russian, not Soviet. Is that all you want?"

"No. I want your skill. Triska said that you were once among the best."

"A compliment, for sure, coming from her. I was never sure which side she worked for. I'm still not sure," Dorff admitted. He continued to study Mick's craggy face and listen to his throaty voice, putting the two together. It was coming back to him. This fellow had been injured in a bomb blast meant to kill him. This man looking at him was none other than Mick Grundy. Dorff took a deep breath, but it was his eyes that gave him away.

"Yes. You remembered, didn't you? I am Mick Grundy. You are looking at me differently now, Dorff. You know my reputation, my past, but the question remains. Will you work with me?"

"I could sell you out to the Russians. There is rumor that they would like to get rid of you."

"True. You might even make a few euros on it. You aren't that kind of man, nor am I. We might kill an enemy, but we wouldn't sell him for a few coins. Would we?"

Dorff shook his head. It wasn't the way to do business, even spy business. "You can pay me for my help?" he asked.

"You will be paid by me personally. I do not represent the American government at the moment. In fact, they are also hunting for me. You may be at risk just sitting this close to me. Are you certain you weren't followed," Mick asked.

"Not even the famous Mick Grundy can follow me," Dorff said, smiling, showing his scattered remaining teeth. "Why are your people trying to find you?" he added.

"My government is full of people who think more highly of Iran's interests than their own. I want to break the link with Iran and root out its agents."

"And how is it possible that I can help?" Dorff asked, leaning forward and talking softly.

"I don't know enough yet to form a plan. Since the Russian leadership seems to be determined to help Iran create a nuclear arsenal, there still must be some who don't agree that it's a good idea. I wonder if they have thought through what will happen if the Islamic Chechen terrorists are given a nuclear device, or any of the other former Soviet satellites along their southern border. This cannot be allowed to happen."

"This has caused me some concern as well," Dorff admitted. "Russia is likely abetting a nuclear exchange in the Mid East, one which will diminish or eliminate the oil output from the area, and since Russia already has the Europeans feeding at the oil teat, they would expect to benefit from conflict."

"If everyone would come to their senses, nothing like this could happen. Tell me whom you know who might be interested in working outside the system," Mick asked.

Dorff became quiet, leaned back in his chair, studying the canteen, while either looking for listeners or thinking about Mick's question. He turned back to Mick and studied his face carefully. "It's not a question that I can answer right here. I have to talk to people and do it very very carefully. It might take some time, and it might be dangerous for me. You have to understand that I gave myself to a cause once before, one that seemed so important at the time, and here I am, abandoned and penniless. No matter how wonderful a cause sounds over a fine marble table, it comes down to brutality and killing in the end, and while you are fighting, you are losing something inside of you that you can't get back when the struggle is over, if it ever is. Yours is a good cause, but for me, in my remaining short life, it will make no difference. And nor will it for you, Comrade."

Chapter 14

"True, Dorff. On the other hand, neither of us has anything to lose any more, do we? They have been hunting me for years, and I have been living a life more suitable for a serpent than a man. You live better than I do, Dorff. While we are still alive, we should do something that matters, rather than just exist. We should do the right thing, even if we die doing it, and no one knows we did it."

"Fine for you, Mick Grundy. You may have your noble cause and mine too. Unfortunately, you will discover that there are no noble causes. Life on this planet will go on and on, ignoring what we do. We are insects, all of us, and our little sand piles will be washed away by time and destructive forces which we can't control."

"Then agree to help just for the thrill of it, Dorff. To bring back the memories of when you were young, and the excitement, the danger, was like a dish of ice cream. You eat it and want more."

"No, Grundy, I am past all that just like I am past lusting over women. I am too old to live that way again."

"Is there nothing I can do or say to convince you?"

"I'll do it for money, Grundy, but it has to be enough."

Mick held Dorff in his eyes for a long moment before reaching into his jacket. He put a thick roll of bills on the table without comment. "A down payment, Dorff. There's going to be more later. You must know, though, that I am not someone who forgets and forgives."

"I have heard of you, Mick Grundy. You will pursue an enemy to hell, and you never hesitate to take your revenge. You can trust me if I work for you, but I haven't decided to come with you yet," Dorff pushed the wad back toward Mick. He needed the money, badly needed it, but he was not about to be pushed into such a project without some thought and not until he discussed the idea with the right people. Likely, the same people who would like to settle scores with Mick Grundy. This would have to be done surgically, one cut and one suture at a time.

"Keep the money, Dorff. I know you need it. Consider it payment for this meeting and no further obligations attached," Mick said and pushed the wad back again. This time, Dorff smiled his gap-toothed smile as the wad smoothly disappeared into his loose clothing.

"How can I contact you?" Dorff asked. "Do you have a place that you are staying?"

"I move around just like you probably would. It would be trusting you too far to tell you where, wouldn't it?"

"A drop then?" Dorff suggested. The old methods that Dorff had been trained to use and did use so many times in the past still worked when done properly.

As if waiting for Dorff to offer this method, Mick pulled out a small metal cylinder and tossed it to him. "Place this in the soil on the north side of the monument above the *Tiergartentunnel*, not far from here. I'll get it."

"Funny that you are using that particular spot," Dorff said. "We often used that one. It's almost under the nose of the American Embassy, and they still watch it."

"We are better than they are. It's so brazen that they will never see us," Mick said.

Dorff laughed hard enough to start coughing, the old cigarette habit still punishing him. "You really play the game! Perhaps I would enjoy doing this with you," he said. "But I need to think this over. You understand." He raised his eyebrows as if to enlist Mick's support. Mick understood, all right. Dorff was going to see which side paid highest for the least risk. It was all about money.

"Remember, Dorff, that Triska is involved. It isn't simply about the money. She will take it personally if you sell me out."

This reminder made Dorff's artificial smile fade. He did remember what happened to those who crossed Triska. They died horribly, extensively tortured, then burned alive. He had even seen the remains of one, and the image of that face frozen in a last scream still made his stomach ache. He never knew if Triska had acted alone or just used some of her many, willing minions. The burned bodies were a message that she was not to be crossed, and she never forgot. Dorff suddenly changed his mind. "I owe Triska, so I'll never sell you out, Grundy. You can count me in, but I still have to put out feelers, and when I do, there is risk for both of us. I would surmise that the Russians don't yet know you are in Berlin, but at some point, they will discover that you are. If I associate my name with yours, they'll come for both of us."

"Your contacts should be told only that Russia is being put at risk, because Iran is arming, and their nuclear weapons will spread beyond their borders with catastrophic results. Call me a rogue agent from the U.S., if you will, but don't give my actual name to them. I will do that later, if they are interested. Your contacts have to understand that all of us will be working outside of any system of government, in fact, in spite of our governments."

"Is there any money in your pocket for them?" Dorff asked.

"No, Dorff. They'll have to do it for Mother Russia, not money."

Chapter 15

Family

Auenbruggerstraße Munich, The Michner Home, 0700 hours

Alfred and Stella sat on one side of the table, April and Triska on the other. Breakfast was prompt, and on time, as expected for this well-run home. They had accepted April and were gracious and correct…but…there remained a wall of unspoken issues. April was sleeping in the guest room, Anna's, and her things were still there, as was the essence of her, the posters, the clothing, the very bed that she had slept in. Strangely, April grew to accept Anna, to think of her as a person not as a competitor. Two photographic portraits of Anna hung in the living room, capturing a radiant young girl, healthy and full of promise. April could easily understand the Michners' grief and how they could blame Mick for her loss. Mick had been true to Anna's memory and beyond doubt still loved her and always would. He and April had known each other for months before they shared their first kiss. More intimacy than a kiss had required being thrown together in a life or death struggle, yet even then, it was difficult for Mick. April realized that Anna couldn't be replaced by anyone, but Mick could learn to love again after all. A fresh new love, one that didn't want to remove Anna from his heart, would do it. What he said repeatedly was genuinely true, that he couldn't lose another woman that he loved. Living with Anna's relatives made April understand Mick better than she ever could have without it.

Stella looked up while buttering her toast, "Kurt is coming this morning. Have you met Kurt, April?" They both watched her face, waiting on her answer.

"At the BND headquarters in Berlin after our last mission," she answered.

"You remember that he couldn't take his eyes off of you?" Triska prodded, her mouth partially full of food.

"I remember."

"I can see why, April," Alfred said. "You are a very lovely woman, and the more I am around you, the more it strikes me."

"It would, Alfred. Now behave yourself. She already is aware of her effect on men, I'm sure," Stella warned, patting his arm.

"Does Mick ever mention Anna?" Alfred asked. His wife looked his way sharply but kept silent.

"It's painful for him to talk about her. He did tell me more than once that he dreams about her every night. I don't bring the subject up with him for that reason," April said.

"Anna was such a wonderful girl…" Stella started to say, then stopped with tears welling up. Alfred pulled her head to his shoulder and patted her back lovingly. He looked across at April and shook his head. They had to stop talking about Anna.

Stella drew herself together and blew her nose. She took a long drink of coffee, and her face became more unreadable. She looked at April, gathering her thoughts for a question that she wanted to ask.

"Careful, Stella," Triska warned. "Don't ask what you don't want to know about." Triska had been waiting for this moment, knowing that it would eventually surface. Though, right now was as good a time as any, she thought, and we all might as well crash ahead and get it over with. "I'm sorry, dear. Go ahead with your thoughts. I won't interfere," Triska said.

"April, there are some things I wonder about. Could I ask?" Stella began.

"I know where this is going, Stella. You both have been kind to me. I feel privileged to share your home and your lives. Of course, you may ask me any question, however personal," April said. She also knew this moment would arrive eventually.

"We haven't seen Mick since their wedding night, but as I recall, he is very handsome." Stella paused to see if there were any comments, then continued. "And, as my husband has pointed out, you are more than attractive yourself." She paused again, looking back and forth at the two pairs of female eyes across from her. They all knew the direction Stella was headed.

"You want to ask if Mick and I are close, even lovers, don't you?" April said what was hanging in the air. She took a deep breath, delaying answering what they already knew in their hearts. "I love Mick Grundy, and I have since nearly the first time I met him. It took a lot longer for him to love me. He felt that he was betraying Anna if he even looked at another woman. On our last mission, there was an impossibly beautiful Russian woman who threw herself at Mick over and over, but he never succumbed to her."

"What happened to the Russian woman? Is she still pursuing him?" Alfred asked.

"I shot her."

"It's more complicated than that my children. Don't take her answer like it sounds," Triska said. Nevertheless, April's answer caused Stella and Alfred to put down their forks. They saw April with different eyes now. Triska and April inhabited a world that couldn't be easily understood by those on the outside. A world where death and violence was commonplace and risk was everywhere.

"Then you know my next question," Stella said with leveled

eyes.

"The answer is yes, Stella. I hope this doesn't offend you in any way," April said.

"Before either one of you answer her, I want to say something," Triska said. "I love this girl beside me. She isn't Anna or a replacement for Anna, she is a different person entirely. I love her, because she is April Chauncy, and she is worth loving, and I love her because Mick Grundy loves her, and I love him as well. I tricked her into coming here so that, I hoped, you would come to love her and she you. Silly old woman, aren't I? What I want most in my remaining years is to have my family, all of them, back in my life. I consider Mick and April part of me, and I hoped you would feel that way also. You both have been missing out in life by letting the past blot out your mind. Please, I beg you, let it go." Triska choked with tears for the first time in a very long time. She blotted at her old faded eyes with her dinner napkin, the bony, speckled hand clutching it, giving away her advancing years.

Triska's little sermon had the intended effect, and it brought her son and daughter-in-law to tears, as it did April. For a moment, the four dabbed at their faces, sniffed and blew their noses, and just as quickly, someone started to laugh at the sight, and they all followed by laughing, quietly, reservedly at first, then uproariously, as they stood together holding on to each other, their heads touching in a circle, their bodies shaking from laugher.

Alfred swooped his small mother up in his arms and twirled around the room, their noses in contact, their smiles lighting the room. "Oh, Mother!" he exclaimed. "How I've missed your bluntness. You've always watched over all of us like a predatory bird in the sky, and you always seem to know what's best for us. I love you, Mother." Alfred started tearing again and put his mother down.

"Then you accept all three of us, April and Mick included, back in your lives?" Triska asked, her small wrinkled face returning to being serious.

"Of course, Mother. We needed our family back again, you and Kurt, and we are most appreciative to have two new family members! This gives us a chance to be grandparents some day," Alfred said, winking at April.

"Well, Grandfather Alfred, not so fast!" April said, raising her hand. "There is a small problem first. Mick hasn't asked me to marry him yet, and he may never do it."

"Don't worry about that April," Triska grinned her sly conspiratorial look while winking her eye knowingly. "Together, you and I can handle Mick Grundy…wait and see."

They all felt relieved to have the past behind them and the future ahead of them as they adjourned to the sitting room to wait for Kurt. A few moments, a carefully thought-out speech, had made all the difference, and suddenly all of them were related as strongly as by blood. April could feel that she was being thought of as not just a beautiful interloper but with pride for what she was as a person, not only how she looked, but also what she thought. She had been raised by her mother and her stepfather, who had little time for this product of a former marriage. Their attitude had been a blessing in disguise, because it forced independence on her, and it helped her to be above all the fawning and gushing about her beauty. Alfred, Stella and Triska suddenly felt like her real parents and grandparent. The love coming from them was a sensation she had never previously experienced, and it was wonderful.

"Triska, you said that you tricked me into coming here. Weren't we being watched and followed?" April asked. She watched as Triska squirmed in her seat, wanting to avoid this discussion.

"Only in our minds," Triska admitted.

"So no one is hunting us?"

"Of course, they are. They just haven't found us yet."

"What about Peter Koffman? Is it true that Mick can't trust him?"

Triska took a deep breath. "BND Director Weisman is an old friend. I helped train him when he was starting. Peter knows this."

"You mean, he wouldn't dare turn on his brother?"

"That's what I mean, but I don't think he ever actually would. He has a lust for advancement, but he only has one brother. He'll be the same old Peter when his head clears."

A knock on the door made everyone jump. Kurt was expected, and the door had been left unlocked for him, but knocking on the front door of his parents' home was out of character. Alfred got up, looking concerned, and headed toward the door. April got up as well, heading for the bedroom and her weapon. Loud voices behind her were of gladness and greeting, and she relaxed, leaving the pistol under her pillow. When she returned, she saw a young couple standing awkwardly beside Alfred, who looked a bit surprised and perplexed. Kurt was changed. No longer a clean-cut boy, he now looked more as if he was a budding rock star, complete with long hair and facial stubble. The girl beside him was dressed to show her figure, and her long blonde hair cascaded past her waist. She had a knowing look, one that gave her away as being too sure of herself, her poise indicating that she felt protected by her youthful beauty.

When April came into the room, Kurt's jaw fell open and his eyebrows raised. *"Ich erinnere mich an Sie!"* he said, stammering a bit as he took her in.

"We are speaking English, Kurt," Triska commanded from the couch.

Kurt looked at his female companion and back toward April. The difference was between cute and world-class. April was a powerful presence when she wanted to be, and at this moment, she very much wanted to be noticed.

"We met previously, Kurt," she said, watching their faces as she drew closer. Before Kurt could regain his footing, April came up to him and kissed him softly on one cheek, then stepped back and smiled charmingly. It was much like churning an ant bed with a stick. The young woman lost her look of self-assuredness and put her arm in Kurt's, both to restrain him and for protection from this unknown woman.

"Your name is April!" he remembered. "Is Mick also here?" he said, looking quickly around.

"He's at least in Germany, just not here. How good to see you again!" she said in a mellow voice. The soft timbre of her words poured over Kurt like sweet syrup, sticking his eyes on her lips as she spoke. His cute companion was growing red in the face. Her previous pleasant visage had been morphed into a Melpomene.

"And you are?" April asked the young lady, while extending her hand.

"Greta. Greta Baddor," the girl said but hesitated to shake April's hand which was slowly withdrawn. Kurt glanced at Greta without hiding his displeasure of her.

"What, if I may ask, are you doing here of all places?" Kurt asked April.

"Frankly, Kurt, I feel as if I'm visiting relatives. They are all so nice to me."

"Forgive me, Mother, Father, Grandmother," Kurt remembered, hugging each in turn before his head involuntarily turned back to regard April.

"Are you some sort of actress?" Greta asked, hoping that she was married with six children or had an infectious disease.

April laughed and held her palms up, shrugging her shoulders in a way that no German could do. *"Comment saviez-vous? Avez-vous vu un de mes films?"*

"I don't speak French," Greta retorted. "What did she say, Kurt?"

"She confirmed that she is an actress and asked if you had seen any of her movies."

Greta looked as if she wanted to throw up her breakfast, and she resumed hanging onto Kurt's arm.

Watching this exchange with a glimmer of humor on his face, Alfred decided to intervene, perhaps hoping to save Greta from herself. "We are pleased to meet you, Greta," he said. "Can you and Kurt stay for lunch? You might know that we haven't seen him for some time, and we have to catch up, as you might expect."

Kurt could see her wishes written in her eyes. What Greta wanted most was to get Kurt away from April as fast as she could.

"We are expected somewhere this morning and can't stay. Sorry," Kurt said to Greta's relief.

"Oh, Kurt!" Stella said. Her face reflecting her disappointment. Kurt held her and whispered something in her ear, then kissed her on her cheek. He and Greta left as rapidly as they had come, and on the way out, Greta regained much of her self-confidence.

"He's going to come back," Stella said, after the door closed.

"That was some display, April," Alfred said. "You chased her away and yet were pleasant to her." He seemed happy to see the young girl go.

"I didn't mean to cause them any trouble, but the fewer people who know where I am right now, the better," April answered.

"Greta was right, though, about you, April," Triska said. "You set his head spinning with just one look at you. Kurt would follow you around like a puppy if you let him."

"Triska, can I ask if Kurt is still…working…you know?" April asked.

"Alfred, Stella, you can be trusted on this?" Triska asked her son and daughter.

"Sure, Mother. You can trust us," Alfred said.

"Kurt is undercover with the BND. Always has been since secondary school. He has become one of the best they have. You noticed that he didn't comment on April being on any wanted list, and you can be sure he knew about it. We can trust this boy and be proud of him."

Chapter 15

Chapter 16

Colonel Dvorkin

Mick had picked the spot himself, and he was there first. He chose a little Russian Cafe on *Samariterstraße* in the *Fredrickshain* district, because it was a place that a Russian agent would feel more at home. It had taken three days to check the place out to his satisfaction. Other than a few small-time thugs, there was no indication of organized criminal activity or of spy networks, though those would be harder to detect in a short time. All he required was a first meeting and the assurance that he was not in the crosshairs of a sniper when he left. There was one main entrance to the cafe from the street, a corner intersection, and no public rear entrance. His motorcycle was parked a block away, nestled between two large trees behind a large church. An exit route would use the small inner courtyard behind the cafe. A sniper would expect him to exit using the entrance, an amateur mistake he was not about to make.

Dorff came in first, pulling off his sunglasses and squinting into the small room, trying to locate Mick. Mick waved briefly and was spotted. Dorff pulled out a chair and sat down stiffly. His back was to the cafe, and it made him obviously uncomfortable.

"Greetings, Dorff," Mick said. Dorff nodded and snuck a look at his watch. He was nervous, not a good sign. "Whom are we waiting for, Dorff?" Mick asked, calmly looking Dorff over.

"English? You are using English in a Russian cafe?" Dorff snarled.

"Of course, Dorff. Around here they speak German and

Russian, not English. Your contact, what does he speak?" Mick asked.

Dorff shrugged. He didn't know. "The contact is Dvorkin, Colonel Dvorkin," he finally answered.

"KGB?"

"They don't use that name any longer, but yes, that is close enough."

"So he is current?"

"Yes, still active."

"And how do you know this man?" Mick asked.

"He had a father. Now dead. I worked with him…many times. Dvorkin thinks old school. Very patriotic to Russia. But…"

"But what?"

"His father was killed by his own side. He knew too much, and they were afraid of his capture or defection. Either way, he had to be silenced. His son grinds away at this memory of the sacrifice of his father. It eats at him. Dvorkin loves his country…not its leaders. He is your man if you can convince him. If not, you should not let him leave this meeting alive. You understand, Grundy?"

"Clearly."

A scruffy waitress brought the tea, strong Russian style, laced with cinnamon and cloves, accompanied by several small sugared tea cakes. She placed several irregular lumps of brown sugar in a small bowl near the center.

"*Tol'ko dva ?*" she asked.

"*Yeshche odin skoro pridet,*" Mick answered. She shrugged and set another cup and saucer in front of the empty chair.

Dorff nervously looked again at his watch, then back at the door. "I don't like it. He's late," he said.

Mick laughed, "If the Colonel is any good, he would bring some of his men with him, and they would, about now, be setting up firing stations across the street."

"Yes, I'm afraid that is plausible," Dork admitted. "You have planned for this?"

"Always," Mick said. Dorff raised his eyebrows. Grundy was well-trained or, at least, experienced. It was what he would have done himself, back in the day.

A figure darkened the door. The silhouette was of a large man, hatted, wearing an overcoat, both inappropriate for the warm ambient temperature outside. Usually, this implied something concealed, a large weapon, armor, perhaps both. The silhouette looked around, his hat swiveling back and forth, then became a man as he entered the room. There was no doubt that this specter was the Colonel they expected. His face and eyes confirmed that he had been hardened over time and that few circumstances would bring him fear. The lines about his mouth were deep, his lips set in a permanent scowl. He loomed over the table where Mick and Dorff were seated.

"*Sadites', tovarishch. Vypey chay,*" [Be seated, Comrade. Have some tea,] Mick said, motioning toward the chair in a casual manner. Dorff stared at the wall, not wanting to look at the Colonel just yet.

Dvorkin sat down heavily and placed his large arms on the table, looking back and forth at the other two men, trying to intimidate them with his ferocious demeanor. After a moment, Dvorkin poured himself a cup of strong tea, and before the first taste, he placed a lump of sugar between his incisors, straining the hot liquid through the crystals.

"*Dal'neyshem posle chaya?*" [What follows after tea?] his deep voice boomed.

"*Voskreseniye mertvykh,*" [The resurrection of the dead,] Mick replied. This question and answer had been a long-held Russian tradition before the Communist revolution. Dvorkin's use of it implied his connection to the old Russia, one that preceded the current hardline administration and its policies. They were off to a good start.

"You speak Russian without accent. Do you also speak English?" Dvorkin asked, pouring another cup of tea.

"I do, and others."

"A talented man. A man of letters," Dvorkin said, smacking his lips after the second cup of tea. He searched Mick's face with his penetrating eyes, not missing any detail. "Your wounds. Your prideful wounds. The result of a noble cause?" Dvorkin inquired.

"*Otritsaniye,*" Mick replied sharply. "The result of a Russian bomb."

Dvorkin's lined face fell, and he shook his head with mock sadness. "I expect, then, that others were also killed or injured?"

"Correct." Mick could feel his anger rising, but outwardly he remained calm, almost casual, as if relaxing in the hard wooden chair.

"This tea should have Vodka," Dvorkin announced and thumped his big fist on the table, making the waitress jump up at the noise. When she arrived, nervously wiping her hands on her apron, Dvorkin said, "*Vash luchshiy russkaya Vodka v chaye. I speshit.*" [Your best Russian Vodka in the tea. And hurry.] The waitress quickly added a pint of Vodka to the samovar and filled a fresh pot for the table.

"*Spasibo,*" Dvorkin said softly to her and affectionately patted her buttocks as she turned away. He quickly consumed a cup of the adulterated tea and turned his attention back to Mick. "And, what do you want with our Russian Security Forces, Mick Grundy?"

"You know who I am, and my history, I see," Mick stated. He looked at Dorff, who wouldn't exchange glances with him. "He told you," Mick said, pointing at Dorff with his thumb.

"Not likely. Comrade Dorff would never betray anyone. It was my duty to find out for myself who inquired about me. You would do the same," Dvorkin said, offering another cup of tea to Mick.

"What are you going to do with your new find, Comrade Colonel Dvorkin?" Mick asked.

"You are legend, Mick Grundy. Every Russian agent dreams of taking you down. I, myself, have had such thoughts in the past. Even now, there are men outside this cafe who would gladly shoot you if they have the chance. If only they knew who I was meeting with that is."

"And, Colonel, what makes you think that I will let you leave this place alive?"

"It would, perhaps, be more difficult than you expect, Mick Grundy. Nevertheless, I am not here to kill you or to have you kill me. First, I want to hear your voice tell me why you sought me out."

Mick looked over Dvorkin once again. He was relaxed, comfortable, showing no signs of preparing for a sudden gesture. An ominous indication that Dvorkin was full of surprises and much more capable than he appeared. Dorff was seated with them but, mentally, was trying to stay uninvolved, acting as an innocent bystander to violence which could erupt without notice.

"My country also is looking for me," Mick said.

"This we know. The reason, we don't." Dvorkin said.

"It's all about the Iranian bomb. Both our sides are helping them. It's wrong, dangerous and foolish. Some people, political appointees, are trying to stop me from becoming involved."

"On this, you and I have agreement, Mick Grundy. It is an unwise policy, at least on our part. Russia weakens daily because of the scourge of its present leadership. They form alliances to sell arms, influence and oil. Foolish things in the long run of history. They should be about helping our people prosper and become healthy instead of allowing the inner circle to become wealthy exporting Russia's blood and draining us of our heritage. Both our countries have willingly elected the wrong people to high office."

"I want to break the chain, the network, which ties some in the U.S. to Iran. It starts with a site not far from here which is a conduit of money and orders from Iran to Washington. I can't do it alone."

"Given your history, Mick Grundy, I would have expected you to kick the door down and shoot them in the head, one at a time. Isn't that your signature method?"

Mick chose to ignore the reference to past events. He wasn't about to be goaded into confrontation with Dvorkin. "Better to humiliate or disenfranchise in this case. Any person killed would rapidly be replaced by another," Mick said.

Dvorkin popped another sweet bun into his mouth, washing it down with his mixture of spiced tea and Vodka. "Yes, now you are thinking like a Russian. By the way, Mick Grundy, my informants say that you are Russian by birth, raised by Russians and speak Russian like a native. True?"

"U.S. Special Forces are my mother and father, Colonel. I speak German even better than Russian, and the only people I care about are German."

"You mean, other than Special Agent April Chauncy, don't you. How could your thoughts overlook a woman that attractive?" Dvorkin chuckled.

"You know too much, Dvorkin."

"Russians are great gatherers of information, Mick Grundy. Pity that we don't often act wisely with our knowledge."

"Do you also know where April is at the moment?" Mick asked.

"And you don't?"

"No," Mick admitted.

"We are keeping an eye on her and your grandmother. No harm will come to them, so this should not worry you."

"Why, then, are you watching them?" Mick asked.

"When Mick Grundy comes, we grow concerned. After all, the last time you were here, we lost two of our top officials. We don't want it to happen again."

"I have been driven to what I have done by Russians."

"Except for the magnificent long distance shot which murdered Anatoly Baranov. As I recall, you had never even met him. It was you, wasn't it?"

"You know it was."

"You did Mother Russia a big favor, getting rid of those two madmen. I, for one, don't hold it against you, nor do I expect that you should not defend yourself. Let me be clear, Mick Grundy. I, Vacslov Dvorkin, hold no malice for you personally."

"But you would still shoot me and claim credit."

"Only if I am ordered to. The trick is to not let my superiors know that you and I are working together."

"You mean that you have agreed to work with me?" Mick asked, surprised by the sudden turn.

"In this, we are on the same side. The truth is that I am relieved that you are not here hunting me at the moment." He offered his thick hand across the table toward Mick. Dorff exhaled noisily, relieved that there would be no gunfire today.

"Now that we are partners, of a sort," Mick said, shaking Dvorkin's hand, "do you have any useful information about the Iranian *hoseiniyeh* by the airport or its Imam?"

"Indeed!" Dvorkin announced and started unbuttoning his heavy coat. Mick reached behind his back, grasping the handle of his automatic as he tensed, prepared for whatever came out of the coat. "Not to worry, Mick Grundy," he laughed. "Dvorkin is a man of his word!" He extracted a thick folder full of papers and threw it on the table. "You read Russian, I expect. There is enough in there to keep you happy until we meet again."

"You knew what I wanted, Dvorkin? How could this be so?" Mick stared at the folder incredulously.

"We Russians do have certain inherited talents, after all. Too bad we can't export and profit from these skills. On the other hand, it might also come to no good in the end." Dvorkin rose to his feet, the meeting obviously finished. "You can use my old friend, Dorff, to contact me. He is trustworthy, but don't forget to pay him either. The drop you are currently using above the *Tiergartentunnel* is fine. The CIA isn't aware of it yet. I'll let you know if you have to change the location. One last thing," he cautioned with narrowed eyes but with a slight amusement around his mouth, "don't leave by the rear exit. I would suggest using the roof, *Micken'ka.*"

"So you thought of that also, *Vacslovovitch.* Thanks for the warning," Mick responded.

"*Beregi sebya,*" Dvorkin said over his shoulder as he headed for the front door. A moment of darkness, then he was gone.

"A worthy meeting, Grundy," Dorff suggested.

"Thanks to you. It was a wise choice of men you made. This one would also be a formidable enemy."

"It is my hope that we don't discover that side of Dvorkin," Dorff said and followed the thought with a large swallow of potent tea diluted with Vodka.

Chapter 17

Exploring Options

Kurfürstenstr, Berlin, 2100 Hours

Mick nodded at the two smiling men flanking the entrance. They were dressed in the particular uniform of the place, a white tank top over black trousers, both were thin, sporting punked hair. The man in the photograph on the door was still entertaining himself with his crotch, and when the door opened, the pulsating music still enveloped Mick, elevating his level of irritation. Zeskie still believed that this gay bar was a safe meeting spot but after hearing Dvorkin, Mick realized that the Russians might have tagged this spot as well. Nothing was absolutely safe from them. A couple of catcalls rang out as Mick made his way through the crowded room, heading for the stairs. Mick chose not to look at his admirers but felt their eyes caressing his body as he passed by. When he opened the door, Zeskie was already busily shuffling his papers, not bothering to look up.

"Greetings, Mick. I trust that Berlin is treating you well. Your accommodations are satisfactory?"

"Excellent, but probably not secure. Thanks for the thought, though."

Zeskie looked up puzzled. "Something I should know?"

"Do you know where April is at the moment?" Mick asked, still standing in the middle of the room.

"Not exactly. She got away from us. Triska is very tricky, you know."

"Well, the Russians know. Dvorkin told me."

"You don't mean the infamous Colonel Vacslov Dvorkin? How did you meet him?"

"Through…," he hesitated, "One of Triska's old comrades"

"I know a lot about your Colonel Dvorkin, but I can't imagine a non-violent meeting between you two. Please…tell me how this happened!"

Instead of an answer, Mick dropped the thick folder in Zeskie's lap and stood waiting for his response. Zeskie started rapidly browsing the sheets, finally looking up in distress.

"Can't read Russian?" Mick guessed.

"Speaking a foreign language is easier than reading one. You can read this?"

"Yes. And the interesting thing is that Dvorkin already knew that. Even you didn't know, Zeskie."

"Everyone in the entire world of intelligence are amateurs compared to the Russians. If only the Americans and Russians would stop thinking that they are adversaries. Generally, we usually like each other on a one-to-one basis. The combined space program proves that our side and theirs can work together. We even have common enemies. But no! There is another Cold War brewing between us. It's so exasperating." Zeskie stopped for a moment before coming back to the current issues. "What did Dvorkin and you talk about?" he asked.

"A lot of posturing, but, in effect, he agreed to help with the Iranian problem."

"And did he explain why he would go against official policy to help you?"

"No, he didn't explain his motives. It's a personal philosophy, I think. I was told that his father was in the KGB and was liquidated by his own people. Likely, Dvorkin carries a grudge."

"I knew that his father was in the field, but as far as I've ever heard, he died of natural causes. While it is possible that your information is something we didn't know, it is just as possible that you are being fed propaganda. A palatable pablum designed to drop your guard. Don't believe anything you hear from them at face value. Remember the old Russian saying, *Doveryay, no proveryay.*"

"Of course, Zeskie, but he has given me what looks to be two years of surveillance work. It appears genuine, and it contains a wealth of information that we could never get ourselves."

"Rather than have you tell me what all this means, I'll have it translated at the Embassy and then check it out. Two days. Don't do anything for two days. Understood?" Zeskie said.

"Can I ask a couple of questions, Zeskie?"

"Whatever. We have no secrets between us."

"Are you very, very sure that this room has not been bugged by either side?"

"Absolutely. I just swept it myself, and, as I told you, those men downstairs are working for me," Zeskie answered.

"You mean all of them?" Mick asked in disbelief.

"Many would be a better answer."

"What do you tell them about yourself and about me?"

"The word is that you and I are lovers. What did you expect?"

"Normal is good enough for me, Zeskie. Of course, I never expect normal from you."

"And I resent that comment, Mick. There is no such thing as normal. Anything else?"

"I want to see April. The Russians are following her around and know where she is. I don't like to have her exposed and not even know it. She needs to come to Berlin where I can keep an eye on her."

Zeskie leaned back in thought, looking at the dirty ceiling. "I agree. Here's what we will do." He dug in his briefcase and pulled out a small phone and tossed it to Mick. "I know you don't trust

Peter at the moment, and I don't disagree. Use this to call your brother-in-law, Kurt, then discard it. Call him from as far away from Berlin as you can manage, in case your location is disclosed to those hunting for you. Ask Kurt to find April by finding Triska. They will be together wherever they are. You can trust Kurt completely."

"Kurt and I haven't talked in over a year, but once we were really close," Mick remembered, looking at the phone as if it were already connected to Kurt. "You still work with him, is that how you know he can be trusted?"

"Kurt is deep undercover, but we keep in touch. He loves you more than you know, Mick, and he will be willing and able to help you, if you ask. Kurt never forgot that you saved his life, and he never blamed you for Anna's death."

As he rode through the cool night, the wind buffeting his helmet, Mick thought about Kurt and his sister, Anna. At times, he wanted to forget Anna because of the pain it caused bringing her image back. Seeing and holding another woman, even one he loved, could not erase his memory of Anna. She was always there, and the one night of intimacy they shared came back to him when he was with April. He never told April, but there were times his mind substituted Anna for her, especially during lovemaking. April was, at those times, just a stand in. It shamed him to admit it. He could never tell her, but he couldn't make his memory go away, nor did he really want it to. At those moments, Anna was alive again and in his arms, merging with his body. He thought at first that it was loyalty to Anna which prevented him from being close to someone else. Not that at all. It was because he felt disloyal to the other woman, in his heart only, loving Anna forever and forever. Even the night he met Anna for the first time, he knew that he was destined to love her. There was something that happened which was beyond physical attraction. It was ordained, inevitable. A match unique, permanent, and the best thing was that Anna had the same experience. They first met eyes across a crowded beer hall, separated by twenty-five meters and innumerable people, but at that instant, it was if he had always known her. She was the part of him that he had been searching for. Together, they made one whole person, but she was taken from him after only one day of marriage, and the resultant scars in his soul were bigger than the scars on his body, and neither would ever go away.

The train to Munich smoothly devoured the kilometers with only an occasional click of the rails signaling that there was something actually holding the train up. Mick adjusted his legs and looked once again around the nearly empty compartment. He had chosen to travel to Munich, because it had been Anna's home, and her family still lived there. And because he decided that it was time that he tried to make amends with them. Surely, at some point, they would forgive him.

There was an advantage taking the night train, other than the lack of crowding. It spared the daylight hours for something more useful than sitting in a comfortable, air-conditioned car. He pulled out the small phone. It would take a lot of effort to discover that his call had been made from a moving train, and by then, he would be far away. Zeskie had given him a number to reach Kurt, and he punched it in.

On the third ring, a muffled voice answered. *"Ja, was?"* Mick couldn't recognize Kurt's voice. Either it wasn't him or some method was being used to change the sound.

"Bruder? Sind Sie das?" Mick asked.

There was a moment of silence and a soft click. "Mick? Is that you?" Kurt asked.

"Hi, Kurt!" Mick said.

"I was just thinking of you, Mick! Where are you?"

"No, Kurt. The question is where are you?"

"You remember where we first met?"

"The party? Sure."

"How far are you from that spot?" Kurt asked.

"I can be there, can you?"

"Two hours?" Kurt inquired.

Mick was there first, and he managed to fold into the shadows near the dormitory entrance. When they first met, Kurt was a college student given to attending parties centered around heavy metal music. It was much later that Mick discovered that Kurt had been working undercover for the BND even then. Through his efforts, a terrorist cell had been exposed which was preparing to indiscriminately kill large numbers of Germans. Following that discovery, Mick had been able to deliver a savage retribution for the death of Anna. One of many to follow. It was a night that made Kurt grow up but nearly had cost their friendship.

A scruffy fellow was stumbling toward the entrance, wearing shabby, loose clothing and sporting an unkempt head of tangled hair. Mick sighed. Another drunk panhandling the young innocent college crowd. The man was just a bit too alert, though, and Mick could see that he was studying his surroundings more than his apparent level of intoxication would seem to permit. Mick observed him closely, and when he finally realized that he was looking at Kurt, he stepped away from the shadows into the light.

"Mick!" Kurt shouted, running toward him with arms extended. They embraced a man's embrace with much backslapping. "I had no idea you were in Munich!" Kurt exclaimed.

"I wasn't. My call was from the Berlin train. It's really great to see you again, Brother! Your disguise fooled me at first."

"You came to get April?" Kurt asked.

"You know that April is in Germany?"

"Of course. She kissed me on my cheek right there," he said pointing to the site, "just yesterday. The spot is still burning."

"Where is she?"

"She and Triska are at my old home."

"You mean with Stella and Alfred…that home?"

"She seems to be well-accepted and happy. I was going to return this morning and see them again. You can go with me. Really, you didn't know she was there?"

"This is Triska's handiwork. The last time I saw April, she was in Triska's apartment in Stuttgart. You know that we are both on the wanted list, don't you?"

"I saw it. You trust me, I hope."

"With our lives, and that is likely the magnitude of it."

"Want to tell me about it?"

"There are Russians involved. A certain Colonel Dvorkin. You might not want to get too close to this one," Mick suggested.

"*Heilige Scheiße!* Not him!"

"Exactly. Him. I am trying to enlist his help with a mission. He seems to be cooperating, but Zeskie doesn't trust him."

"Nor would we. Dvorkin is a dangerous man, Mick."

Chapter 17

Chapter 18

Anna's House

From the street, the house was just as Mick remembered, as if time had stopped. In his mind, he could see Anna walking with him to his waiting motorcycle, love in her eyes and sorrowful to see him leave again. He felt his eyes moisten and wiped his face clumsily with his sleeve.

"Hard, isn't it?" Kurt asked. "It took a long time for me too. It was her bedroom door that always brought out my tears. I would walk past it just knowing she was in there, then suddenly remember that she was gone forever."

"Don't, Kurt," Mick asked.

"Sorry." Kurt stopped in front of the house and switched off the motor. "April is going to be happy to see you again, and I will be happy to see her again. She destroyed my poor date in five minutes when we were here previously. I couldn't tell if it was intentional or not. It's just like a force comes into the room when she arrives. She takes the focus away from anything but her."

"Especially for men," Mick agreed. After a pause he added, "I am worried about how Stella and Alfred will react when I walk in."

"You can be sure that Triska has softened them up for you. Just be yourself and trust those two women of yours," Kurt offered, while leading the way up to the front door. Mick loomed behind him feeling awkward and exposed. A dangerous hulk that most people rightly feared. "While we are alone, Mick, I have one question for you. Something that I've wondered." He noticed that Mick was waiting on his question, but other things were foremost on his mind.

Kurt cleared his throat and looked sideways and smiled. The question was an awkward one. "Being with a very beautiful woman…is the sex any different?" he asked quietly.

"You've obviously never been in love," Mick responded. "When you are in love, you are looking inside, not outside. You'll get it someday."

Kurt nodded and rapped sharply on the door, and they waited silently, listening for footsteps.

The door opened suddenly and as it swung wide, they were treated to the sight of April standing there with tears in her eyes but with a broad smile, joy radiating from her face.

"I peeked," she admitted, "after you turned the car off." She seemed to leap toward them and enveloped Mick with her arms and her kisses, her feet left dangling in the air. "The sight of you is most welcome," she whispered into his face.

"Where's my turn?" Kurt said petulantly. They ignored him so he proceeded past them into the house.

"I've only been away from you for a few days!" Mick said, feeling a little embarrassed about her show of affection. He put her down carefully, as if he was afraid of breaking an expensive glass vase. "You have been accepted here?"

"Completely!" April said in an excited whisper. She spoke with her face close enough that he could only see her eyes. "I have found a new family, just like you. We are like two orphans who have been adopted by wonderful people. It's such a marvelous feeling!" She led him in by the hand as if he were a stray animal being shown into a strange place. They were all standing there, all four of them, looking at him with love in their hearts.

Triska was the first to come forward, and she nestled softly into his waiting arms and looked up at him and winked. No words could have conveyed her meaning and feelings better than that little wink.

"I get confused, Triska. Are you my mother, grandmother or another girlfriend?" He patted her affectionately behind her head and kissed her forehead softly.

"I have claims on being called your mother," Stella said, walking toward him with her arms extended.

"That's all I could hope for, and I can't express how grateful I am to hear you say that," Mick said and embraced her, noticing that Alfred also was coming toward him.

"And I want to be known as your father!" Alfred said, choking back his tears. The four stood there in a bundle with arms intertwined like some strange effigy of an Indian deity.

"And your brother has already hugged you," Kurt shouted from across the room, causing all of them to laugh. "And if you don't break it up, you'll find your brother hugging April!" he added, to more laughter.

"Mick, could we ask a big favor from you?" Alfred said, blotting his face with his handkerchief and pushing away so that he could see Mick's expression.

"*Sie können mich alles fragen, mein Vater,*" Mick said, also tearing from the moment.

Alfred looked around at the others' faces who seemed to understand what he was about to ask. They were in agreement, he could tell by telepathy. Alfred gave April a quick telling glance, but her face was blank. She didn't foresee what was coming.

"We…I…all of us would love to be present when you ask that lovely woman over there to be your wife. Could you ask her…*bitte*? For her and for us?"

April's hands shot to her mouth, and her eyes widened. She had been a bystander in this love fest between Mick and his German family, but now they were all looking at her as they started moving away from Mick, letting them face each other across the room. They locked eyes for a quiet moment, and acceptance went in both directions. Mick slowly descended to both knees and extended his hands toward her. She came to him and clasped both hands, tears streaming down her face.

"April," he said hoarsely, looking up into her face, "with full understanding of what you are getting into with me," he paused, gathering the will to ask her the question they all knew was coming. "Would you agree to be with me the rest of our lives? To be my wife?" Even before he finished, she collapsed into him, covering his head with her body and her arms, sliding down to her knees in front of him, holding his face gently between her hands, while shaking from sobs and little gasps. She held him like that for a long moment, just looking back and forth between his eyes before pulling his face into hers for a long tender kiss.

"If I could only tell you how I feel right now. This moment is one I will treasure for always," she said, kissing him again and again, while they pulled each other into a firm embrace, rocking from side to side in rapture.

"If that is not a yes, April, then can I ask you to marry me instead?" Kurt asked from the side, once again causing everyone to laugh. Triska started applauding, and they all joined in with whoops and cries of happiness. Mick and April rose slowly to their feet without letting each other go and keeping their eyes fixed on one another.

Alfred slapped Mick on the back, saying, "This is a proud moment, my son. Welcome back to our family. Both of you. And may many happy days await you both. We are so pleased to have been here to witness this moment."

After an enjoyable dinner, they remained around the dinner table, chattering back and forth in small conversation. Mick relaxed and looked around during the small talk, observing the home of his wife and her parents in detail. On first looks, everything was in the same place, just as he remembered, but…older, worn at the edges, even Alfred and his wife. Stella had preserved Anna's bedroom as though her daughter would someday return, just as before, and they could continue their interrupted lives. It was always there in their eyes, the sadness and longing for something which could never happen. Time had passed, and for all of them, especially for Mick, Anna was starting to recede into the years, even though they all fought to preserve her.

Mick took a deep breath and looked at April. She instantly responded with an expression and smile which told him that every fiber of her being loved him. The dreams about Anna had to stop. Yes, it was his fault that Anna had died, and it was also still true that he loved her. Nevertheless, he had to carefully fold her memory and put it away and go on with life. All of them had to do the same.

Alfred wanted to ask a question. It was obvious that something was on his mind and he kept trying to catch Mick's eye, hesitating to actually say what he was thinking. "*Ja, Vater?*" Mick asked, anticipating him. Everyone's attention was on Alfred's face.

"Are you staying with us tonight?" Alfred asked hesitantly. The reason he wanted to know was obvious. April was sleeping in Anna's room. The question was delicately asked but very deep emotions were attached to its significance…and Mick's answer.

"Where are you staying, Kurt?" Mick asked, turning away from Alfred.

Kurt was waiting for this moment, understanding how impossible it would be for everyone for Mick to be with his new love in this of all houses.

"I hoped that you would be staying with me tonight, Mick. We have a lot of catching up to do," he said.

Mick turned toward the others and asked, "Kurt is right.

Would that be acceptable for everyone?" The answer came quickly and with relief in their faces. Except April's. Mick saw her smile and nod approval but, at the same time, wipe away a tear.

"I might as well say this in public, Mick," April said. She paused for a long moment and then, dry-eyed and firmly, she spoke again. "You are not leaving Munich without me." It was a declaration, an order, a statement of fact.

"Of course not," Mick responded. "Leaving can wait for a few days, though. We owe our family the time it will take to feel comfortable with us. The world's problems will have to be solved, for the time being, without us."

Chapter 19

Finding Allies

Kurt's Apartment, Munich

Now can you tell me what you are doing in Germany, Mick?" Kurt asked from his bed. Mick had insisted on sleeping on the floor in the small apartment and had his back to Kurt.

"I don't really know myself. There hasn't been much of a plan so far. We are going to try to discover what connections the Iranians have in Washington and then figure out how to break them. Later, I suppose, we will be obliged to deal with our American traitors in some fashion."

"Didn't you read the documents the Russians gave you?"

"I only scanned them. The CIA has been going over them in detail. Zeskie would know by now if they are real and are of any use."

"Well, call him!"

"Not that easy, Kurt. I have a dedicated CIA phone with me, but I was warned that the conversation might be monitored. Officially, I am on the wanted list, so you can understand that I don't want to be tracked down, and I don't want anyone in Langley to know what we are up to."

"I can call him. No one is tracking me, and I can use the official BND systems to do it."

"You will get pulled in. This is going to get very dangerous, Kurt."

"As an active agent, it's my job to get involved. This obsession that Iran has with nuclear weapons will affect all of us in time. They have to be stopped."

Mick turned and looked, in silence, at his brother-in-law for a long time before answering. "I couldn't stand to see you hurt, Kurt. I just can't put you at risk."

"I should tell you that I got an official call from the BND office in Stuttgart yesterday. They are looking for you. I told them that I didn't know anything, hadn't seen you, hadn't talked to you and so forth. At the time, I was telling the truth. Peter Koffman runs that office, you know. Your brother."

"Yes, my brother. My only known blood relative. The best man at my wedding. The one person in the world that I thought I could count on no matter what."

"Why would he turn on you, Mick?"

"It defies my understanding to answer that. What promotion would be worth the life of your only relative?"

"You should talk to Triska about him."

"She knows all about it. In your opinion, Kurt, how likely are they to be able to find me?"

"They are very good inside Germany. In time, they will find you. Another question is: can you avoid the long reach of the CIA?"

"Ron Zeskie would never allow that to happen. Never," Mick said. He paused for a moment, lost in thought, then added, "April and I have to get back to Berlin soon. Zeskie can tell both of us in person what's next in his plan."

"You are going to let the girl you just became engaged to get involved in a dangerous operation, and you won't let me?"

"April, Triska, and probably you, are being watched by the Russians. She will be safer with me than here.

"You shouldn't trust the Russians. Colonel Dvorkin has a reputation equaling yours. He must have ulterior motives to have made any contact with you. He might be laying a trap, getting you to let down your guard by making you think you are allies."

"I trust very few people, Kurt, and I don't trust my new allies at all. The other reason April is going with me is because I can't really order her to do anything, so I might as well get used to the idea of doing what she wants."

Kurt exploded with laughter, slapping on the bed for emphasis. "To see the notorious and feared Mick Grundy being led around by the nose! It's too much," he roared.

Mick turned his back and ignored him, trying without much success to grab some much needed sleep. He became aware that Kurt was using his telephone but couldn't make out what the conversation was about or whom he was talking to. Mick rolled back over and sat up.

Kurt saw Mick and held up his finger, a pause, a signal to wait.

"*Danke*, Triska," he said and clicked off. Mick's eyebrows went up.

"Something wrong?"

"I put Triska to work on your problem. By morning, things will have changed, so we'll discuss it then," Kurt said and pulled the cover over his head.

The phone beside Kurt's bed started ringing at six sharp. Vibrating and buzzing like a distressed, oversized cockroach and just as welcome. Kurt picked it up, his hair going in every direction, "*Ya?*" He sat up and became more alert "*Ja, Kommandeur,*" he said, standing up, nearly at attention. "*Ja, Kommandeur,*" he said with more snap. "*Ja, Kommandeur,*" he said again and punched off the call. Mick rose to his feet, expecting an explanation. As he pulled on his shirt, he saw that Kurt's forehead was beaded with sweat.

"All right, Kurt. Let me have it," he ordered.

"Well, as I promised, things have changed. The call was from the head of the BND…himself. I am ordered to assist you personally with anything you need and to accompany you to Berlin. He specifically stated that you are not to leave my sight. The next part might be a problem." Kurt paused for a breath.

"I'm waiting."

"Your brother, Peter, will also to be ordered to Berlin to assist. He is bound to consider it a demotion, and the command seems to be intended to have that effect."

Mick started to laugh. "He should have made friends with Triska. Now he's paying the penalty! When is all this to take place?"

"You are directing the show; it's up to you."

"I'll call Peter later today, and we'll work up something." Mick sat down and thought things out. They had a first rate team in place…if they could all work together. Two Americans, two Germans…three if he counted Triska, an East German and a Russian. Zeskie would be astonished to learn that an experienced international team was at his disposal. All they needed was a plan of action.

On the way back to *Auenbruggerstraße*, Mick tapped Kurt on the shoulder. "Let me use your phone." Kurt asked no questions and handed it over. Mick quickly dialed a number and waited. The phone clicked twice, then Mick said, "Greetings from an old friend. Same place, same day." He handed the phone back to Kurt. "We will meet Zeskie on Friday night in Berlin…three days."

As soon as the door opened, they were greeted to the aroma of grilling sausages and coffee. The sounds of laughter mingled with muted voices, drifting from somewhere distant, enveloping them in the arms of home. Mick felt as though he belonged here. All the people he loved were assembled in this one place, and all the happy memories of Anna were also still here and no longer painful to recall. It was where he belonged, the only place he had ever belonged. He respectfully pushed the dining room door open and stuck his head in. Alfred was seated at the head of the table with his newspaper spread in front of him, a fresh coffee in his hand. Stella was just coming in holding a big platter of steaming food, and through the other door he caught a glimpse of April in a white apron, her back to him. Just as he was wondering about Triska, he heard her voice in the kitchen. They were all there. A German version of a Normal Rockwell painting.

"Hi!" Mick said and pushed the door open as they came into the room.

"Right on time, my boys!" Alfred said and pushed his paper away from the table.

"Sit, sit!" Stella commanded. "We eat now."

After Mick sat down and drew up his chair, he felt April's warm hands on his neck followed by her kisses, working their way along his cheek toward his lips.

"Oh, Mick. I am so happy. Thank you for making all this possible," she whispered in his ear. He didn't answer but reached up and stroked her arm. He saw Alfred's wink toward them and Kurt's smile.

"So, did you boys work things out last night?" Stella asked, her back to them.

"All is well, *Mutter*," Kurt answered for both of them. Triska appeared and pulled up her chair opposite Mick. She studied his face to find out if he knew what she had done during the night. His eyes told her that indeed he did know and that he was grateful. There was a special relationship between them, a bond, a link from the past to the present. Not only love was shared by them but also respect, a willingness to do one's duty to society, to protect and serve where few would dare. It was if he always had known her, as if he had looked into those eyes the day he was born and knew that she would always be there for him.

"When do you leave," Triska inquired. They all drew a deep breath waiting on his answer, the date which would end their collective happiness.

Mick glanced at April. Her perfect almond eyes were full of emotion. She no longer wanted to leave this place. The world's problems no longer mattered to her, her previous duties had been done with honor but no longer called to her any more. She wanted to live this life of love and family that she had previously only known in her dreams. Her eyes telegraphed a clear message that she didn't want either of them to go back to trouble and danger. She had what she most wanted in life, and there was no longer any destiny but this one.

"We leave Friday…early," Mick said with his head down so that he didn't have to look at her face. The room became dead silent, the air leaden with emotion, a weight placed on the delicate scale pushing the fulcrum heavily toward unbalance.

"April, please let the boys go without you. Stay here with us," Stella pleaded. April's eyes were rimmed with moisture, and she didn't look away from Mick when she answered.

"My place is with Mick. Where he goes, I go."

Chapter 20

Surprise!

Kurfürstenstr, Berlin

The red Porsche rolled slowly by the entrance like a bird inspecting a branch before landing. The same two men were lounging by the entrance, their right leg up with its foot against the wall. Guards, of a sort, but more likely they were waiting on personal opportunities. Mick parked the car and shut off the motor. He was stiff from driving in this little car. At least on a motorcycle, he could extended his legs as needed.

"This is it?" April asked. "Looks seedy," she remarked, looking at the drawing of a male sex act covering the entrance door.

"You don't know the half of it. On the other hand, this is one of the few places in Berlin that I don't have to worry about you," Mick chuckled.

"I can see why," she said. "Now what?"

"We are waiting on Peter and Kurt. Then we'll all go in and upstairs."

"So you expect Zeskie is already there?"

"He has been the other two times I've been here."

They sat in silence, watching the people pass both on the street and in front of them on the sidewalk. It was a personal show of humanity in nearly all its many forms. A theory circulating for years states that there are only several dozen human body forms, and personality is tied to the morphology of one's body. After some pondering, most come to believe that there is some truth in it.

Mick and April were coming to the same conclusion as they watched people pass. Some were hurrying along, some sauntering, some fat, some thin. Each one, in some way, was like another person they had encountered previously, and they expected both would be similar and familiar.

A car door closed, almost too quietly, causing both Mick and April to look toward the sound. Peter waved and smiled at them, and Kurt got out of the other side. They were both dressed casually and inconspicuously. Mick pointed to the bar entrance as he and April got out. He pointed up to indicate that they were to go upstairs after entering.

The two thin men flanking the door stopped them, blocking the entrance. Both were leering a thin smile at Peter and Kurt but preventing them from entry. Mick arrived just in time, because he could see Peter's patience wearing thin. He signaled to the men who recognized him and backed away from the entrance. They both carefully inspected April, when she passed by, as if she was an unusual variant of human species. The foursome made their way up the creaking and dark stairs, Mick following in the rear. "Second door to the right," he said from behind.

Peter Koffman pushed the door open without knocking. "Peter?" Zeskie exclaimed, followed by "Kurt! You also?"

They were shaking hands when Mick and April came in and closed the door. Peter and Mick exchanged embraces as the others watched.

"No hard feelings, Peter?" Mick asked.

"None, my brother. None. I was getting too soft. This will be good for me and my future. By the way, I never would have allowed anyone to pick you up. I was just keeping up appearances. You and your beautiful fiancé…yes, Kurt told me…were never in any danger."

"Thanks, Peter. The last thing I wanted is for anything to come between us."

"But there is something, Mick. I will be eternally jealous regarding your future wife. I am putting you on notice."

Zeskie sat heavily on the bed, surveying the room. "Someone tell me why this room is so crowded."

"Simple, Ron," Kurt said. "Peter and I were ordered to take part by the *Kommandeur*. We are just following instructions."

"Great. Any more surprises other than April is no longer in Stuttgart or Munich?"

"Yes. A big one. April and I are getting married."

"Congrats. Now let's get to work," Zeskie said and snapped open his briefcase. Mick and April looked at each other with some surprise but remained quiet. Zeskie pulled out a thick folder and opened it.

"At first glance, this Russian information is the real deal. It represents intensive, intrusive, spy work of the first quality. And it has taken two years of painstaking work to assemble this masterpiece. Your informant is genuine, that is, if his documents have not been adulterated; however, his motives are obscure. Our Colonel Dvorkin is about the last person in Russia that we would expect to turn, so we are forced to surmise that Russia is playing both sides, seeming to support both by supporting neither. This could turn on us when we stick our necks in the trap Colonel Dvorkin might have laid for us."

"What part of that information is useful to us?" Mick asked.

"All of it. The documents show that the Iranians are doing exactly what we thought all along. Information is flowing in both directions, from Washington and from Tehran. They use code names, but there could be several people in Washington involved and, apparently, at least one in the White House itself. That one is the ideologue. The others are being paid large sums of money.

"Is the President involved?" Mick asked.

"I wish I could say no. On that issue the information is not helpful."

"Exactly what do you see as our mission?" April asked from behind Mick.

"We have to discredit this Iranian source in the eyes of the Germans. Force them to close the facility and eject the Iranians. If we instead just kill them all, others will replace them, and the violence could damage German-American relations."

"Another possibility, if I may?" Peter spoke up, holding his index finger in the air and smiling. They all turned toward him.

"We have a classic, ancient struggle between the two main fractions of Islam going on throughout the world. That's why the Iranians are keeping a low profile in Germany, and it's also why they want the bomb so badly. They most fear being overrun by the Sunni Arabs, not the Americans or the Russians and certainly not little Israel. What we need to do is to let Arabs do the dirty work for us, or at least take the blame for any deaths."

"A possibility," Zeskie said, not looking up from his papers. "Any other suggestions?"

"The same idea as Peter, except blame it on the Russians," Kurt suggested.

"Also, something we should consider," Zeskie said quietly. "From my study of these documents and our own findings, I have found a significant weakness which can be exploited. Want to hear it?" The murmurs indicated that everyone was interested. "Sex," Zeskie said flatly. "This nest of terrorists and spies masquerading as Holy People are obsessed with sex. Back in Tehran, it's likely not so easy under the penetrating stare of the Ayatollah, but here in permissive Berlin…anything goes, and has. The Russians have observed prostitutes being entertained as well as underage children being sodomized, all within that one building. One man is acting as *Zuhälter*. He procures women who are brought in and passed around for a couple of days at a time. The children are of both sexes and are a different story. Most of them originate in Russia and are smuggled across various borders. I suspect that is the real reason why Dvorkin is involved. Russia's ally is abusing her children, and it puts them in a difficult position. They would like us to solve their problem and then, I'm sure, blame us for the solution."

"What happens to the children after they..." April couldn't finish her thoughts as she fought back her tears. Zeskie looked up at her with sympathy, but just shrugged. He didn't know.

"They are committing an illegal act! Germany won't stand for it!" Kurt swore.

"I'm afraid that we will, Kurt," Peter said and put his arm across his shoulder. "German industry is dependent on imported fuel of all kinds. A lot of it comes from that part of the world. Besides, they will accuse everyone of trumping up false claims against them and encourage our many Muslim citizens to riot against us."

"Then, I'm all for shooting the whole bunch," Kurt rejoined.

"I have some additional information you might want to hear first," Zeskie said. "The children, for the most part, are gathered up in Russia's southern areas including Chechnya. Most would be Sunni Muslim. I might remind you that our Iranian spies are all Shiite. See where I'm going with this?"

"Not so fast," Mick interrupted. "If it were as easy as just getting out the word, the Russians would already have done that. We need a trigger, a flash point."

"All that is a diversion, Zeskie. We need to know who their contacts in Washington are. That should be our priority," April said.

"Agreed. And I am already working on that. The Russian data suggests that the Iranians in Berlin are only acting as a conduit for information, and they don't know whom they are dealing with or why. That is, if you believe the Russians. We need to intercept the Iranian communication stream directly, and it's not electronic, or we would already know about it. I think they must be still using the old-fashioned hand-carry method. A diplomatic case full of goodies."

"I don't see the entire picture, Zeskie," Peter said. "It seems that a lot things have to happen nearly at the same time. Complex plans often go awry."

"Especially if your only source of information comes from your enemy," Zeskie admitted. "As soon as possible, we are going to plant our own bugs so that we can verify what the Russians have told us." He paused, waiting for the group to digest all the information. "Kurt, Peter, please wait outside for a moment with April. I need to discuss something with Mick."

After their steps faded down the stairs, Zeskie stuck his hand out for a handshake. "Congratulations on your wedding plans, Mick. I am truly happy for you, because April is a wonderful woman and very much your equal. But…" he stopped and looked more stern. "Don't you know why every agency in the world does not permit lovers to work together in dangerous situations?" Without waiting for a response, he continued, "Because it affects your judgement and puts at jeopardy the success of the mission. You know this is true, yet you have committed yourself to April, and as a result, the mission and your very safety is at stake. I don't like it one bit."

This was the first time Mick had ever seen Zeskie angry, and it took him aback. "I know you are right, Zeskie. Of course you have reason to be angry, and I assure you that I intended to leave her with Triska, but things happened which I couldn't control. April has met and been accepted by Anna's family, and for the first time since Anna's death, they have welcomed me back in. April is the real reason. It's like having Anna back again…someone to love and produce grandchildren for them. I couldn't deny everyone their happiness this time. They have been hurt enough."

"My advice to you is to make sure that April comes out of this healthy, because you couldn't face another loss any more than they could. Keep her out of harm's way…do you hear me?"

Chapter 20

Chapter 21

Setting Up

They watched the power pole intently, not taking their eyes off the transformer hanging innocently below the wooden crossbar. A stray bird or two passed by, mindless of the unseen power surging through the black wires which delivered a steady energy supply to the *hoseiniyeh*, just visible in corner of the visual fields of the binoculars. Right on time, the grey transformer seemed to vibrate, then violently expanded before erupting in bright sparks and flames. Mick swung the binoculars toward the *hoseiniyeh*, which was now shrouded in darkness.

"Exactly, perfectly done, Peter," he said aloud, even though Peter wasn't there to hear him. He turned to Kurt who was already in uniform waiting for the next step. "Got what you need?" Mick asked.

"All on the truck," Kurt replied. Mick patted him on the back, the signal that he was to go.

Mick watched as Kurt stopped in front of the darkened building and walked under the still smoking telephone pole, looking up and shaking his head. Momentarily, a man joined him and started wildly motioning with his hands and pointing to the darkened *hoseiniyeh* nearby. Kurt pointed to his truck and then, seemingly reluctantly, walked with the man toward the building.

When he passed into the darkened room, a flashlight beam hit his face like a slap. After lingering for a moment in his eyes, it passed down to his name tag, which read Herman, RWE. The bright light played over his rather dirty uniform and shoes before returning to his face.

"*Wer sind Sie?*" a gruff voice asked from behind the menacing light.

"*Rheinisch-Westfälisches Elektrizitätswerk,*" Kurt patiently answered.

"*Warum sind unsere Lichter aus?*" [Why are our lights out?] the voice asked in accented-German.

"*Defekter Transformator. Ich muss einen Stecker prüfen Sie, ob Sie eine Welle der Spannung hatte.*" [Defective transformer. I need to check a plug to see if you had a surge of voltage.]

The first man motioned for Kurt to proceed and led the way with a flashlight. Kurt quickly found what he was looking for… an electrical outlet near the center of a wall. It was the site he would have selected for a bug, and he was confidant that the Russians had the same sharp eye for location. Kurt bent over the plug and unscrewed the cover, letting it fall to the floor then looked up to the man beside him.

"*Haben Sie ein Problem finden?*" [Did you find a problem?] the man asked.

"*Es scheint, ein Abhörgerät in Ihrem Stecker installiert sein,*" [There seems to be a listening device installed in your outlet,] Kurt answered, pointing out the small white device at the corner of the receptacle box.

The man let out a whoosh of air and stood up, chattering in Persian. Several sets of feet descended on their location, and the room was pierced by shafts of yellow flashlight beams and angry voices speaking foreign curses. The first man grabbed Kurt by the sleeve and escorted him to the door, nearly pushing him across the threshold.

"*Bevor ich gehe, muss ich Ihnen sagen, dass ich morgen für Reparatur zurück. Vielleicht haben Sie Schäden an Ihrem Schaltungen.*" [Before I go, I must tell you that I have to return tomorrow for repairs. You might have damage to your circuits.] Without answering, the man slammed the door in his face. Kurt shrugged and headed toward his truck.

"He did it!" April said. "Are you sure the Russian devices have all been disabled?" she asked Zeskie who was standing next to her.

"I'm never one hundred percent sure but just very sure. The voltage surge was enough to wipe out every single electrical device in the building, sort of a lighting bolt effect. We'll make them wait on the new transformer until morning," he said.

"Peter is putting that one in?"

"Perhaps not Peter up the pole, but he's sure to be there while it's being done."

"And that will give us audio of the building?"

"After the new plugs are in place. Some of them even have video."

Two days later...

The armored Mercedes swept around the corner effortlessly and nearly silently except for some tire noise. Its occupants knew the roads to the airport by heart, and this trip was like all the others…except for the recent discovery at the *hoseiniyeh*. Over twenty bugs of Russian origin had been discovered, thanks to the accidental explosion of the high voltage transformer, and the place had been in near total confusion since. The Russians had previously been so helpful or at least did a good job pretending to be allies. The Americans or the Israelis would be the usual suspects, but the Russians? A team was there now taking the place apart, looking for any other devices, and Bahadur had been given a large stack of folders to transport back to Tehran as quickly as a flight could be arranged. This was information the Imam did not dare to transmit electronically, even in code.

Bahadur adjusted the metal cuff on his wrist and shifted the satchel to take the pressure off his leg. He hated this long boring trip and hated to return to the dark world of Islam back in Tehran. He liked women…too much at times, and he was starting to like the way they dressed in the Western world, their faces and heads uncovered, and their bodies invitingly on display. The big car slowed unexpectedly, and reflexly, Bahadur looked forward, just in time to see a blinding series of flashes erupt from the left, nearly picking the car up by the front and pushing it sideways. One of the right side wheels hit the curb forcefully, pivoting the car around violently to face the opposite direction, tossing Bahadur around like a rag doll, before coming to a jerking halt. Bahadur was confused and fear suddenly welled up in him. The trip was so simple. Get on the plane, sleep, get off, be driven overnight to the Jameh Abbasi Mosque. This can't be happening he thought. It's not part of the plan. But it was happening. A shadow was standing beside the car, and its weapon was pointed at the driver who had his hands in the air. Bahadur expected the gun to burst into flames again in any second, blowing the hardened glass window all over the car along with parts of Rahim's face and brains. He felt his bowels trembling and thought for a moment that he was going to soil himself, but a sudden bright light from the oncoming traffic lit up their assailant who seemed to hesitate. The weapon's muzzle hovered just outside the glass for a breathless, eternal moment, deciding what it was going to do. A police siren came on, the sound close, piercing, causing the gun by the window to evaporate as did the shadow holding it. Bahadur never thought he would be glad to see the stuffy German police, but he was now more than grateful. A car stopped just in front of the wrecked limo, its bright lights blocking out anything other than the immediate interior of the car. Another car joined the group, pulling up in the street beside the limo, its blue light flashing hypnotically, changing his world from white to blue and back again.

The back door opened and a uniformed man wearing a brimmed cap pushed his head inside. *"Sind Sie verletzt?"* [Are you injured?] he asked.

Bahadur was trembling, and his mouth was dry. He looked around the backseat aimlessly, trying to recover his senses, not really knowing what he was looking for. He looked back at the policeman but realized that he couldn't speak in German at the moment, his brain still blocking any intelligent response. The officer reached in and snapped Bahadur's seat belt off and tugged forcefully on his arm.

"Aussteigen," he said, helping Bahadur to his feet. A thick column of smoke was pouring from the hood of the car and around its front tires. Bahadur vaguely recalled a previous warning about the danger of fire or explosion in a similar situation. The officer led him to the patrol car and helped him into its backseat, closing the door with a firm and authoritative slam. Bahadur realized that the attaché case was still attached to his wrist, and as far as he could tell, he was uninjured. The patrol car lurched forward, pressing Bahadur into the backseat. He knew that he should protest, but there was a thick glass separating him from the driver. A quick look around informed Bahadur that there were no handles on the inside of the backseat doors. He started thinking again, more clearly now that he was safely out of danger. As soon as they arrived at the police station, he would protest vociferously. The plane was scheduled to leave, and he had to be on it. He would demand to be taken to the plane…or the Iranian Embassy. That was it, become loud and angry and demand his rights. The car turned hard, and accelerated into the night. Wherever it was going, Bahadur was going also, and without his bodyguard.

The car stopped and Bahadur was jolted back to reality. When the car was switched off, there were no lights at all, no way of telling where it had stopped. An unsettled feeling came over

Bahadur, and his fear resumed its progress into his throat. This was clearly not a police station, more like a cave. The back door snapped open, and a big hand grabbed a fistful of his clothing, and he seemed to float out of the car into a standing position. The same big hands patted his clothing in a typical police search for weapons or anything else hidden from view. In the dim light from the car interior, Bahadur saw the uniformed policeman accepting what looked to be a big wad of cash. The one handing over the cash was much larger and layered in black clothing. Then Bahadur remembered the ghost outside the car window. The one with the lethal weapon which had destroyed the limo. It was him! The transaction complete, Bahadur was now an official possession of this killer, owned by him and at his mercy, if there was to be any mercy.

"*Vy ! Poydemte so mnoy,*" his captor croaked, and pushed him forward toward the darkness.

Russian! The man is speaking Russian! Bahadur's brain screamed at him. First the bugs and now this! Bahadur feared the Russians. They weren't soft or liberalized like the Americans and the other Europeans. Russians were old style, blood and steel…and pain.

A door was opened, letting light trickle out of the building looming in the darkness, and Bahadur was pushed, stumbling, into a grim interior full of trash and grime. The path led toward a room down the hall to the left where more light was spilling into the hall. An object the size and hardness of a gun barrel was being pushed into Bahadur's back. It guided him toward and into the lit room which contained a single table and one chair.

"*Nasazhat',*" the raspy voice commanded, the gun barrel pushed him toward the chair. After he sat down he had a look at this apparition who was in control of his destiny. The man dropped his black coat on the floor and laid his weapon on the table in front of Bahadur as if defying, daring, even encouraging him to reach for it. Bahadur had been trained in weapons by the *Pāsdārān* before becoming a courier, and he recognized the weapon on the table as a Bolkov PP-2000, a late model submachine pistol of devastating power, even given its small size. Only Russian special forces had this weapon and not many of them at that. The man carrying the weapon moved with the confidence and fluidity of an athlete, one trained in combat for many years and who would probably enjoy a one-sided contest with his captive. No matter how close the weapon was, Bahadur wasn't about to make a lunge for it. The eyes of his captor were those of a poisonous snake, hard, black, full of hate, hoping for an opportunity to strike his victim. Bahadur started to shake, slightly at first, then enough that it made the chair move along the floor.

The man picked the satchel up and placed it on the table roughly. Bahadur's wrist was forced to follow along, and he knew enough not to resist.

"Dayte mne klyuch," the man demanded. Bahadur was afraid that was the reason he was captured. But there was no key, just for this reason. Even Bahadur wasn't to be permitted to read what was in that case. He wanted to appease his captor, really wanted to, and would have given up the key…gladly given it up…if it would spare his hand from being severed. The thought was enough to let his bowels finally win the struggle, and the resulting odor started ascending in choking clouds encircling his nose. His captor laughed, his teeth lighting the room with dark humor. There was a metallic sound as a ring of keys appeared, and one after another, the lock was tested. Finally, mercifully, one was found that opened the bag. The thick bundle of documents were withdrawn, and Bahadur's eyes followed his captor as he left the room, the weapon still in reach on the table.

Bahadur's eyes bulged at the weapon lying on the table. He

quickly looked the room over to see if there was any way he could be observed…there wasn't. The room was a small sealed box with two doors. The temptation was strong. The tables could be turned with this weapon…but…it was too easy. The man wanted him to pick it up. There was a trick! He quivered with indecision. Pick it up or not? Terror replaced anxiety as he understood that his life was really on the line at this moment. However, when his superiors learned that the precious contents were missing… Either way it was going to be bad, very bad for Bahadur.

After a long while, the door opened, and the thickly muscled man returned. Bahadur was watching his eyes, and he saw surprise in them. He had forgotten the gun! It was not intentional but accidental. That moment gave Bahadur new energy, and he stood up at the same moment he grasped the potent weapon, causing the table and chair to be thrown clattering to the concrete floor. Now he was the one armed, lethal, and he pointed it at the chest of the Russian. "Click…click…click." The Russian smiled and methodically took something from his waist. "Pop." The dreaded sound of a large switchblade knife opening. The Russian held it up, turning it slowly so that the light could play along the slender pointed blade. He smiled and Bahadur's blood froze. It was in the plan all along.

"Khotite zhit' v noch', tovarishch?" [Want to live the night, Comrade?] the Russian asked. Bahadur nodded that he did and dropped the weapon to the floor, then kicked it away toward the Russian. A door opened and an insanely beautiful woman came in holding Bahadur's folders. She ignored him as she moved directly to his satchel, slipping the folders back in place and snapping the lock closed. Her perfume was soft, fragrant and lingering, but the woman, who had her blonde hair tied back into a tight bun, gave the impression of being as hard as her companion. Bahadur doubted if he were a match even for this small woman, and he

became aware that his feces were spreading down his leg toward his shoes, inching their smelly way past the hairs on his legs, drop by drop.

"*Nikto ne budet znat', ob etoy nochi, no ty i ya Ne govorite, i vy budete tselymi i nevredimymi. Pogovorite i umeret'. Vy ponimayete?*" [No one will know of this night but you and I. Don't talk, and you will be unharmed. Talk and die. Do you understand?] Bahadur understood very well and nodded that he did. He also understood what the consequences of this night would be if he told his story in Tehran.

The German policeman held the rear door open, and Bahadur climbed in gratefully, clutching his bag. There was still time to catch his flight.

Chapter 21

Chapter 22

The Briefing

Kurfürstenstr, Berlin

Zeskie shook his head up and down with taut lips and narrowed eyes. "It was as I suspected. The Russians populated the data with fantasy and lies sprinkled with truths. An excellent example of good spycraft on their part but of limited use to us. This new information is exactly what we were looking for." He lowered the briefing paper and looked around the room, finding Kurt's eyes. "And you, my young spy! Excellent work getting our devices into the *hoseiniyeh*. All of them are working perfectly and likely will for years."

"I am gratified, Ron, but to be truthful, I couldn't even spot the devices. Can you tell me where they are?" Kurt said from the end of the bed.

"Common enough electrical plugs, right? Molded inside the plastic, the bugs are undetectable even by X-ray. They are powered by the electrical fields generated by the plugs which also masks the signal. The real work is done by the transformer outside the building which codes the signal and sends it to a satellite. The projection beam is collimated, and you would have to be above the transformer to detect it."

"You should know, Ron, that I didn't actually put them in. The Iranians wouldn't let me back inside, so I just handed them a box full. It's funny that they did our work for us!"

"Actually, that is what I expected them to do," Zeskie

explained.

"Now tell us about the papers we copied from the messenger case," Mick said.

"That's the best part. They were clearing out their files in case of a raid or a close examination by the German BND. We have a good deal of information that we couldn't have discovered by any other method, including two of the Iranian contacts in Washington, their code names and how much they are paid every month. It makes me sad to see so many Americans willing to sell the future of the world for only money."

"What happened to the courier, Bahadur?" April asked.

"He has returned to Berlin seemingly not worse for wear. If he had told anyone about being forced to give up the documents, we would have never seen him again. The confirmation is that the *hoseiniyeh* has returned to normal, business as usual."

"What are we going to do about the American traitors?" Mick asked.

"Remember Major General Adams of U.S. Army Intelligence?" Zeskie responded, eyebrows expectantly raised.

"Sure, great guy!" April ventured.

"I asked that he and his agency start processing the names. That means surveillance of all kinds, physical and electronic. We have to start building a case against them, and given that their supervisor is in the White House, it will have to be airtight and then some."

"If I may, Zeskie," Peter said holding up his finger. "What is the name of this person you just spoke of?"

"The toughest one of all. Code named Maggot by the Iranians. A true zealot who was indoctrinated as a child and who has lived an entire life with one ultimate purpose. To bring down the United States of America. It will be nearly impossible to prove anything against this person, and Maggot has the ear of the Press. I am withholding my suspicions regarding Maggot's identity for now to prevent any of you doing something rash until we're ready."

"Does this mean that our mission is over?" Kurt asked what everyone was thinking.

"No! The *hoseiniyeh* is still functioning, and we still need to bring it down. Besides, there are some names we don't yet have. I am working on a plan right now which will require the same kind of teamwork that you just accomplished, and I need all of you in order to carry it out. Mick, you'll have to bring Dorff into this and tell him that he is going to need some of his old buddies. We will pay them well for their services."

Zeskie looked at their faces, studying their reactions before speaking again. "And some bad, but really not surprising news," he began. "Mick, you are a high priority for the Iranians…you even have a code name. They know what happened in Tacoma, and they know you are in Germany. They even offer a cash reward for your death or capture."

"I'm wanted by everyone. It couldn't get any worse unless the Pope gets upset at me also. So, what, pray tell, is my Iranian code name?"

"Elapid."

"I never heard that word before. What does it mean?" Mick asked, his brow furrowed.

"It's the name of a group of viper snakes. They are referring to you as a poisonous snake," April said.

Kurt broke out laughing. "Ha, ha…it fits! They are right! I kind of like it!"

Peter interrupted the laughter and stood up. "The Berlin police impounded the Iranian limousine and studied the damage done during the attack. The utter destruction of the motor and the shells collected at the scene were described as "caused by a Russian weapon" and a report has been given to the Iranians at the *hoseiniyeh* and to the Iranian Embassy in Berlin. We can assume that our friend Dvorkin will realize that we are trying to frame him even after he helped us."

Zeskie laughed. "The information he gave us was mostly invented by the Russian security forces. They wanted us to stop the sex abuse at the *hoseiniyeh* but not the spy network in America. Some friends."

"They will deny involvement, but the Iranians still won't trust them from now on. There is also the matter of the Russian listening devices they found, and Bahadur will eventually be forced to admit that a Russian was looking at their secrets," Mick said.

"In short, no more cooperation from the Russians, such as it was," Zeskie concluded.

The little Porsche turned into the corner, tires chirping noisily, then accelerated with engine screaming as Mick prepared to break and fling them to the left across traffic. April was holding on with one hand on the dash and the other on the grab bar overhead.

"Mick! Slow down…please! They couldn't possibly be following any longer!"

"Just a few more… just to be sure," he said as he turned the wheel hard, sliding the car sideways before the tires caught again.

April pushed her feet into the floorboard, trying to prevent being ejected under the seat belt strap as the little car braked again, shivering as the tires hopped at first then dug into the pavement. Mick studied his rearview mirror carefully before allowing the speed to drop back to posted limits.

"No more tail," he said. "Wonder who it was?"

"Hope we never find out," April said, adjusting her clothing and also looking behind them nervously. "You have a place to stay tonight, I assume? One that is slightly better than the snake holes that you usually select?" Mick didn't answer, his attention still on the mirrors. They slid through the dark streets with purpose, their path no longer random. Ahead, a brightly lit complex beaconed to them, and to April's surprise, Mick turned in suddenly and came to a stop within reach of a uniformed doorman who instantly grabbed the door on April's side.

"*Guten Abend! Willkommen im Plaza. Sie brauchen Hilfe mit dem Gepäck?*" [Good evening! Welcome to The Plaza. Do you need assistance with luggage?] he said politely, accompanied by a small bow at the waist.

Mick accepted the claim ticket and passed the man a folded bill. "*Wir werden registriert. Mein Auto parken, wo es nicht gesehen werden kann. Verstehen Sie?*" [We are registered. Park my car where it cannot be seen. Do you understand?] The attendant nodded that he did, and Mick gave him another bill.

At the door to the lobby, Mick paused, holding April back with pressure from his arm. With narrowed eyes, he studied the people and the place through the glass for a long moment before holding the door open for her. They made less than a grand entrance and walked toward the elevators using an indirect approach, talking together with their heads down.

Room 314 was spacious and clean, and in the center was a group of hand fitted leather luggage awaiting its new occupants.

"Have you been here previously?" April asked as they settled in.

"First time. Zeskie had the luggage delivered, not me. I'm sure we will find more than clothes there.

"And now you can tell me what Ron Zeskie and you talked about after he kicked us out."

"You…and me…and why it's a bad idea for us to be in love. He's right, of course."

April came to him and enveloped him with her arms, looking up into his eyes. "No?" she said and smiled.

Chapter 22

"And you are right, of course. I can't live without you," Mick said and kissed her waiting lips.

Chapter 23

Hard Encounter

The Reichstag Cafe, Berlin

Mick saw Dorff's eyes snap on his as soon as he turned the corner. This time Dorff had his back to the wall, and his face showed concern as his eyes darted toward each corner of the cafe. Dorff was nervous, which made Mick nervous. Something was going wrong, and there was some danger hanging around the room like the scent of a wolf before he jumps the chicken wire.

Mick pulled a light wire chair out and sat down, his arms crossed on the table facing Dorff. They didn't talk at first, at least with words. Dorff was intently watching the door behind Mick as if expecting someone or something to come in.

"Being tailed?" Mick asked, intently watching Dorff's face.

"I think so. They are good, very good."

"How many?

"Two teams…perhaps three."

"Why did you lead them here?"

"Didn't see them until I was entering. Sorry. Thought you and I together could take them on."

"Armed, Dorff?"

"An old Luger. Still works, though."

"Know how they got onto you?"

"I expect it was the Russians. Payback of some kind. It's the only way. No one else could tail me, I'm not an amateur." Mick rubbed his chin and pressed his back into the chair to reassure himself that his 45 was still there.

"Well, we need to talk before the action starts, Dorff. We want some more men for a job. Your old friends. We'll pay well. Know any who speak Persian?"

"If we…you and I…live to see tomorrow, Grundy, I can get some. Even Persian is no problem. How many men?" Dorff said as his eyes continued their methodical and relentless scan.

"Dozen, two of which should be fluent in Persian. That should be adequate."

"Can I ask what they will be doing?" Dorff asked.

"Not yet. Shouldn't be dangerous, but it won't be legal." Mick could tell by the uplifted brows that Dorff had more questions, but he kept his silence. He slowly, slowly sat up more in his chair, his eyes fixed on something behind Mick's back.

"See them?"

"One. He is standing in the door looking at us. Dark skinned, not black. Black eyes, longer beard. Wearing a tan overcoat, his hands in his pockets. No doubt he's after us…or you."

"Can you hit him from here?" Mick asked.

"You mean shoot him right in the open?" Dorff asked incredulously.

"Of course. Can you do it?"

"No. Another one is now standing beside the first. They have the door blocked. There could be others in the hall."

"Follow my lead, Dorff," Mick said, then turned to look directly at the new arrivals. Meeting their eyes told him that Dorff had sized it up for what it was. Someone wasn't going to leave this room alive. One of the men shifted his stance causing his long coat to partially open revealing a short automatic weapon just starting to be brought up into firing position. Mick dove toward the floor, drawing their eyes toward him as he drew his pistol. Before he had the first man in his sights, Dorff's gun opened up from behind the table, and the first target was thrown up and back by the impact. Mick's gun fired at the second man, who was taken by surprise, two bullets entering his brain before it could give the signal to return fire. The room erupted with screaming, people noisily fleeing toward the corners of the room as Mick sprang to his feet, his weapon still pointed at the empty doorway. Mick sensed that Dorff was also advancing toward the door, his forward pointing pistol leading the way. Endless combat training sessions had made Mick's reflexes conditioned to expect another pop-up target and right on cue, another head appeared around the corner as the man's gun sprayed the room with automatic fire. A quick discharge from Mick's gun spun the new assailant around, and he fell heavily across the threshold into a spreading pool of dark blood. An ominous shrieking grew in intensity, drifting into the room from somewhere down the long hallway. Mick picked up one of the fallen Iranians and tossed the body over the threshold into the hallway. Almost before it hit the marble floor, submachine gun fire erupted from the hall, twisting and hurling the body backward into the opposite wall. Mick dropped to the floor, sliding into the opening with his pistol pointed upward. As soon as he saw the other men, he started firing from his low position, catching them too quickly for reaction. Over his head, he heard the Luger bark three times. The men in the hall were not as well-trained as Dorff had thought, because they were grouped together and fell together, all four of them. Alarms in the massive building started ringing from several directions, and sounds of shouting could be heard closing in on the cafe.

"You injured, Dorff?"

"No. You?"

"No. Let's move and quickly. Follow me," Mick said.

"Instead, Grundy, follow me. I explored this building before you were born," Dorff said and started running back into the cafe. In the corner of the room, barely noticeable, was a narrow doorway, painted exactly to match the wall, and therefore hard to spot.

Closing the door behind them, then locking it from the inside, they felt their way along a dark narrow corridor which led down steep stairs, one set after another. Behind them they could hear pounding coming from the narrow steel door, sending drum waves of sound cascading threateningly against their backs.

With a squeaky turn of a rusted steel handle, Dorff opened the lower door allowing the light of the outdoors to welcomingly wash over them. Mick quickly looked around. They were at ground level, outside the massive building looming over them. They walked casually away, not looking back, as if they were on a lovers' stroll in the woods. Police sirens were moving toward the Reichstag from every point on the compass. Mick and Dorff smoothly blended into the crowd gathering to watch the emergency in the very building which had always represented the heart and soul of Germany. As the crowd increased in size, they faded silently away.

"You are better than I expected, Dorff. Age hasn't slowed you very much."

"And you, Grundy, are a worthy partner. Your military training comes back nicely."

"Well, our former Russian friends have shown their true colors, haven't they?"

"Did you expect anything different, Grundy?"

"I hoped things would change. Actually, I like Russians even though I've been forced to shoot some of them from time to time. We have so much in common, you know."

"Like the fact that you are genetically Russian, you mean?"

"That's not been proven to me," Mick said.

"That's what they are saying, that you are a Russian by blood."

"Even if that's true, I'm an American by choice."

"The Americans are also hunting you. How does that make you feel?"

"Sick. The ones doing it are going to be very sorry, that I promise you."

Chapter 23

Chapter 24

This Time, Sincerity?

 id you hear about the ruckus over at the Reichstag?" Peter asked, eyebrows lifted. The question was friendly and inquisitive, not threatening or accusatory. Mick knew his brother better than that, Peter knew something that he was holding back.

"Were there any surveillance cameras working?" Mick asked.

"No. Our big surprise was that someone, a very skilled person, disabled them…in advance. We got nothing. The witnesses were too frightened to think and didn't remember clearly, so it's hard to know what actually happened or why. All we have is seven very dead foreign nationals who are in the morgue being processed."

"Well, do tell!" Mick exclaimed.

"From what we do know, two men killed seven heavily armed assassins in under ten seconds. Every shot they fired was a fatal one. Highly skilled and well-trained, I must say."

"Real pros?"

"Yes, but not perfect, however. A news camera came on the scene in minutes, and there was some interesting footage taken from outside the Reichstag that day."

"And?"

"I confiscated their memory cards before the broadcast, just in case…then I accidentally destroyed them."

"Good work, Brother," Mick said.

"You need another weapon. The old one could be evidence," Peter nearly whispered. Mick withdrew his pistol and handed it to

Peter without a word. Peter took a brown paper package from his bag and handed it to Mick, also without a word.

"There are two in here," Mick commented, judging the heft and size of the package.

"One is for you from Zeskie. The other one is from my personal collection of Lugers."

Mick nodded then loaded the new 45 and put it behind him. The Luger was tucked into his pants to be given to Dorff later.

"Was it you who disabled the video in advance?" Peter asked.

Mick didn't answer. He didn't need to. Peter correctly guessed that Mick was the one.

"How did you know?" Peter asked.

"I have been intermittently followed in the last few days. I knew that they would catch up when I stopped moving. They were Iranian, weren't they?"

"*Richtig.* Quds Force. Straight from the Supreme Leader of Iran, just for you."

"I'm complemented. Can't you people over in BND round up the rest, assuming that there are more out there?"

"Working on it. Don't drop your guard, though."

Dorff accepted the Luger silently, but checked the action and the cleanliness of the rifling. "Meet with your approval, Dorff?" Mick asked from across the table. Dorff didn't answer but instead buried the new Luger into his loose clothing.

"The old one, the one that ties you to the shooting, Dorff. You must get rid of it."

"No, Mick Grundy. Never give up something useful. You have much to learn."

Mick shrugged. It wasn't his risk, and therefore, none of his business. He looked around the cafe again and glanced at the time. He expected to be kept waiting, par for the course. When you are forced to wait for someone, it is supposed to be humbling, but it wasn't doing any such thing for Mick, because he was slowly getting angry.

"He's late," Mick observed to his tea cup.

"Of course," Dorff returned.

"You sure they are ready?" Mick asked.

"Absolutely. They will never be seen until it's time," he said reassuringly, smiling a crooked, tight smile.

They waited in silence, sipping Russian black tea, in the back corner of the ethnic Russian cafe on *Samariterstraße*. It was Dvorkin's turf, but it showed defiance meeting him here. Mick suggested it, Dorff hesitating at first, but after Dorff's old spy network was in place, all heavily armed and scattered strategically around, Dorff felt more at ease, but also knew that the Russians could gain the upper hand if they wanted to badly enough. It was another gamble, but Mick wanted to face down Dvorkin and put an end to the surrogate war.

The doorway darkened, and their eyes turned toward the shadow. Dvorkin stood for a moment, looking over the cafe and into each little corner. He was dressed in jeans, short lace-up boots and a short-sleeved collared shirt, exposing his muscular forearms and his thick neck. His bushy hair was speckled with gray, but otherwise full and virile. He and Mick locked eyes, two poisonous snakes staking out turf. Dvorkin made straight for their table with long measured strides.

"*Privet, Mik Grandi... Tovarishch Dorff*," Dvorkin said with his rumbling voice, while his deep set eyes peered from under his embossed frontal bone.

"Sit, if you will, Dvorkin," Mick said and nodded toward the chair. Dvorkin twisted at the waist catching the eye of the barmaid. He snapped his fingers and pointed to the table. She understood and immediately started bustling around behind the bar. He sat down in the chair and put his arms on the top, a signal that he was unarmed and peaceful.

"And what brings us together today, Mick Grundy?"

"You know, Dvorkin. You put the Iranians on our trail. Why?" Mick said, keeping his hands under the table.

"You tried to turn the Iranians on us. I had to even the score."

"Having us killed would not have solved your problem with the children, would it?"

"You are having a joke? Would I expect that ragtag bunch could take out Mick Grundy when my fellow Russians couldn't after many tries? Of course I knew you would prevail!"

"And the valuable documents you gave me were mostly Russian invention."

"And I knew that you would pick the wheat from the chaff. My comrades would never permit full cooperation. This was my personal gift to you, and I imagine you have developed your own source by now for comparison. Has this enabled you and Ron Zeskie to develop a plan?"

"We have some ideas, but there is little to thank you for," Mick said.

"*Moy novyy drug!*" he laughed. "What do you expect of me?"

"I expect that you should put aside our problems and, instead, concentrate on our common enemy."

"And I plan to do just that if you will stop trying to implicate Russians."

"I so promise. You have my word, Dvorkin."

"My solemn oath, Grundy, is that we will put aside any hint of conflict between us until this is over, and after that, we may continue to try and kill each other!" he laughed loudly, slapping the table for emphasis. The little barmaid jumped at the noise, rattling the tray she was bringing to the table. She sat it down and made a little curtsy before backing away nervously. Four cups, filled with black tea and Vodka, with a pile of sugar cakes in the center were arranged thoughtfully on a black lacquer tray, and Dvorkin was the first to help himself.

"So what is your little plan," Dvorkin said with a mouthful of cake, his eyebrows elevated in either wonder or amusement.

"You should forgive my reluctance to tell you," Mick replied.

"Well, if I were doing something similar, Mick Grundy, then I would try to cause conflict between the rival sects of Islam. That way makes everyone happy. You could, for instance, kidnap children from one faction and blame it on the other. More effective if the children are harmed or degraded in the process."

Mick sat back looking at Dvorkin with intensity. He knew even before the plan was fully hatched. How could he know?"

"And, I would try to recruit some of the older but highly trained East Germans to do the dirty work. Of course, they would have to be paid well…very well… enough to buy their silence if not their loyalty."

Mick looked at Dorff. His men had been turned for Russian money. Dorff met his eyes and shrugged. It was expected after all, there was no cause here, only money.

"But, not to worry, Mick Grundy, because I like your plan, such as it is, and I will keep silent about it like a good partner would do," Dvorkin said and drained his second cup of Vodka laced tea.

"Dvorkin, do you know the name of the Iranian asset in the White House?" Mick asked.

"That, my Comrade, is your problem, not ours. After all, your people freely elected that bunch. You must deal with that issue without our help." He reached for his third cake.

"What exactly does my new ally propose to do to help us?" Mick asked bluntly.

"We will stay out of your way, if you leave us out of it. That's a lot of help, Grundy."

Mick sipped his potent tea, looking across the table at his potent adversary. "Pity," he finally said.

"I agree," Dvorkin said. "Americans and Russians should not always be on the other side of things. Let's, you and I, at least, come to terms and be at peace with each other." Dvorkin offered his big hand across the table toward Mick. After a slight hesitation, trying to discern if Dvorkin was sincere, Mick accepted his hand. "After all, you are a Russian by birth, my new friend, and I am willing to forgive and forget," Dvorkin added before letting go.

"Again the birth thing. I've heard that before, as you may know, and I'm tired of hearing that fabrication. I have a brother, a German, and we are related according to our DNA. It's my belief that my father was an American soldier."

"Perhaps, *moy brat, moy tovarishch,* I know more than you about this subject," Dvorkin said. He turned to Dorff and grinned, "About your men, Comrade. Two have fled, but the rest are in place, all ten of them. They would do their not good enough best, but they and you are outmatched. If we meet again, we should do so without need of armed forces. Agreed?"

Dorff nodded acceptance and slunk further down in his chair.

Dvorkin rose to his feet and threw a wad of euros on the table. "My treat today, Comrades. *Otpravit' privet po Aprel'.*" Again a deep laugh as he turned and darkened the door on his way out.

"You have leaks, Grundy," Dorff said, observing the obvious.

"And so do you," Mick retorted. "Can we trust this man?"

"Of course not. But do we have a choice?

Chapter 25

April's Turn

In the far distance, she could hear a ringing. Turning her head to localize the sound didn't help, but the ringing seemed familiar, persistent and growing louder. April opened her eyes and squinted at the bedside clock. 2:00 AM. The phone was ringing loudly beside the clock.

She pushed her arm above the blanket and reached out blindly for the receiver, bringing it back under the covers to her ear. "Yes?"

"April!" the excited voice said into her ear. "Are you there, April?" it persisted.

"Yes," she answered sleepily, rubbing her face with the other hand, bending her nose back and forth in the awakening ritual. "Who is this?" she asked while yawning widely.

"It's Peter, April. Are you awake now?"

"Sort of," she said as her mind spun up like a disk drive awakening. "Something happen to Mick?" she asked, her voice registering some agitation.

"This is about you," Peter said, then hesitated for a moment while her brain came fully alert.

"Tell me. I'm ready," she said and sat up, feeling for her pistol under the pillow.

"First, we are on the way to you right now. Ten minutes out, no more. We just got word moments ago that you are the target. Get ready and hold on. Are you getting this?"

"Target? Who are…"

"We think about twelve. Probably, they are already in the hotel and on the way up to your room. There is no time to talk. Arm yourself and take cover. We are coming."

April dropped the phone and rolled off the bed on the side away from the door, pointing her Beretta across the bed at the only entryway into the room. She listened for any unusual noise, now alert and focused. The room was small, the bathroom behind her, the window drapes closed. She tried to recall if there was any way to open a window to the outside but remembered that they were sealed, and the modern outside structure was flat with no sill. There was only one way in and one way out. They would come through the only door. She flipped the gun safety off and lined up the sights just above the handle of the door when she heard the first sounds. She decided to lower herself below the bed to effect maximum surprise, just as the door handle turned softly, emitting a click. Whoever was there was using an electronic passkey.

The door squeaked softly as it opened, while April held her breath. Peter said that he and his team were on the way. Ten minutes he said. She had to hold out for that long…at least.

"We know that you are in here. Come out, and we will not harm you," a deep, accented voice said. April heard a soft footfall as he and others came cautiously into the room. The bed was mounted to the floor with a wood perimeter, so she couldn't shoot under it. From far away, sounds of sirens were now decidedly audible. Help was on the way.

"We are prepared to kill you if necessary. You don't want a grenade to be tossed over the bed, do you?" he said. The sirens grew louder.

"I am unarmed. What do you want?" April said.

"You will come with us," the voice demanded. He was just on the other side of the bed, and the room was very dark. They must have closed the door, April surmised. That would mean two or three men at the most. Where were the rest?

"I'm afraid. Tell me what you want with me?" she said, whimpering a bit.

"You are only a hostage. We would prefer a live one. Come out right now."

"No," she said. She felt the bed move as if someone had mounted it from the other side. He was on his way across. April rolled to her back, her pistol gripped by both hands. In the dark, his head was hard to see when it started to appear above her, but she knew she was even harder to see in the shadow of the bed. When the man's head was directly above her, she fired directly into his forehead, sending his body up and slightly back. She extended her arm so that her pistol was pointed across the bed and toward the door when she opened fire. She spread out eight quick rounds in a fan shape toward the presumed intruders. There was a shriek before an automatic weapon poured fire into the mattress resulting in a huge plume of dust and fabric. April's hearing was gone, but she could feel the vibration of a body hitting the floor on the other side of the room. She started moving around the foot of the bed as quickly as she was able, pausing to look before becoming exposed. At the end of the bed, she peeked using one eye, pulling back quickly. A man was crouched in the corner to the side of the door, his weapon pointing over the bed. Two bodies were on the floor and motionless. Legs extended out awkwardly over her head from the one on top of the bed. She began to hear the sirens outside as her hearing returned. She took her time aiming her weapon at the last man, determined to hit him in the head in case he was wearing armor. Five rounds were left in her magazine, and four were sent toward the hiding man's head. He suddenly stood and, in a final death spasm, gripped his trigger while his weapon discharged all its ammo toward the concrete floor creating a massive fireball. April didn't move, waiting for the next man through the door. One round left, but she was going to make it count.

She didn't have long to wait. A terrific explosion erupted in the hall, blowing the door inward as smoke curled devilishly into the room, backlit by hall lights.

"April?" a voice called. "Don't shoot, it's Peter. Are you there?" he asked.

"Here."

Several big men pushed into the room, all heavily armed. "April?" Peter called softly. April slowly stood erect, tossing her pistol on top of the body on the bed. Peter rushed to her, wrapping his big arms around her and pulled her into his chest.

"We got here as fast as we could after they were spotted. I'm so sorry it wasn't in time. Are you injured?"

"No. What happened to the others? Twelve you said." She pushed away from him and surveyed the fallen bodies.

"You got four. One in the hall blew himself up trying to toss a live grenade at us while a bullet tore through his chest. The rest got away."

"Don't stand here coddling me, Peter. Go chase the others down, or they will be back."

"Not to worry, April. I have thirty men outside, and they are tearing out the shrubs looking for them. We'll get them. Did they say anything to you before the shooting started?"

"The one on the bed said that I was going to be a hostage…or dead."

"You would have been bait to attract the most dangerous man in Germany to his death. I'm afraid that there will be no end to this. No matter how many we kill, there will always be a new supply."

"It's like the end of worlds, Peter. The fanatics have penetrated Washington and are already acting as if they own Europe. They have managed to reverse the old order of things and now have all our backs to the wall."

"What we should have learned from the origins of World War II is that you have to kill your enemies, not allow them to grow in power until it is nearly impossible to stop them. You can't play by your own rules, you have to play by theirs."

April stood still, watching Peter's face as he grimaced, thinking about the epic struggles starting to again envelop a sleeping Europe. "Where is Mick?" she asked, interrupting his thoughts.

"Meeting with Zeskie and Dorff, I believe."

"Why weren't you and I invited?" April asked.

"Because Dorff was part of the East German Stasi. As an officer of the BND, I couldn't be expected to ignore his long history of atrocities against fellow Germans. I would have to shoot Dorff on sight."

"Didn't you provide Dorff with a new pistol?"

"Yes. Because of my brother. Dorff saved his life. But that doesn't change reality or history."

"Has it occurred to you that Dorff may be playing both sides? After all, I have no obligation to shoot Dorff, and he could have worked it so that I would be alone tonight instead of at the meeting."

Peter stroked his chin thinking it over. "But Dorff killed four Iranians at the Reichstag Cafe. It wouldn't seem possible that…" Peter stopped, his mind running down the possibilities. "On the other hand, it would be a perfect cover. Only the BND knows whose bullets killed which Iranians. It could mean that Dorff set that one up also."

"Don't forget about Dvorkin. He may be controlling Dorff, just like the KGB and the Stasi did years ago. This is starting to look and smell like a Russian chess board to me."

Peter sighed, "I don't know what to think any longer. My original training was as a simple soldier…you see the enemy, and you kill the enemy. The real world of lies, half-truths and strange allegiances is not what I thought I understood. I'm sure that my brother feels the same."

"He did…once. Now he is part of that dark world and is better at it than nearly anyone. Don't discuss what you suspect with Mick. Let him figure it out by himself, because he will. I do have one suggestion for us, though," April paused, making sure that Peter was listening. "We have to talk this over with Triska. We need her advice."

Peter had forced that thought back into the hidden places of his mind. Triska. The old spy. Yes, Triska might be useful after all. She knows Dorff, suggested Dorff, and now should be made to assume responsibility for Dorff. "I agree, April. It's painful and humiliating for me to admit, but this sort of thing is right up her alley, not mine."

"Then it's settled. I know that you don't want to deal with Triska so I will go to her for all of us. All I need is a safe trip down to her, wherever she is at the moment."

"I am going to take you into protective custody tonight, April. This will allow you to travel with a heavily-armed escort, and I will call Triska myself to tell her that you are on the way."

"Zeskie," he answered, then, as he listened to the caller, his eyes roamed the room, settling on Dorff. Mick noticed that Dorff wanted to squirm but, instead, kept extraordinarily still, holding his breath while trying to listen to the small voice on the phone. Zeskie grunted and hung up.

"Problems?" Mick asked.

"Indeed. A big shootout at your hotel. Five dead and the entire area has been cordoned off." Zeskie looked at Dorff as if waiting for a response.

"Why are you looking at me? Do you imagine that while I was

here I could have had anything to do with whatever happened?" Dorff responded, raising his voice and his eyebrows in protest.

"I didn't say any such thing, Dorff, but I do remember the effort you went through to keep this meeting between the three of us. Makes me wonder."

"We are here to discuss the abduction of toddlers and small children. The fewer who know, the better. You agreed as I remember," Dorff said, pointing his finger at Zeskie.

"Is April involved?" Mick asked.

"Sure. That's what it was all about. They tried to take her hostage or kill her. She shot four of them in her room. One blew himself up. Some apparently got away," Zeskie said. "She is uninjured. An entire unit of the BND was dispatched to the scene, and they are still there with Peter in charge."

Mick stood up, agitated, angry, clenching his jaw and his fists. He stared off into space, already calculating his revenge.

"Wait, Mick. Not yet. Let Peter and his men handle this for now," Zeskie pleaded.

Mick turned slowly toward Dorff, hovering over him, rage written on his face. "Dorff, I was beginning to like you."

Dorff jumped to his feet and backed away, both palms up toward Mick. "No, Grundy. They want you to think that. I had nothing, nothing at all, to do with this. We are on the same team, Grundy. You are angry, and I don't blame you, but Dorff is your friend, not your enemy." He continued to retreat until his back was against the dirty wall. Mick stood, rigid as a statue, his mind racing back and forth over the facts.

Ron Zeskie stood and moved in front of Mick. "Listen for a moment, Mick. Doesn't this sound like a Russian strategy to make amends with the Iranians by providing them with critical and timely information, knowing that Dorff would be suspected? Dorff would seem to have no motives, not true with the Russians. You have to calm down while we think this through."

"Where is April?"

"Peter has taken her under his wing. You have absolutely nothing to worry about, because she is safe." Zeskie would say no more than that with Dorff present, and Mick sensed as much.

Mick's eyes said it all, words were not needed. If Dorff was involved, there was no hiding place small enough or remote enough to conceal him. Mick would take a horrible revenge on him, no matter how long it took.

"You will discover, Mick Grundy, that I am telling you the truth. We must get back to the plan. Can you do this?" Dorff asked and returned to his chair to show his confidence.

Reluctantly, Mick sat down, but his face was dark and his eyes mean. Clearly, there were going to be retributions, it was only a question of time.

Chapter 26

Old Spies, Young Spies, Forever Spies

BND Headquarters, Stuttgart

Triska was waiting, already seated behind the big polished table when April was ushered into the room. The door closed softly behind her just as Triska got up to exchange hugs with her.

"So glad to see you again, my dear April. I heard about your adventure! You impressed everyone, even me!"

"And I am glad to see you again, Triska. Thank you for always being there when we need you."

"I'll be there for you both as long as I live." Triska dropped her smile, "It must be important for you to travel all this way for a conversation."

"I had a close call the other night. Zeskie was right. I shouldn't be where Mick has to look after my safety and his while running a mission. I was in the way, and I have nothing to add to their mission."

"You are right to get away from Berlin. The people after you won't quit until they get Mick Grundy, or he gets them. You will be safe here in Stuttgart."

"You remember a man named Dorff?" April asked.

"Gruber Dorff. Sure do. Is he involved?"

"He is working with Mick. I think Mick got his name from you, didn't he?"

"He is one of the several I recommended. Have you met him?"

"No. Mick and Ron Zeskie are the only ones who have. I get the feeling that Dorff is dangerous."

"And you are correct. Gruber Dorff is a methodical killer, at least in the past he was. We thought of him as the hit man for the Stasi. He was always reliable when I asked for favors, and of course, I made a point to return favors when he requested them. Within limits, I always trusted Dorff."

"Colonel Dvorkin. Know him?" April asked.

"Know his history. So what is this about, April?"

"I know you keep up, Triska. You already likely know more than I do, so you know the question."

"You wonder if Dorff is answering to Dvorkin and if Dvorkin is playing everyone, is that it?"

"Yes, exactly."

"Simply put, you can't trust Dvorkin, even for a moment. But Dorff doesn't like the Russians, never has. I don't believe that Dorff would do that, especially since he knows I'm involved."

"Do you have an opinion who tipped the Iranians off about me?"

"Sounds like Dvorkin's work. He enjoys playing havoc with the Americans."

"If Mick finds out, Dvorkin won't live to see another day," April observed.

"Dvorkin is one tough customer. Easily as hard as Mick. I hope it doesn't happen that way."

"Have I been arrested? Am I free to leave here?"

"You have been listed as a witness in protection. No name was entered. When I leave, you go with me to my apartment. Satisfactory?"

"I love you, Triska," April said, becoming emotional.

"And I love you, my dear future *Enkelin.*"

A Small Cafe, East Berlin

They waited while the cell phone lay helplessly and silently between them, inanimate for the moment.

"He's always late. You know this," Dorff repeated. Mick grunted, a sign that he agreed that it was true. Dvorkin would keep God waiting if he could. It was a sign of his superiority, his importance, to keep people he considered under him waiting.

"I won't wait much longer, Dorff. After today, I have to assume that Dvorkin wants war between us, and that he never intended to become allies."

Dorff shrugged. Conflict between the Russians and Americans was an old story. It was no skin off of his nose if they went at it again…as long as he wasn't connected in some way.

"Are you satisfied that I had no hand in betrayal of your FBI Agent?" Dorff asked.

"I still have questions, Dorff. You have proven to be resilient…and dangerous. You are not yet above suspicion." Dorff sighed and resumed staring at the small phone.

When it rang, the long awaited sound startled both of them, and Mick resisted the temptation to pick it up first. Dorff sat and watched his ringing phone but didn't pick it up. It rang over and over until their nerves could no longer take it and finally Mick snatched it up.

"Grundy here."

The familiar voice on the other side speaker laughed. "Well, my new friend, Mick Grundy. Is this call you requested from me an act of friendship or a warning?" Dvorkin asked.

"A question, Dvorkin. There was an attack on the hotel where April was staying. My feeling is that it was your piece of nasty work."

"And is this a question or an accusation, Mick Grundy?"

"A question."

"Then the answer is simple. I, or my colleagues, had no part in it. My word on it. Will you believe me is my question to you?"

"Then who?" Mick asked.

"Well, on this side of the street, we feel that Americans were involved. The same ones who are hunting you right now. Their Iranian allies were only too willing to do their bidding, to their tragic end. By the way, that is some woman you have hooked up with. I would love to meet her someday."

"Not the CIA?" Mick asked, his face coloring. Dorff was listening intently to the one side of the conversation and putting the pieces together.

"Not the CIA. Zeskie knows nothing about this, and he will be mortified to learn that there are paths around him. Are you prepared to believe me yet?"

"Yes, Dvorkin. In a way, it would be less messy if it were you, I'm sorry to say."

"Not at all, Mick Grundy. I am a rather messy person, and I am glad that you don't have to discover this for yourself. Another issue, my friend. You and your people have managed to turn the Iranians against us. They are secure with their new American friends and think that they can manage without us. Congratulations on a small but temporary victory."

"All in a day's work. *Do svidaniya i byt' v bezopasnosti.*"

"And you, Mick Grundy."

Mick put the phone back on the table and felt the eyes of Dorff on him, expecting an explanation. "It wasn't you or him. My people did it," Mick said.

"You have a big problem, Grundy."

Chapter 27

An Alternative Plan

Kurfürstenstr, Berlin

April looked up at Mick, waiting for him to hold the door open, smiling as he did so. He looked down and smiled back. "Too grubby to touch, my tough little FBI agent?"

"Special Agent," she corrected as they entered the bar. Again, all eyes were on them, and the ambient conversation diminished. Mick couldn't tell if he was the one being scrutinized or if it was April. He didn't want to know, really. They headed up the creaky stairs with Mick's hand affectionately on the small of her back.

Zeskie was waiting, briefcase open on the bed, sandwiched between Peter and Kurt. When Mick and April entered, they saw the worried looks all around. Mick drew up a chair for her and stood behind it, his hands lightly, protectively, on her shoulders.

"At last, and safely back," Zeskie said. "Welcome, April. I can't tell you how good it is to see you again. We never talked after your episode at the hotel, but among those few of us who know what happened, we are all deeply impressed with you."

"I second that," Kurt joined.

"What happened to your CIA phone?" Zeskie wondered.

"It's taking a trip toward Italy in a southbound train. They'll have to tear the train apart to find it," she answered.

"And yours, Mick?"

"Mine is being carried by a feral city cat. It's amazing how well duct tape works."

"I'm really sorry about this, you two. They went around me and nearly cost both of your lives.

"Please explain, Zeskie. What are you talking about?" Peter asked.

"Their CIA phones. They were being monitored by Washington, and their conversations and locations were disclosed to our enemies. Have any of you heard of INR before?" Even April shook her head no, as did the rest. "A little history lesson then. It started with the OSS or Office of Strategic Studies of World War II. At the end of the war, a branch was separated, given to the State Department and titled the Bureau of Intelligence and Research. Lately, their official publication lists under four hundred employees and a budget of under one hundred million dollars. Those are preposterous figures as everyone in the intelligence service knows. Their actual budget is controlled by the White House, and their employee list is very, very long. It's all so secret that even the CIA doesn't know how big the INR is. The current directors are appointed by the present administration. You know the rest. There is the source of the Iranian connection, just a few blocks from the White House."

"How long will it take them to figure it out about the phones?" Mick asked.

"I don't know if there are boots on the ground here in Berlin. If there is a physical presence here…then not long. Two days max."

"Why is April back here where she could get hurt," Kurt asked Mick what he and Peter were thinking.

"Because she had to leave. They knew where she was, so there was no choice," Zeskie answered for him.

"But, that's not why you called us together, is it?" Peter surmised.

"No. Our listening devices at the *hoseiniyeh* have started paying off since the attempt on April. The ones who escaped Peter's dragnet turned up there, and we were privy to their conversations. We even managed to take a few photographs. To summarize, there are at least ten men, fresh from Iran who are determined to kill any enemy of their version of Islam and more on the way. Mick and April are high on the target list, as we already knew, but there is a surprise also. They blame the Russians not only for spying but cooperation with Americans, and Colonel Dvorkin has become public enemy number one."

Kurt started to laugh. "It's exactly what we wanted. A wedge between the Russians and Iranians! How perfect!"

"No so fast, Kurt. Any rift is likely temporary, because the two sides need each other for different reasons," Mick noted. "Both sides are in conflict just short of war with us in the West. It will be our side which loses if we all don't wake up soon."

"And that won't happen with the present administration in Washington. The West usually looks to Washington for leadership, as it has done since the War, but no longer," Zeskie noted.

"All of that is interesting, of course, but what are we to do about any of it?" Peter asked loudly.

Zeskie looked up to Peter to make his point clear. "You, Peter, should alert the BND to start more rigorous screening at the German borders to prevent large numbers of Iranian fighters from entering. We will provide your office with what we have on the ones here already, and your people can try to scoop some of them up. The rest we will have to hunt down and kill before anything else happens."

"This is another distraction from our original purpose which was to cut the link between Washington and Iran," Mick said.

"There aren't any rules against doing two things at the same time, Mick," Zeskie answered. "I have prepared a list of Muslim children from Sunni families for Dorff and his men. They were selected from influential, wealthy homes, and when they go missing, we will be sure to disclose to their parents the pattern of child molestation which has occurred at the *hoseiniyeh*. The resulting uproar will ensure the destruction and elimination of the Iranian presence in Berlin, and our hands will be clean."

"I'm sorry, Ron. I just don't understand why the children won't just tell their parents that nothing happened to them."

"They will. But it will be too late to save the Iranians."

"I don't like the plan, and I don't believe in it," April stated.

"And I agree with April," Mick added.

Zeskie slumped visibly, tossed his papers on the bed and threw up his hands. "All right, I have been pushing this agenda, but I'm open to suggestions. Everyone here will admit that the *hoseiniyeh* has to be shut down, but more importantly, the Americans who are in sympathy with them have to be found and stopped. I'm listening."

"First item," Mick said with his finger in the air. "Another kidnapping of their courier. We got by with it before, and we learned a lot."

"They are better prepared than last time. Now, they are using three cars, all bristling with well-trained and armed terrorists. It would never work like last time," Zeskie said.

These guards are from the same bunch who attacked our hotel?" Mick asked.

"I presume so."

"Killing two birds with one stone. It's the way I would want it." Mick said. "Any other changes?"

"Yes, they are using a different route and traveling to the airport during the daytime."

Mick mulled it over. Zeskie was right, it was going to be hard and bloody…plus it was an open attack during broad daylight. The German and international press would descend like ravens on the scene. He glanced at his two brothers and saw that they were conversing together and shared a look of concern.

"You two have anything to add?" Mick asked them.

Peter sat up, frowning. "There is something troubling me, Mick. Zeskie has his list of children to kidnap, and from here, it looks extensive, but I have concerns that we are not being told the entire truth. There is reason to think that the process has already started before this meeting."

"I don't know what you are referring to Peter," Zeskie bristled. "We haven't agreed to start as yet, I've only put down some names as suggestions. You have to explain your remarks."

"In the past three days, there has been a spate of child kidnappings across Germany. I saw the list myself, posted in the Berlin office. There is a lot of talk about it because of the ethnicity of the children…all Arab. Frankly, I assumed it was the work of the CIA or Dorff's crew. Are you saying that this is not true?"

"We, to my knowledge, haven't been even close to grabbing a child. So far, the matter is still under discussion," Zeskie answered.

"Two were from the Berlin area north of here," Kurt added. "I, too, assumed that it had started."

"In the last three days, huh?" Zeskie said absentmindedly as he reached for his phone. After it connected, he said, "Jones…Zeskie here. Are there any reports of children at the *hoseiniyeh* recently…in the last several hours?" He listened silently for a moment, then hung up looking saddened and perplexed.

"And?" April prodded.

"Yes. They are back at it again, even at this moment. The whole thing is being recorded by my staff. I guess they did our work for us. We don't need to worry about picking children up after all."

"Something's not right here," Mick said. "Previously, they were using children from a remote area who had no protection whatsoever. They are too smart to start using local children, because the consequences would be terrible for them when they are caught."

"This information will authorize a raid by the German police assisted by the BND. I will see that it happens tonight." Peter said.

"Not to disagree with you, Peter, but like in America, you have to have probable cause. We can't openly admit that we bugged the place. You'll have to post surveillance first or capture them with the childen as they leave…after the fact, I'm afraid," April said.

"I have a better idea," Zeskie said, rubbing his chin. "I'll have our Ambassador's office alert the respective Arab representatives. Let them do what we wanted them to do, and it shouldn't take too long."

"Agreed. Nevertheless, I have to act to save any children I can, and as quickly as I can," Peter said and stood up motioning to Kurt to follow. After goodbyes, they quickly left.

"Well, it's started," Zeskie said. We won't get any more information from that place, and we will have to act on what we have so far." He sat back down and looked at April and Mick across from him. "Have a place to stay tonight?" he asked.

"All taken care of," Mick replied. April nodded yes as well.

"Got your BND phones?"

"Yes. Got yours?" Mick asked.

"Sure. Funny that the CIA station chief would have to depend on Germans for communications, isn't it?"

"Not funny. Sad," Mick replied.

Chapter 28

A Uniquely Arab Solution

Jalal al Din shifted gears during the lumbering turn as the massive concrete truck responded lazily to its accelerator. The drum behind them was turning slowly and was noisy about it but, of course, so was the big diesel motor. It was another example of hiding in plain sight. Jalal al Din wondered if the efficient German police would be inquisitive about a concrete delivery during the night, but, so far, no one even looked at them twice. He glanced at Siddiq who was studying the map again. He didn't appear in the least distressed about the night's work. Siddiq was cheerful and talkative as if they were going to visit family or even a lover. Not so for Jalal al Din. He hands were sweaty, forcing him to use extra pressure to turn the big steering wheel.

"How much further?" Jalal al Din asked over the din of noise. His voice was high pitched and fast.

"Two more blocks. After the next turn, you have to gather some speed." Siddiq looked at him hard for a moment, wondering if Jalal al Din had second thoughts or had lost his sense of mission. "It is a good cause, Jalal al Din. Do not think otherwise," he shouted and patted Jalal al Din on the shoulder.

"The children. Any there will die. Does that not concern you?" Jalal al Din asked, keeping Siddiq in his vision too long. Siddiq gently pushed Jalal al Din's face forward toward the oncoming road.

"The children have been violated. Their parents would not accept them back. They will be cleansed by fire." Siddiq smiled broadly at his wisdom, his assurance of the appropriateness of their actions. He was proud to become a martyr for Allah. Proud that he could take the lives of so many foul Shia at the same time. It was a vision of completeness of his life come true. "Do you not share my happiness for this holy mission?"

"I was just thinking about all that I am giving up," Jalal al Din said over the noise. "Do you want to give up the pleasures of women or fresh food, or of even seeing your brothers again?"

Siddiq looked surprised. "We are all to be reunited in the afterlife. Allah will provide us with many virgins. You know this but still you fret?"

The last turn was accomplished, and the big truck labored heavily to gain speed. The bounding and jostling in the cab grew more violent as the speed slowly increased. Jalal al Din was too involved in driving to answer Sidduq's questions. The one story *hoseiniyeh* was just in sight now, and the truck was making a direct line for it, the only obstacles a short curb and one small car. In spite of his fears, Jalal al Din smiled broadly and started to laugh. Nothing could stop them now, and in a few moments, they both would be in the arms of Allah. He pushed the button starting the arming process and held the accelerator to the floor.

A terrific explosion shook the southwest side of Berlin as an orange fireball rose high into the sky, casting a flicking light and diverting two commercial aircraft from their landing pattern above the nearby airport. A rolling shock wave broke windows for several blocks and overturned dozens of cars in adjacent streets. Smaller fires were burning briskly in nearby buildings still standing. Later, the death toll would be counted at nearly fifty and that would not include anyone vaporized in the target location of the explosion. Berlin had not suffered a bomb of this magnitude since the war.

The bed shook slightly, and Mick patted the other side. She was still there. He glanced at the bedside clock which displayed 4:10 in glowing red. Turning over, he snuggled into his pillow, determined to get at least two more hours sleep, when, in the distance, he heard the first sirens. He started listening in spite of himself, now more awake, and he could hear them from several locations, the sounds filtering into the hotel room. Something was happening.

"What it is, Mick?" April asked, patting him softly, mostly to reassure herself that he was still in bed with her.

"I don't know. Just some sirens. Hope I didn't wake you."

"Something did," she said sleepily and rotated her wrist to look at her watch.

Mick wrapped his arm over her and pulled her close, just as the cellphone started ringing. He picked it up and held it between them so that they both would hear the caller.

"Mick!" Peter boomed. "You hear the explosion?"

"We heard something. What was it?"

"The *hoseiniyeh* is now a smoking hole…vaporized and spread all over Berlin."

"You're kidding! Who could have organized a retaliation this fast? How was the weapon delivered?" Mick was imagining a cruise missile or a targeted weapon from a fighter jet.

"Truck bomb…a very big one. We are expecting some party to claim credit soon, because it looks like a suicide attack."

Mick sat up, pulling the phone away from April's ear. "The planning would have to have been in the works for a while, wouldn't you think? I mean, you only received reports of missing children three days ago. I don't understand," he said.

Peter cleared his throat, "We were under the false assumption that a clamor would arise from the Arabs forcing the German Government to eject the Iranians, or perhaps shoot a couple of them. This is like the Mid East; we are in the midst of a vendetta. Clearly, we don't have a clue what is really going on."

Nikolay and Pavel each got out from the front of the car at the same time. Nikolay reached for the rear door handle but stopped, remembering that Colonel Dvorkin didn't want or need favored treatment. He wondered if the Colonel didn't want a potential enemy to see how important he is, or did he actually feel that all men were equal? The door opened, and the large Colonel got out more easily then would be expected for his size. The car seemed to sigh relief and slowly decompressed by twelve centimeters. Dvorkin slammed the door and motioned for his bodyguards to walk behind at a respectable distance. They could see that he was thicker than usual and surmised that he was wearing body armor and even more likely, carrying an automatic weapon under the heavy coat. Pavel caught the eye of Nikolay and shrugged. Neither man knew where they were going or the reason, and there was nothing new about it. They were there to protect, not advise. Pavel checked his weapon again, fingering the safety on and off, and patting his pockets for additional magazines. After watching this familiar routine, Nikolay did the same. Given the well-deserved reputation of Colonel Dvorkin, bodyguards were largely superfluous, but that is what the high command demanded.

The streets were dark enough, but this area had suffered with the influx of poverty-stricken immigrants from Turkey and Syria and who knows where else. Some of the street lamps had been intentionally broken, and some were just stolen. There was danger here, you could feel it in the sounds of echoes and the litter on the sidewalk. A meeting was scheduled, but Dvorkin never kept appointments punctually. It was bad form and indicated weakness. He would get there when he got there. Besides, this group was just another Islamic terrorist organization wanting weapons from

Russia. Tiresome. Dvorkin hated these rabble, their cause, their beards, the smell of their food, in fact, everything about them. Russia was playing Russian Roulette by dealing with them. Look what happened to the Americans who supported the *Mujahedin* in their fight against the aging Soviet Union in Afghanistan. It came back to haunt them and still does.

The small parade turned the corner. A long row of tall windows above street level indicated the south corner of their destination…a warehouse full of imported food destined for the growing Mid Eastern population of Berlin. Dvorkin rolled his eyes and inhaled deeply, trying to prepare his body for the assault on his olfactory centers. He laughed to himself. They all had heard the explosion earlier as the fanatic Sunni had evened the score against the equally fanatic and morally depraved Shiites. A brilliant piece of maneuvering, if he did say so for himself. The idea, of course, was created by the Americans, but they weren't up to implementing it as well as he had. All it took was a little bit of nearly simultaneous efforts. Kidnapping and, at the same time, informing and alerting the right people. The filthy Iranians were careless in determining where their last load of children were from. It was their responsibility, their appetite for sex with children that had enabled the plan to work. And it had worked! From this day forward, no children from the Russian provinces would be abused, and their reward of immolation was well deserved and earned, child by helpless child. And the best part was that Russia would not be blamed. The Iranians remaining alive in Berlin would be led to believe that the CIA was behind the entire plot, and there was at least some truth in this fabrication. The Persians always believe that every rock covers a CIA operative, and every reversal is a CIA victory. The Americans might yet figure out that Dvorkin was the mastermind and had accomplished what they were helpless to achieve. There could be no harm in the cooperation that would ensue from a reduction in tension in this new old Cold War.

The still night air split with the sound of machine gun fire, lasting at least four continuous seconds. Dvorkin dropped to the pavement as he had been taught so long ago by his *Stárshiy Serzhánt*, a tough man devoted to tough training. The gunfire stopped as abruptly as it had started. Dvorkin glanced around behind him and saw his bodyguards lying in lifeless heaps. He rolled to his side and pulled his weapon up while looking for the assailants.

"You are about to be shot. Do not move," a voice came from the shadows in accented-British English. Dvorkin lowered his gun and tried to look toward the sound of the voice. He needn't have bothered, because the owner of the voice was standing close enough to see his shoes.

"Get up, Polkóvnik Dvorkin, and raise your hands as if you meant it," the voice commanded. Dvorkin slowly rose to his feet wondering if he could still get at his weapon. A pair of hands grabbed him from behind, holding his arms as another pair quickly cut the strap holding his machine pistol. They frisked him, finding two additional pistols and an automatic knife. "You will remove your coat, Polkóvnik," the same voice commanded, then added, "and your body armor." Dvorkin was starting to feel vulnerable, and the feeling grew when he felt the hard muzzle of an automatic weapon in his back. "Walk," the man commanded. Dvorkin silently counted the men in view. Five, all armed with stubby black weapons. Perhaps more in the shadows across the street. The group headed for the same warehouse door Dvorkin had been headed toward. It opened from the inside just as they arrived, and they passed two more men on either side of the door, a weapon hanging under their shoulders.

Dvorkin knew enough not to ask questions. If they had wanted, he would already be dead. It was something else…perhaps an interrogation…or hostage. Time would tell. He was outwardly calm, confident, but not defiant. The direction led into a small side room where a chair was waiting for him, and he was thrust toward it. After being seated, he studied the faces of the five men in front of him. He could see anger and hatred radiating from them. Their obvious commander was the only one clean-shaven, as the others had nearly identical dark, abundant, facial hair making their exposed teeth gleam as if they were wolves ready to feast on meat…him. Dvorkin was sure that the men were trained soldiers from a special forces unit, and their appearance and the few words spoken indicated that they were Iranian.

"Just who are you and what do you want?" Dvorkin asked, looking at the man in charge.

"We wanted you, the man responsible for the bombing and murder of Iranian Holy men."

"Me? I am Russian. We don't use suicide bombers, never have, never will. Might I suggest a radical Islamic group such as yourselves as the suspect?"

"Don't insult us. This was your work, Dvorkin. Your men, under your instruction, made sure that fanatics would come after our peaceful people."

"And why would I do that to former allies in the struggle against the West?"

"You may have personal reasons, I suspect, but there is also the probability that you believed your own lies about criminal sexual activity at the *hoseiniyeh* and acted in concert with agents of the CIA."

"Lies? This declaration of innocence is from the perverted lips of your 'holy people', isn't it?" The commander struck Dvorkin in the abdomen with his foot, knocking him and the chair to the floor. No one rushed to help him up, and there were grins of satisfaction all around. He slowly stood, glaring back at the men in the room and, just as deliberately, sat down again.

"I will tell you men that each of you will pay a terrible price for my capture. May you enjoy your moment of dominance for as long as you can. You have been severely misled by your superiors. The fact that your people, in the now-smoking *hoseiniyeh*, were given to sexual predation with minors is a truth, like it or not, and believe it or not, none of you will live to return home again." As soon as he finished speaking, one of the guards used his weapon to strike a violent blow to Dvorkin's head, rendering him unconscious.

Chapter 29

Exposed

Tiergartentunnel Park, Berlin

Zeskie squinted at a distant building, shielding his eyes with his hand. "Frankly, Mick, I can't think of a more exposed place to meet than this one. The American Embassy is only two blocks from here; I can almost see it." Mick didn't answer and was looking around slowly, taking in every human form within view.

"We're not leaving until Dorff shows up. Just keep watch and tell me everything you know about the bombing."

"No group has taken credit thus far, but it clearly is the signature of al-Qaeda or a spin off. Over fifty Germans dead. The whole city is in a state of panic."

"Who precipitated this?" Mick asked without looking at him.

"I would say that the Iranians did it by their actions, but some other party put the process in motion. It reeks of Russian spycraft, but I am at a loss to supply any facts."

"A comment that Dvorkin made to me the last time we met. He remarked that our plan would be 'Effective, more so if the children are harmed or degraded in the process'."

"Well, that's exactly what happened. Think he did this?" Zeskie asked, looking at Mick for comment.

"I do, but something went wrong with the plan. He would have wanted the blame to fall on the U.S., but so far there has been no accusation."

"Wait for it. It's coming."

"Not, I think. This business was tightly engineered. It should have happened by now." Mick looked over his shoulder expecting Dorff to show at any moment. "I'll bet the Iranian forces discovered who was actually masterminding this. They lost not only their link with Washington and all their personnel, but they also suffered humiliation inflicted by Arabs. They are bound to be angry."

Zeskie was silent, thinking things over. "We have been compromised by the State Department. They have been monitoring everything we did up until last week, even your meetings with Dvorkin. They told the Iranians everything. That's how they suspected Dvorkin, and that's why they knew that we hadn't acted yet."

"The phones," Mick suggested.

"Yes. State didn't bother to read the adulterated reports my office filed, but instead were listening to the source directly. I never thought I would live to see the CIA compromised by our own country."

"So, probably without really meaning to, Dvorkin did us a favor. He shut down the *hoseiniyeh* for us while also stopping predation on children. He did what State would have never allowed us to do. To bad we never discovered all the names of traitors operating out of Washington, including the main link...the one they call Maggot," Mick said. He pointed with his chin at Dorff who was making his way slowly up the path toward them.

"Greetings," Dorff said, giving a slight bend at the waist and looking over Zeskie with his peripheral vision. He sat on the end of the bench next to Mick.

"Any news of the bombing from East Berlin?" Mick asked.

"For sure. A much discussed topic and you might be interested that our Russians friends are running around like ants."

"For what reason?" Mick inquired.

"Our erstwhile ally, Dvorkin, has gone missing," Dorff said without emotion or excitement.

"Surely the Russians can find him, and quickly," Zeskie observed.

"If they really want to," Dorff said.

"Why would they not want to find their Colonel, pray tell," asked Mick.

"The Americans, at least the former Americans, would never let one of their own fall into the hands of the enemy. With the Russians, there is not so much a case of principle as a matter of competition."

"You are saying that if Dvorkin goes missing forever, some other Russian is anxious and willing to take his place?" Zeskie said.

"It is always the way," Dorff shrugged.

Mick and Zeskie exchanged glances. An opportunity, they sensed. "Dorff, I know that you know more than that. Spell it out for us," Mick demanded.

"Since there is no more *hoseiniyeh* for you to worry over, there is no more opportunity for Dorff and his friends to…you know…have a little cash for a rainy day. My poverty keeps me silent."

"How much?" Zeskie asked, his voice carrying some volume.

"Ten thousand euros. Not much when you spread it around, you understand."

"And what do we get for ten thousand?" Zeskie leaned around Mick to watch Dorff's face.

"Just where Dvorkin is, that's all." Dorff mumbled. "At least my suspicion."

"Your suspicion! Do we get the money back if you are wrong?" Mick asked.

"For that amount, I will confirm the address by this afternoon.

If you want expert help…help that you don't want the other U.S. agencies to know about…then we will want another ten thousand…in advance."

Zeskie nudged Mick with his elbow. "If I pay, and Dorff actually can find out where Dvorkin is…well, what are we going to do with the information? The Russians might not really want him back, the Germans would like to see him gone, and he has been a thorn in our side for years. Do we really want to see him loose again?"

Mick ignored the question, concentrating on Dorff instead. "My good friend, Dorff. What is your opinion regarding who took Dvorkin and why?"

Dorff was silent, looking with squinted and wary eyes around the park, always searching for hidden danger.

"All right. Zeskie, agree to pay Dorff the twenty thousand euros," Mick said.

Zeskie grunted, neither a yes or no, and Dorff leaned out to look at his face. "I'll pay you Dorff. Now tell us everything," Zeskie hissed through his teeth.

Dorff allowed himself a small smile. A victory, however small in the scope of things, felt good. "There is a food warehouse near *Krumme Straße* in the far east side of Berlin. My sources say that a disciplined group of men have been seen going in and out recently. I have not seen these men myself but, for the moment, assume that they are part of the Iranian Quds Force who remain in this area. If they discovered, or even suspected, that Dvorkin was acting as a contact man for al-Qaeda, they might want to take him back to Iran to answer to the Ayatollah in person. The Russians are anxious to restore goodwill with Iranians and will look the other way. Dvorkin has no friends who will come to his rescue. None."

"How fast and far the powerful shrink," Zeskie mused. "You know we could have figured that out more cheaply on our own,"

Zeskie quipped, patting Mick on his shoulder, "What are we going to do with this expensive information now that we have it?"

"We are going to rescue Dvorkin," Mick answered.

"Why would you risk life and limb for a Russian operative who was, until recently, ready to kill you on sight?" Zeskie was exasperated and threw up his hands.

"I met with Dvorkin twice. He is much like me, a kindred spirit, so I have sympathy with his plight right now. Other than you and April, my own countrymen would not fight for me either. But there is another reason. Restore Dvorkin to power without letting the Russians know who did it, and we will have made a valuable ally. For me, it might be the way to stop the Russians from hunting for me once and for all."

"I see your point. Anything I can do?" Zeskie offered.

"You can't help. The CIA has been compromised, don't you remember? Dorff and I will handle it, and we have to act soon before Dvorkin is moved."

"What are you going to tell April?" Zeskie asked.

"She's safe where she is for now, and Peter is watching the hotel. What she doesn't know won't hurt her. If we tell her anything, she will want to take part."

"Yes, she will, and she has a right to. If you value her and respect her, you will figure out some way she can contribute. My own view is that her chief asset, her jaw-dropping beauty, is intensely distracting for men. Use that."

Mick stopped to think. He didn't want April remotely close to danger or violence even though she had proved herself over and over to be capable, even ruthless, when it was required. Still, he had to live with her after this was all over. Any plan to free Dvorkin would involve killing, and it would be better not to expect his two brothers to work outside of German law. That left April, and her talent could make the difference between success and failure.

Reluctantly, Mick had to agree that Zeskie was right. April would take part.

Chapter 30

Scouting

Krumme Straße, East Berlin

"How many did you count?" Mick asked, not taking the binoculars from his face.

"They are all dressed alike and moving in and out. I'm not sure. I can only manage to tell two of them apart," Dorff answered. Mick and Dorff were lying hidden behind a decaying brick parapet on the roof of a building two blocks from the warehouse. Dorff's men had been watching the building on and off for two days and as yet no one had actually seen Dvorkin. If he had ever been held inside, he was still there they reasoned. The guards were well-disciplined and altered their positions constantly, moving in a seemingly random pattern. Mick thought he had counted seven of them, but still not only wasn't sure but didn't even have a guess how many were inside the large structure.

"The trucks, Dorff. He could already be inside one of them."

"Yes, I know. We can't explore the trucks, because they are in full view of the guards, and we can't continue to delay action like this, they could move him at any moment."

What Dorff said was obvious, and Mick didn't bother to answer. The guards were largely in the open and could be easily killed by sniper fire, but Mick knew that would cost the life of the hostage inside. One or two could be silently taken with a knife, but killing several would be noisy, no matter how it was done.

Dorff put down his binoculars. "They never seem to eat and

never stop moving. There must be a lot more of them than we can see."

"We need a diversion. Something which will draw them off without making much noise. Where are the men that you promised?" Mick asked.

"Look carefully in the bushes behind the trash bins," he said, pointing to the area just off the pavement of the parking lot. Mick concentrated on the area and saw a foot slowly moving under a branch.

"How many are there?"

"Two. There are three on the other side, hidden in tall grass." Again, he pointed and Mick followed his finger.

"Yes. Very good. That makes six of us, five or as many as seven of them. If we could make them all look the same way for a few minutes…it might work," Mick thought out loud.

"There is something which will work, but I hesitate to tell you about it," Dorff said. Mick studied his face in the dwindling light. It must be something dreadful, if Dorff was holding back. Dorff continued, "There is product developed some time ago by the KGB called Kolokol-1. It has only rarely been used. Ever hear of it?" Mick shook his head that he hadn't. "Remember the Moscow theater crisis of 2002?" Dorff asked.

"Vaguely," Mick answered. "Didn't a lot of innocent people die unintentionally?"

"Yes, but the scheme to knock out the terrorists worked, and it still will work. Kolokol has been weaponized into canisters. The later versions are called Kolokol-6."

"And why are you telling me about….are you saying that we could lay hands on one?" Mick asked. Dorff backed away from the edge and shrugged, an indifferent reply. "Does that indicate that we could get a canister?" Mick persisted.

"If we are willing to steal it from the Russians," he answered.

"It's a matter of time, Dorff. We don't exactly have a lot of it, if we are going to save Dvorkin."

"Two guards, that's all, and only ten kilometers from here. It's in a hidden depot left over from the Cold War. The site was maintained by crack Soviet troops at one time, but now guards are paid a salary and don't even know what they are guarding."

"How do you know what's in there?"

"It was my job as a *Stasi* operative. The items stored there were for my use."

"What else is in that bunker?"

"Poison gas, fragmentation grenades, explosives."

"How many people know what is in that site?"

"Truly, I don't know. I may be the only one left who remembers. The guards are only told that it contains data, sensitive data."

Mick didn't have time to think this through, he had to decide. "Where is it, exactly, and how would you go about getting in?"

"It's in a bank. Off the main vault in a side corridor. The two guards are there to keep people from entering the area, and they sit outside the security door drinking coffee."

"And you know the combination?"

"Of course."

"Then you go over there and steal the canister, and your men and I will wait here. Tell them if I start shooting, they are to do the same," Mick said. Dorff nodded but didn't get up.

"Something else, Dorff?"

"I need your FBI girlfriend. I understand that she is attractive, and I think she will be perfect for getting the attention of the guards."

Chapter 31

The Canister

Petersburger Straße

Dorff checked his wristwatch. They only had a few minutes until the bank closed. Zeskie had called and connected him with April Chauncy, but a telephone was no substitute for direct contact and coaching. April spoke only broken German, but they had worked out a hurried plan, which did not depend on her language skills. He felt in his pocket for the key, the one to the safety deposit box which would allow entry into the vault, only meters from the storage site. There was no time for failure, and he wasn't yet sure of a plan. There were just too many variables. As soon as this woman, April, appeared, they could begin. The danger of something going wrong and being found in a Russian illegal weapons storage site was on his mind. There would be news coverage and prison time…not to mention vengeance by the remorseless Russians. Events like this didn't bother him at one time. He had rather enjoyed the thrill of stress, but he was getting too old for this game.

A black car jerked to a halt at the curb, and a woman slinkily emerged from the backseat. She had long swaying hair and wore a deeply cut, tight sweater in nearly transparent soft wool. There was a wide glossy belt at her waist over a tight, high skirt. She was a traffic stopper, and Dorff, despite his age, couldn't stop gawking at her as she swayed on her high heels toward him.

"Dorff, I believe," she said and enveloped him with her smile.

"Yes. I am Dorff, Gruber Dorff. You will do nicely. Shall we?" he asked and extended his bent arm. They entered the bank at five minutes before closing time, arm-in-arm, attracting eyes which went back and forth trying to comprehend the relationship between the older man and the young beauty. Dorff headed for the far corner where a clerk was still behind the window for the safety deposit boxes. Dorff put the key on top of his yellowed identification card and slid it across to the woman. She looked at the number on the key and pulled a card out of a long tray.

"*Hier unterschreiben,*" she said, sliding the card across and also offering a pen. The clerk's name tag said that she was Brena. No last name. Brena was in a hurry, because she wanted to leave the bank promptly, and she knew from experience that people could dawdle once inside the safety deposit box room. "*Können Sie Ihr Unternehmen schnell abzuschließen, bitte?*" [Can you complete your business quickly, please?] she requested politely.

"*Sicher!*" Dorff smiled back at her. Brena led the way toward the vault, and they passed through a huge circular opening with the massive vault door hanging from one side. The corridor continued on toward another similar vault door which was closed. They came to an intersection, the left corridor led to a room arrayed with small lock boxes in long rows and columns. The other one led toward two guards who were watching from their chairs outside a smaller vaulted opening. Brena used her key and the one supplied by Dorff and retrieved a box, placing it on the center table.

"*Sie haben vier Minuten,*" she said, tapping her watch with her long nail. Dorff busied himself with the contents of the box leaving April to look at the guards who had not taken their eyes from her. She gave a little wave, and they both did likewise, both beaming smiles toward her. She smiled back and slowly strolled toward them, her curvy figure exaggerated by her clothing and her swaying walk. As she got closer, both men stood up eagerly.

"*Und was ist Ihr Name?*" one asked while the other continued to look longingly at her figure.

"Colette," April answered, batting her eyes at them. She placed a hand on her waist, thumb forward, which gave a favorable view of her ample breasts. They watched intently, nearly drooling. "*Je ne peux pas vous parler avec mon papa observation, vous savez,*" she said quietly, conspiratorially.

The men looked confused by her use of French. Neither spoke a word of it. Their faces fell until the second guard asked hopefully, "Can you speak in English?"

"A small bit," she puckered on the pronunciation of 'bit.' "I said that my Papa watches me. Come out, and we talk." She walked away from them with her buttocks swaying hypnotically, their minds captured by what marvels could be found under her thin clothing. The two guards watched as she turned the corner, heading back into the bank lobby. They looked at the overhead clock and back at the older man still bent over the lockbox. One minute to go. They both had the same thought at the same time. The girl was waiting for them just outside. Her older escort was still occupied and wouldn't interfere for a few moments. They hurried to catch her before she got away. Opportunities like her didn't come every day. In the lobby, she was waiting for them, smiling and leaning on the center island, her impressive cleavage arranged to have maximum effect on the two men as they walked toward her. Behind the counter, Brena looked at the clock. Only a few more seconds. She noticed that the old man had remained inside while his attractive companion was loose in the lobby. Disgusting. She looked at the threesome engaged in close conversation, the men hanging on every word the woman uttered while trying to look between her fine breasts. She waited until the second hand crossed the twelve before getting up. Just at that moment, there was a loud 'slap' and angry voices. She looked at the threesome and saw that one of the men was holding his face, and the woman had squared off at him, both hands on her hips. It was interesting, this spectacle, and it promised to get even better. She wasn't sure that one of the guards wasn't going to grab or even hit the woman, but they just stood in place and argued with her. The bank manager was headed in their direction, drawn by the angry shrill voice of the woman. The two men were trying, unsuccessfully, to calm her down when the manager arrived. Brena could hear the woman yelling in French at them. French women, so excitable, she said to herself as she remembered the old man still in the vault and glanced again at the clock. Two minutes past. She sighed, resigned to trying to evict the man as quickly as possible. She turned the corner just as the old man was walking toward her.

"*Danke, Brena, für Ihre Unterstützung,*" Dorff said, bowing slightly at the waist. He walked past her, toward the growing melee in the center of the lobby. Without saying a word, he took the young woman's arm and led her toward the door, leaving the bank manager and the two guards watching her hips as she paraded toward the exit.

"Did you get what you wanted?" April asked. Dorff grinned and patted the canister inside his coat.

Mick rose on one elbow, watching Dorff's progress toward him in the evening twilight. He knew from looking at Dorff that his mission had been successful. When he was alongside, he pulled a slender metal cylinder from under his clothing and laid it on the roof between them.

"Total unconsciousness in two seconds," Dorff said. "Hard to believe but it's true. It's released as a fog and usually they instruct that the cylinder should be placed in a ventilation system. Now there is one very important item you have to understand." He pulled out a small leather case and placed it beside the cylinder.

"This is the antidote. It reverses the effect of Kolokol, but it must be rapidly given or the victim will die. If we find Dvorkin alive, he has to get this drug as fast as possible. You understand?"

"You mean that I am the one who is destined to place the gas, and I am the one to administer this antidote, don't you?" Mick asked.

"This is your mission. Yes, you are the one," Dorff confirmed.

"Got any ideas how to do it?"

"If I were younger, I would enter the warehouse at the far end and work my way toward this end. Expect to encounter armed men stationed along the way. After that, you have to make it up. When you have put the inside men down using the gas, break a window, and we will open fire on the ones outside."

"Just how am I going to avoid being overcome myself?" Mick asked.

"There are two syringes in the case. One is for you before you release the gas. I'm not sure that it will work, but it's the best we can do for the moment."

"I have developed a healthy respect for you, Dorff. Back in the day, you must have cut a wide swath."

"So some say. If I heard it from Triska, though, it would mean more."

Mick checked his pistol and felt for spare ammo magazines. He was carrying the cylinder and the antidote in a small makeshift sling on his back. From the bushes, there were no visible guards near the rear door, but he knew that a well-trained army unit would not overlook something so fundamental. He didn't want to resort to gunfire and alert the others before he was ready. A careful study of the rear door area did not detect any obvious surveillance cameras, and Mick reasoned that the Iranians had gathered here, because it was available and remote, not because they had possessed the building long enough to fully equip it with electronic gear. They would be gone soon, possibly during the night, and use one of the available trucks parked in the rear to attempt retreat toward Iran.

Attempting to break the door in would be the signal that the building was under attack. Mick elected to simply knock on the door and see what happened.

Mick knocked softly, as if someone who knew what was behind the door was knocking. It was a request to open, not an order. He readied himself as he heard some muffled conversation on the other side. At least two. The door opened slowly, a brow and dark eyes peering through the slot. A gun barrel was visible in the lower opening, still pointed downward. Mick hit the door with all his explosive force, pushing the guard backward and against the wall and allowing the door to fully open. There was a pop, just before the knife entered the man's throat, and in a blur of motion, Mick kicked the other guard in the neck, swinging his foot with maximal effort. The first one sagged to the floor, blood gushing from his neck, his eyes wild and his hands grasping futilely at his hemorrhaging neck. Mick didn't intend to kill the second man who was now lying on the floor struggling to breathe. A quick visual search showed that they were in a hallway at right angles to another hall. He could hear voices murmuring from the other hall. So far, he was undetected. After picking up one of the automatic weapons, and slinging it over his arm, he took the bundle from his back. Roughly, he turned the still gasping man on his stomach and tied the bundle in place using the man's belt loops. He took the antidote pouch out and opened it. Two syringes, both labeled Naloxone, lay side by side. An alcohol prep was thoughtfully provided. He took one out and quickly stabbed it into his deltoid as he was taught in Special Forces training.

Mick picked the man up and placed him on his feet. He put the muzzle of his pistol between the man's eyes and held it there, so that it would be very clear what was going to happen. The man started to sag, still fighting for breath, and Mick slapped his face hard and shook him by his shoulders. He spun the man around and started marching him toward the intersection of hallways, pushing the man ahead with the barrel of the machine pistol. As they rounded the corner, Mick pushed the man down the long hall. As he stumbled forward, there was a scramble of alert from several men gathered at the opposite end. Mick waited, calmly watching the proceedings from the corner of the hall, and as the man stumbled closer and closer to the opposite end, two men rushed out to help their injured comrade, one on each side. Mick stepped out in plain view and opened fire, striking the three at waistline level and rupturing the canister on the back of the man in the middle, and just as quickly dove back out of the line of fire. There was instant return fire from the other end, and the edge of the wall erupted in dust and fragments. Suddenly the firing stopped, and Mick could hear new voices calling out in alarm, but shortly, they also were quiet. He cautiously reentered the hall and saw a cloud hanging at the other end from the ruptured canister, mixed with smoke from the guns of the guards. There were two piles of bodies. The first, the three that Mick had shot, were intertwined together in a spreading pool of blood. Farther down the hall were several more, one half out of an adjacent doorway. The dust was beginning to affect Mick, and he suddenly felt dizzy. From his fog, he could hear gunfire begin from outside the building, close and violent. He stumbled forward, making his way over the bodies of the fallen into the side room. Lying in a cot on the far side was the thick broad back and shoulders of an unmistakable man, Dvorkin. His unconscious burly head rested on a dirty pillow. Three more bodies were scattered on the floor and an assortment of weapons stood along one wall in a neat, perfect row. He remembered that he had to save Dvorkin and made his way slowly as if the progress of time had slowed. He took out his remaining syringe and stabbed it

Chapter 31

into Dvorkin's thick shoulder.

Chapter 32

Comrade!

Her soft hands were holding and supporting his neck and head in her lap while she leaned over him protectively and studied his craggy face. Mick's eyelids fluttered and his breathing was regular, a welcome change. It was only a question of time before he emerged. Dvorkin was alive but out, really out. Dorff explained that he was really fortunate to be alive, because the way Mick had released the Kolokol, everyone close had received a massive overdose. After the last Iranian went down in the courtyard, they had rushed inside and opened the doors and windows so that Dvorkin and Mick could be pulled out before it was too late, and without the rescuers also being overcome. The resourceful Dorff had requisitioned one of the panel trucks in the lot, and they had all made their getaway before German police descended on the area.

"You should put his head on a pillow and take a rest, April," Zeskie suggested. She had been in the same position for two hours, and Zeskie knew that she had to at least get up and stretch or take some nourishment. As before, she ignored everyone but Mick's sleeping face, her full concentration, her immense love of him, pouring forth like an endless fountain.

"What's going to happen now?" Dorff asked Zeskie.

"I don't know, Dorff. Mick and I are rather out of the loop, more or less outcasts like you. We are all in the same boat now."

"Not a good place," Dorff said. He knew what was going to happen. Nothing, that is if they were lucky. It was the start of a new life…outside of the inner circle. In the past, at least, the CIA had not been given to assassination of their former agents. The new America which had emerged in the last five years might be different, he suspected. He watched with envy the care that April was pouring onto the unconscious Mick. "Some woman, that one," he murmured to Zeskie.

"Yes, that she is. They have each other fully at last, and there is some hope for their future. They are both very lucky."

Mick moved, trying to turn over, and April restrained him as she spoke to him quietly in a soothing voice. "Not too much longer," Dorff predicted. Mick had given himself partial protection, but the dose of Kolokol he received included other anesthetic agents not reversed by the antidote.

They had tried to clean Dvorkin's face of blood while he slept, but there were too many lacerations, some of which should be closed by a surgeon. He was also missing his front teeth, likely broken by repeated blows during interrogation. Dorff shook his head. It was hard to imagine what path of vengeance Dvorkin would take when he was back on his feet. Without doubt, Dvorkin would punish those he could and would relentlessly take back all he had lost. Mick Grundy was, at least, free of retribution from him. Grundy had his woman and his German family to return to. Dorff had a rented flat and little else.

Dorff had parked the truck in a seldom-used area of a small city park, and Zeskie's car was nearby. As the morning light grew brighter, just before the sun rose to wake the part of Berlin that was still sleeping, April sighed relief that this night was over. This adventure, this life of worry, loneliness and fear, it was all over like the night. Just as the sun rose, so did her confidence and hope that the future was to be brighter than their past, especially Mick's past.

Mick's eyes opened fully, but his vision remained unfocused. He felt April's touch and heard her voice as she caressed his head.

He blinked a couple of times, finally becoming fully aware.

"Can you help me sit up?" he asked.

"Sure you are ready?" she asked. Mick started struggling without answering. He was obviously ready. He looked around, still somewhat dazed, and saw Dvorkin lying close by.

"He alive?"

"He is, thanks to you. A bit beaten up, but he will survive to drink Vodka again," Zeske said.

Mick looked around and saw Zeskie, Dorff and April, his mind clearing rapidly. He reached for April and drew her in. "I could hear your voice in my sleep. It brought me around. Seems like you said that you loved me."

"Why would I say that? You must have dreamed it!" she teased. He hugged her closer and kissed the top of her head.

"I'll say it for you. I love you," Mick said. He noticed the two men who were both smiling. "Can you tell me what happened?" he asked them.

"Simple," Dorff said. Our side won, the other side lost. Comrade Dvorkin is saved. There is nothing else you need to know."

"Yes, he does," Zeskie said, throwing his CIA issued black phone on floor of the truck. "I…we…have been cut off. No more money, guns, information, and most of all, no more support."

"No matter, Zeskie. I no longer care," Mick said, still enveloping April with his arms.

"Well, I do. There is unfinished business across the pond. Bad guys are in charge over there. We can't just let them run the country into the ground."

"Look, Ron, they have all the cards now. We have none. They won."

"Not by a…" he saw April looking at him and stopped before expressing a vulgarity. "This isn't over, Mick, for me or for anyone else who loves the U.S.A."

"Then you are on your own, my friend. That was my last mission. I'm used up. My own countrymen have put me on their wanted list. No one over there cares if I live or die, never did really. The only thing I want, I already have right here in my arms, and I'm not taking any more chances that could change that."

"I am an expert on being cast out," Dorff injected. "You get used to it. There are times you miss the excitement, but when you think about it, you are tired of getting shot or shot at. The world will go on without you. I promise you that will happen. Your absence will be filled by another more quickly than you can imagine, just as our sleeping friend here will soon discover. My humble opinion, for whatever it's worth, is that the four of us should go fishing and enjoy the remainder of our lives."

"Dorff, I like you better all the time," Mick said and offered his hand. Dorff took it, and they enthusiastically shook. "Thank you, Dorff, for saving my life. You are a worthy partner."

"And you, Grundy. We were born to work together. Except for age, we are just alike."

Zeskie sighed. "The fact is, that all five of us are just alike. Dedicated, trustworthy, dependable and, oh yes, expendable. The only difference is that April is decidedly better looking." They all laughed, except for Dvorkin, who was still asleep.

Mick rolled Dvorkin on his back and looked at his torn face. "Can't we do something for his face?" he asked.

"I'm cut off, Mick, and I'm sure you don't want him taken to an emergency room where his Russian competitors can get at him before he can defend himself," Zeskie said.

"No, but I'll bet Peter would know someone who could keep his mouth shut." He felt in his clothing and pulled out the BND cellphone he had been promised was secure from the CIA.

"Peter! Your brother calling," Mick said.

"*Mein Gott, haben wir uns Sorgen um dich!*" Peter exclaimed.

"You needn't worry. We are all safe and sound," Mick assured him.

"There was a massive killing last evening. Was that your work?"

"I've resigned from anything connected to violence. It's all in the past."

"And April? Is she safe?"

"Safe in my arms."

"Then, do you need anything from me or us?"

"Yes. There is one of our party who was beaten rather savagely and needs some care. He is currently unconscious, and it would be better that his treatment be kept very quiet. Understand?"

"Yes, I think so. Would this person possibly be the one being sought by some from the East?"

"Among others."

"I see your need very clearly. You want to help this fellow regain what he has lost?"

"Yes, I think that would work out for everyone," Mick answered.

"I'll give you an address and meet you there personally. My promise is that the matter will be handled very discreetly," Peter said.

Dr. Elbers had a kindly face, but an efficient, German disposition. He studied the still sleeping Dvorkin and then looked back at the others who were standing by. "What has this man been given to make him sleep?" he inquired authoritatively.

"Unknown," Peter answered. "That is not the issue. We are here for you to repair his injuries. Proceed, please." Dr. Elbers let a moment of anger flash across his face. He detested being forced to attend to the rabble of the spy world just because of his former

GDR employment. After all, he was not responsible for crimes against other Germans as his countrymen and the Red Soviets were. Nevertheless, he was to be a captive of the West until he died or was too old to practice. He sighed, resigned once again to his fate. He pushed an intercom button to signal his nursing staff to join him.

They all watched quietly as the talented Dr. Elbers repaired Dvorkin's face. During the procedure, Dvorkin stirred, slowly emerging from the anesthetic weapon's effects. Dr. Elbers removed the drapes just as Dvorkin's eyes fluttered open.

"The tooth repair is not part of my skills," Elbers stated. "And the sutures will need to be removed in a week or so. Other than that, he is back in your hands, or on your hands as the case may be." He took his leave and left the room along with his two nurses. The five were alone for the moment, and their next move awaited Dvorkin's recovery. They didn't have long to wait, and it was obvious that he was becoming aware as he looked around the room trying to place where he was. Mick got up and moved to his side, looking into his face.

"You will be more handsome than ever, Dvorkin. The scars will complement your visage nicely. The teeth are another matter," Mick told him.

"Grundy? Is that you Mick Grundy?" Dvorkin asked, blinking his eyes rapidly trying to clear the fog.

"Yes, it's me. Welcome back to our nasty world."

"And you saved me, Mick Grundy? Saved me?"

"Yes, with help from others. I only claim a small credit."

"Comrade!" Dvorkin said, and grabbed Mick's arm with his massive grip and pulled him in. "I thought I would never again breathe a free breath. You of all people! The sworn enemy of the Russian people rescuing Dvorkin. It makes me want to weep!" He tried unsuccessfully to sit up. "How could this happen, Grundy? I expected the GRU, and I got Mick Grundy!"

"You are worth saving, Dvorkin, or we would not have tried." Dvorkin rubbed his face feeling the bandages, then stuck his tongue between his teeth, feeling the missing parts. He looked around the room and saw April. He blinked, then smiled.

"April Chauncy, FBI, in person. Let me look upon you, because I have only had the privilege of seeing your photographs previously." He struggled to a sitting position, hanging on to the cart with both hands to prevent falling off. "Yes, you are as beautiful as they say. You would make an excellent Russian spy. We know the value of beautiful women in Russia!"

"And I have heard as much!" she answered, rewarding him with a smile.

Dvorkin attempted to return the smile but put his hand to his face. "I can see that I have to forgo smiles for a little while, but I won't forget." He look at Dorff and Zeskie and nodded to them. "We make strange companions, my friends. This is a new world Dvorkin has awakened into, and changes will have to be made." He attempted to stand, and Mick was there to steady him.

"Look, our new friend, you have to stay with us for a short time. You will need to be fully in control when you rejoin your people. They will be surprised to see you again, I'm sure."

"Meaning that I was replaced in a single night. I might have expected as much. Some will pay dearly for their switch of allegiance, that I promise." He noticed Peter standing quietly in the corner. "Ah, I am honored *Heerführer* Koffman that you also lend your assistance." He extended his hand toward Peter who, after a momentary hesitation, took it.

"I might have refused if I had known for sure whom I was helping, Dvorkin. This does not make us allies."

"Oh, but it does. Things will be different. I know more clearly who my enemies are and who my friends are." He put his arm over

Mick's shoulder and patted him on his stomach. "His friends are my friends. You can owe no greater debt than your life, and I'm sure that his was on the line for mine as well. We are comrades, we are even related, a fact that Mick Grundy didn't know until this moment. Another secret should be shared. I would have never harmed a hair on his head myself!" He tousled Mick's hair with his thick hand, then pulled him closer with the other arm.

Mick pushed away from him. "Too much too fast, Dvorkin. You owe no debt to me for your rescue. It was the right thing to do, that's all. Don't treat me like a spring bride, I'm not used to it."

Dvorkin stood without assistance, swaying just a little. "One more question, comrades. What happened to the ones who took me?" The set of his jaw told everyone that his first thought was for revenge.

"They are no longer with us. You need not worry about finding them yourself," Mick said.

"Did you shoot each of them in the head?" Dvorkin asked, a sly smile on his lips.

"Not a one. I have changed also."

"*Nebo!* Tell me that it isn't true. The Mick Grundy trademark. The world will never be the same!"

"We can see that your recovery is nearly complete, Dvorkin. May we leave before the *byk der'mo* gets too deep?" Zeskie said.

Peter tapped Zeskie on the shoulder. "I hear that things have changed for you. Temporarily, I hope. May I provide a safe place for all of you for a short time?"

"That is an offer we can't refuse," Zeskie said.

"I can," Dorff said. "I prefer my former life, if you don't mind. None hunt me, because I'm not worth anything, so I will say my goodbyes here." He turned toward April first and extended his arms. "We may never meet again, lovely April, but I want to tell you that it was a joy for as long as it lasted. You make me want something that I can never have again…my long lost youth."

April embraced him and kissed his cheek. "Anyone could tell that you are a spy master who still has usefulness. I enjoyed it, and thanks for the compliments," she said.

Dorff stood in front of Zeskie and looked him in the eye. "Don't forget, Zeskie, that you still owe me twenty thousand euros."

"No, more than that, Dorff, and I always pay my debts. You will get it shortly, my promise."

"And neither do I forget, Dorff," Dvorkin said in his deep voice. "And I owe you much."

"I could not have done this without you and your advice, Dorff. It's been a privilege to work with you. Triska was right about you," Mick said, shaking his hand.

"Yes, Triska," Dorff said and seemed to look in the past for a moment. "How I long to see her again. Be sure and talk me up to her. Her high opinion of me is worth gold."

"Triska!" Dvorkin exclaimed. "She is legend. I can tell you all the truths about her that you do not know. She worked for our side not yours! A well respected spy, a near myth, yet I have never seen her, even a photograph."

"I have," Dorff said. "In her prime, she was a match for the beauty of this woman, but had the heart of a demon. No side owned her. Triska worked for Triska."

"So she fooled all of you," April observed. "I know her, and she is no demon, and no person ever had such a big heart."

Dorff raised his eyebrows but didn't comment further. He gave a little bow, a nod of his head and silently left the room.

Chapter 33

Hiding in Luxury

Seminaris SeeHotel, Potsdam

A not too soft knock on the door caused April to sigh out loud. "It's him again. Can you get it this time please?"

Mick grinned at her and patted her arm affectionately on the way to the door. Dvorkin was a little too much company, and he had a bad sense of timing, but this time was better than most he had chosen. Mick opened the door to the grinning face of Dvorkin, who immediately pushed his way in. His big fist was holding the neck of a large bottle of Vodka which he held aloft like a prize turkey.

"Did you get your swim in today, my friends? Such a pool! I love it here. We ordinary Russians are not given to such luxury! I might as well switch sides right now!" he exploded as he headed for the couch. "Two, no, three glasses for the Vodka!" he called out in his booming voice. He sat down to wait and grinned at them.

"Good morning, Comrade," April said. "You should know by now that I don't drink raw Vodka, but thanks for the invitation. May I ask what brings you so early?"

"It is a beautiful day, one that nearly matches your magnificence, my dear April. A joy to be alive. If only I had a woman like you to share it with!"

"You might consider a woman a bit more sturdy than I am, Comrade. She will need to have very thick skin also." Dvorkin gave one of his huge laughs, the kind that nearly shook the windows.

"No, no, my dear April, I have a tender side also. Pity that you will never know that about me." Dvorkin seemed to grow serious for a moment. "Let me say that I have enjoyed knowing you both…and I don't want to shed a tear over it right now…but it has been very meaningful for me."

"I sense that you are about to separate from us, *Vacslovovitch*," Mick said. "Is this a drink of Vodka among former friends?"

"Not at all. Among permanent friends. I love you both, and I insist on coming to your wedding, that is if you ever get around to it."

"We are still in hiding. The air has to clear first," Mick explained.

"Is that where the infamous Ron Zeskie is at the moment? Clearing the air?"

"He would say that you are on the opposite side and not want me to tell you that," Mick responded.

"As I hear it, Zeskie or you or the heavenly beautiful April, doesn't have any side any longer."

"True for us, but Zeskie has other plans. He is working on something, but he is not confiding or burdening me with it any longer," Mick responded.

"I have something which may change your mind, *Micken'ka*. Are you interested?" Mick didn't answer but instead looked at April. No, he didn't want to know or be compelled to do anything which would separate them. He shrugged for an answer.

"First the Vodka. You are going to need it," Dvorkin said, reaching for the two glasses. He filled both to the top and smacked his lips, offering one to Mick. "*Dlitel'nyy srok sluzhby*," he said and raised his glass to them. He took a long deep drink and exhaled mightily, settling back into the couch. Mick took a burning sip and tried to keep from coughing. Dvorkin reached into his shirt pocket and pulled out a folded sheet of paper. He extended it to Mick and patiently waited until it was accepted. Mick unfolded it, looking at it in silence while the others watched his face for emotion. He handed it to April, and after a moment, they heard a 'whoosh' as she expelled air.

"I think I need the Vodka now, Comrade Dvorkin," she said, picking up Mick's nearly full glass and taking a deep drink. She looked at Mick who seemed impassive. "Did you know this?" she asked.

"He is the one the Iranians called Maggot. It fits with what we suspected. A piece of paper is not proof, but we both know that it is the truth, and I don't believe that Vacslovovitch Dvorkin has any reason to deceive us."

"We knew for a long time. You Americans should have known because of his actions, his previous speeches and his associations. It represents a complete failure of the greatest democracy in history, and it disappoints the world. Your system is no better than ours or the Chinese system. You have more radicals in your universities and in your press than are in North Korea."

"Yes, *Vacslovovitch*, your assessment and condemnation are valid. It's true," Mick said and got up and looked out the window, studying the extensive patio surrounding the pool and the distant hills heading toward southern Germany. It was no longer his problem, and he refused to deal with it.

"At least you have to tell Zeskie," April said.

"He knows," Mick said facing away from them.

"What is he going to do about it? Or you. What are you going to do about it?" Dvorkin questioned.

"I'm not about to shoot the President of the United States. The people elected that monster. They can un-elect him. It would be the only way to get rid of him because of his support by the Left. The funny thing is that the Left has also been betrayed. He sold all of us out to a sect of Islam, but his supporters still sing his praises. I am out of it, forever. I no longer claim to be an American."

"You could easily be Russian, if you want," Dvorkin said softly.

"I don't want, thank you. I feel German. I have German family, and I love this place, but I am done fighting for anything except the persons that I love. That includes you, you big bear. I love you also, not that I exactly know why."

Dvorkin launched to his feet and quickly picked Mick off the floor and squeezed him from the back. "And I love you also, Mick Grundy. And I love April also, but I wouldn't dare pick her up like this!" He put Mick back down and patted his back. "You love me because we are related. We have some of the same cells floating around inside of us. We are much the same, only I like Vodka better than you, and you have a better woman than me." Mick turned and hugged Dvorkin, and they exchanged kisses on the cheeks.

"Are you leaving us?" Mick asked.

"Today. It is time that I taught a few lessons. Want some target practice?"

"No, thank you. I've had enough to last a lifetime."

"Give me a few days and watch the news. You will know when it's over, and then you two can go back to Triska without worry. I will never let any Russian near you again. My oath. Send me an invitation to the wedding. I'll bring the Vodka!"

After a few tears and a couple more belts of Vodka, Dvorkin excused himself, leaving Mick and April alone for the first time in weeks. They sat down and held hands.

"Is this what being married feels like?" Mick said and studied her face.

"We'll find out, won't we?"

"Yes. I like it, very much like it," Mick whispered and took her in his arms while smoothing her long hair from her brow.

"How are we going to live, Mick. I don't have very much money, and I'm sure not going to apply for benefits from the FBI. Did you manage to save any?"

"Once, Anna's father told me that I would make a good male model. I am hoping that he still feels that way."

"That will help, but it might take a while yet. What do we do until then?"

Mick reached over and pulled his jacket from the back of a chair. He withdrew a small leather folder and put it in her lap without comment. She opened and studied if for a moment, her eyes getting bigger.

"This is ours? All of it?" she gasped.

"Wedding present from Ron Zeskie. It's from a CIA slush fund, a very big one. Zeskie said he needed the rest for something he is planning back home, or he would have given us all of it."

"With this, you don't need to work…ever."

"Of course I do. Your lips would tire of me. You have to have a break now and then. Besides, I don't want the people's money. That's only security until we can get on our feet."

April pulled him toward her and touched his cheek with her nose. "I'll never get tired of you."

Chapter 33

Chapter 34

Vengeance, A Little At A Time

On The Train to Stuttgart

April took another newspaper off her stack and opened it noisily. The slight motion of the train caused the newspaper to float softly back and forth. "There is another one in here. This time in Bonn. Two men shot to death and left in an alley. Both are Russian. The paper speculates that it was a mob hit, drugs and all that."

"And it may have been," Mick said sleepily, his eyes still closed.

"This is an epidemic of Russian deaths all over Germany. The Russian mafia can't be that extensive. I think it's Dvorkin cleaning house and making it look like a mob war." Mick was very proud how quickly she was able to read in German, and her accent was diminishing daily with his coaching. Soon she would be indistinguishable from a native speaker. They were starting to work on regional accents as well, and April was a quick study.

"Whatever you say. Remind me to ask Peter. He would know."

April rattled another newspaper. Mick opened one eye and squinted at it. It was in English and from the U.S. "Now, what are you reading?" he inquired.

"Zeskie said to watch the paper. I'm watching. This one is a Washington paper. I figure if anything happens it will be in Washington. So far though…" she trailed off, distracted by her reading. He opened the other eye and studied her face in profile. He loved to look at her when she wasn't aware, because her features were so natural. Her lip curved in a different way without expression, and he took in the sinuous curves of her face with his eyes.

"I thought you were sleeping," she said without looking his way.

"Your face caught my attention. I am admiring it."

"When my face sags from age, will you still love it as much?"

"The way I see it, my eyes will age along with your face. I'll still see you the same."

"Silly. Say, here is something buried on the back pages which might be relevant. Want to hear it?"

"If you want me to."

"It's another sex scandal. This one is about molesting women in the office. A senior State Department official. There was an arrest." She put down the paper and looked at Mick. "I should think this would be on the front page. It's big news." Mick opened his eyes again and looked at her funny.

"What was the name?" he asked.

"Herbert Rollings. Know him?"

"He was on the list I took from the Iranian diplomatic pouch. That's what Zeskie was telling you. He wasn't going to shoot anyone to bring them down. It's going to be nastier than that. The reason it's not on the front page is because the leftist newspapers are trying to suppress it." Mick leaned back and looked at the ceiling of the train car. "It's going to get really interesting when he figures out how to take down the President. He'll have to go into hiding, because he's going to have every single government agency after him using some trumped up charge."

"Almost as dangerous as bullets," April agreed. "Do you miss the action?"

"No. I was trained as a soldier. You find the enemy and kill him before he kills you. It's pretty simple in some ways. This business of discrediting someone takes a different sort of person. It's Machiavellian or Russian, and it's quite the same as techniques the Left uses constantly."

"What are our plans in Stuttgart?"

"To find Triska. I'll call her when we get off the train. Want to rent a car?"

"You mean, instead of a motorcycle for two?" April sparred.

"Silly. Big one or little one?"

"Do we have to plan on running away in the middle of the night?"

"Hopefully that is behind us. Big one then."

"Yeah, and no spaghetti and chocolate ice cream. Promise. That last time almost got us killed."

The door opened on the first tap, and Triska was standing there beaming at them, her arms extended and tears in her eyes. "I knew you would come home to me," she said. "Welcome back, and don't ever plan on leaving me again!"

Mick, then April, kissed her on her cheeks as she did for them. On the table behind her was a big spread of food and wine resting in coolers. "My, you were expecting us!" April remarked. She started to ask how Triska knew but thought better of it.

"I stay connected, my dear children. Please sit down, and we can plan the wedding while we eat."

"Triska, no one would expect that a little grandmother would be so pushy! You have to give us time to catch our breath. There are still a lot of plans we have to make and decisions to be reached," Mick said.

"What are you talking about? Nothing matters as much as the wedding. Don't you think I'm right, April?"

"You are always right, *Großmutter*," April answered.

"Well, about where we will live after the marriage, or which country we will settle in, and how to make an income. Big little things like that," Mick said.

"It's all settled. You will live right here in Stuttgart so that I can keep you close. You will both become German citizens. Mick will become a clothing model, and April will be a liaison for the BND to the FBI. See? Nothing to worry about. I even have a little house picked out."

"So, *Smartyhosen*, do you also know how many children we are going to have?" Mick asked.

"I won't be happy until you have two. Either sex is fine with me as long as one is a little girl."

"We love you, Triska," April said, while laughing and watching Mick's face.

Supper was simple but started with *Burger Knäckebrot* with *Würchwitzer Spinnenkäse* and two kinds of *Feldkieker*. The dessert, on the side table, was a low but tempting *Schwarzwälder Kirschtorte*. After the meal, Mick leaned back, watching the two loves of his life discuss nearly everything under the sun, switching between English, German and French. He could tell from the glances that Triska was allowing April to show off for him and that she enjoyed doing it.

Triska was quiet for a moment, then pursed her lips and furrowed her brow. She got Mick's attention quickly. "Triska?" he inquired, a request that she discuss what was bothering her.

"Dvorkin has assumed control of Russian Intelligence this side of Moscow. To accomplish this he has dispatched an unusually large number of Russian agents, all of them suspected of allegiances to the wrong side. It has been nearly an undeclared war between the factions, but we think it has finally come to an end."

"We have been noticing a large number of Russian deaths in the papers," April said. "Drugs, they said."

"That happens also, but not on this scale. No, it was mostly Dvorkin's work. He is a man to be feared and is quickly rising in power."

"I wonder, does the BND know what is happening across the Atlantic? Any news?" Mick asked.

"We try to follow what happens in America very closely, because your fate and our fate are linked. There is scandal after scandal over there right now, but nearly all of it is low-key and never makes it to the national television networks. Under the covers, it is causing a rising political storm. We are worried that your President will suspend Congress or even declare martial law to hold on to power. He has ignored your Constitution for years and nothing ever happens to him for it. The world can't afford another American Civil War which seems to be the direction it's all heading."

"The people made a poor choice at the polls. Now they are stuck with their choice," Mick explained.

"We're not sure that your people won't do the same next time. Our Adolf Hitler discovered that the people usually will believe what they are told and are reluctant to think for themselves. In addition, voters usually choose the easier way or listen to campaign pledges. Hugo Chávez kept winning elections because he promised the poor more and more entitlements. The same strategy is working in your country right now." When Triska finished, Mick was silent for a moment, thinking about what she said.

"I'm positive that you are right, Triska. There really is no doubt…but this President has captivated the liberal press who withhold truth and print his lies. There is nothing to do but hope for a change at election time. Ron Zeskie went back home to try to straighten this mess out, but he is only one man," Mick said.

"Look, you two," April interrupted. "We can't solve the world's problems, even though we would like to. I feel like Mick does, we dedicated our lives and our commitment to America most of our adult lives. It's enough. Now I want nothing more than to live a normal life with our new family and without risk or fear or hiding."

Triska nodded that she was in sympathy, but added, "I hate to mention this to you both, but you may have eliminated the Iranian terrorists for now and pacified the Russians, but what about your own country? They still have both of you on their wanted list, and sooner or later they will find you, especially when Zeskie's replacement takes over. This isn't over yet."

"Triska, we are counting on Ron Zeskie to make things right. He is making progress over there, and by our count, he has taken out six of them and hasn't even resorted to gunfire to do it," Mick said.

"Well, let's hope," Triska said. Just as she finished speaking, there was a soft tapping on the door.

"Expecting anyone?" Mick asked, getting to his feet. Triska shook her head, and Mick headed for the door with his pistol in his hand. He stood to one side of the door and asked, "*Identifizieren Sie sich.*"

"It's Peter! Open the door, *bitte.*"

Mick opened it, and Peter stepped in, grinning and holding a large bouquet of roses. Under one arm was a box of French chocolates. "Greetings. May I come in?" he asked.

Triska looked grim and hard and fixed Peter in her narrowed eyes. "And is this an official visit?"

"Certainly! I have come to bury the hatchet between you and me, and I bear gifts to make it official!" He offered the chocolate in one outstretched hand and the flowers in the other. "I wish to state publicly and in front of my only relative that I have been a fool, and I wish to bow down at the alter of Triska." Peter gave a slight bow at the waist and grinned at her.

"Don't be *der esel*, Peter. I never cared that you thought ill of me because I am old. Before you were born, I had the respect of our intelligence service and theirs. Your admiration is something I can live without."

Mick stood between them, looking both ways. "I don't have many people in my life that matter to me, but both of you do. Please, for me Triska, accept Peter's apology, and let's move on."

Triska got up slowly and came to stand in front of Peter, looking up at him with her faded blue eyes. "You mean it?"

"Yes, Triska. I have changed. Your skills and resources are beyond mine, and I admit that you are an asset to Germany. I even heard Dvorkin sing your praises, and Dorff…well, he thinks you are a movie star, although a dangerous one."

"Dorff," she said, looking far away for a moment. "Dorff was an attractive man at one time, and there was always an air about him, a hint of danger and mystery. A lot of women were attracted to him back then. I haven't seen him in many years, and I've wondered about him on occasion."

"I worked with him," April said. "He is still impressive. Dorff is smooth and efficient, a real spy from the past."

"And Dorff was indispensable dealing with the Iranians. In fact, I was astonished by him. He is a good man to have in your corner," Mick added.

"Where is he now," Triska wondered.

"He slipped back into the shadows where he likes it. Zeskie made sure he had a big wad of euros in his pocket, so he will likely be very hard to find again," Mick said. Triska didn't respond, but they could tell that she was thinking and working on something that was bothering her.

"Now that I am welcome here, I need to fetch the Schnapps I left just outside!" Peter said, moving toward the door. "I also came to tell you that I am ready to help plan the wedding. You must be working on an arrangement by now."

"You are to be best man," Mick said and patted him on the back.

"I knew that already. You wouldn't dare to replace me, unless you want me to give the bride away instead." His comments caused Mick and Triska to exchange quick glances. It was a touchy subject, and there were only so many possibilities.

"I have to be consulted on that one, boys," April said. "Don't dare presume to speak for me, because I already have plans."

"And can you tell us who it will be?" Triska asked.

"When the right time comes."

Chapter 35

Shadows

Triska's Apartment

What are your plans today, *meine geliebten Kinder?*" Triska asked. She passed around the coffee and set down another platter of buns.

"We should go on a long run to use up all these calories you have been feeding us!" April laughed. "Instead, we are going shopping. Want to come?"

"I have a meeting this morning, but I can meet you somewhere for lunch," Triska replied. "Might I inquire what you will be shopping for?"

"A ring. Actually a pair of rings. One diamond," Mick said, watching April blow him a kiss across the table.

"And?" April encouraged.

"And a wedding dress," Mick said. Another kiss was passed over the table, accompanied by a big smile.

"I see. No, that department is up to you two. Let me know when you want to see the house I have picked out for you," Triska answered.

By the third store, Mick was already fatigued, but April remained enthusiastic and energetic. "I need to stop for coffee, April. These decisions are giving me a headache." He pulled her toward a small outdoor cafe, and they sat down, waiting for the waitress. Mick leaned back, stretched and rubbed his eyes. He saw

April looking at him and knew what she wanted. He reached into his pocket and handed her the box, and she opened it with delight on her face. It was a pair of matching wedding bands, both highly engraved and crafted in rose-colored gold.

"My these look marvelous! Look at them in the sunlight," she offered, holding the box so it caught a stream of light. It was true, the rings were special and meant for a lifetime of enjoyment. The sight of them made Mick's heart jump, especially when he could look at her happy face and her almost childlike joy while holding them. The new diamond ring she wore sparkled in the shadows like a beacon announcing their commitment to each other. He was having a difficult time adjusting to seeing April as his wife-to-be and not his partner and agent of the U.S. government. They were free of all that. It was behind them for good. All the subterfuge, the planning and the feeling of sudden and lurking danger was gone. April was going to be his constant companion from now forward, and they were going to grow old together after a fabulous life of happiness. Mick hadn't dreamed about Anna for weeks now, and he was sleeping better. The large handgun was still at his back where he could easily get at it should the need arise, but it was looking more and more like he was done with that also. Dvorkin had changed things as he promised, and both Triska and Peter said that tensions with Russians in general were markedly improved. There had been reprisals and counter-reprisals all over the Middle East as the two main branches of Islam fought it out as they had been doing for millennia. The Iranians were likely still in touch with Washington, but they were no longer doing it from German soil. Likely, they had forgotten about their enemy named Elapid and moved on to more pressing issues.

After years of field work, the reflexes of spy work come by second nature. The slightest unusual noise or movement causes the eye to take another look, a harder look. The gut tightens and the pulse rises…the fight or flight response. A family dog sleeping in the kitchen is oblivious to all the usual noise and conversation. He ignores it, but if the handle to the outside door makes a soft click, he is instantly on his feet barking. Mick didn't know what caused his attention to suddenly be riveted to a car parked nearly a block away. He studied it carefully for a time as his antenna for danger rose, pointing toward that very spot. The car was ordinary, parked correctly and looked much as all the other cars in sight. What was it about this car that his brain found interesting, riveting? He kept watching but tried to appear uninterested. It's perhaps the highest art of spycraft, watching without appearing to be interested. Again, he had a sudden flicker of intensity as he caught sight of what his subconscious brain had known all along. It was the brief flash of optical glass reflecting from the interior of the car. A brief, blue glint of sunlight. The reflection of a telephoto lens, either on a camera or a rifle scope.

"April, dear, better put away the rings," he said in a level tone accompanied by a tight-lipped smile. Instantly, she looked at his face, reading what he was thinking.

"What did you see?"

"A lens inside a dark car about two hundred meters from here. Can't make out what or who is also in the car. Again. Some party is interested in us," he said under his breath. Her eyes widened a little, then her face went back to unreadable.

"Got your weapon?" she asked.

"Sure. You?"

"Of course."

"Here is what I want to do. We will go out the back of the cafe and head toward the river. There is a *Stadtbahn* stop about two blocks from here, and if we time it right, we will ride the train north toward Hofen. If they manage to follow us, we'll take them on. Ready?" he asked.

The plan was a good one and well-timed. They stepped on the small commuter train just before the doors closed. Mick sat on one side, April on the other so that they could watch for followers. It only took four kilometers before Mick spotted the black four-door Audi trying to follow the train north. There must be more than one car in pursuit of them, he guessed. This surveillance was professionally executed, but the list of potential adversaries was small. The BND was not one of the parties pursuing them but would have to be brought in, Mick thought. The Russians, Iranians or…Americans, and Mick was sure he could bet which one it was. It was not what he wanted to happen, but whomever it could be was forcing him to consider violence as a first resort. Killing Americans was something he really did not want to do, because it went against what he believed for his whole life. Those were the people he had fought for and had pledged to protect. If it was just him, he would disappear like the snake he was at one time, killing would be the last resort. But now there was April, and whomever it was would not be allowed to attempt an arrest of her and live to tell the tale.

He signaled to April to get ready to get off. There was a stop ahead which was not close to a street, and they could get away unnoticed. As long as they blended into the crowd and took an unexpected direction, they would be very hard to follow or detect.

The train slowed and stopped in the middle of an art fair full of street vendors and shoppers. As they disembarked, Mick led her toward a gelato stand, and they sat down, sharing a cone, but also watching the crowd carefully. Either no one was looking, or they were very professional and hard to detect. Mick tossed the cone in the trash, and they suddenly rushed toward another train which had just stopped, the doors being flung open with a hiss. They followed the same technique of separating and watching from both sides, communicating by glances. As the train gathered speed toward the north, Mick relaxed a little and winked at April. His plan appears to have worked for the moment. It all depended on the scope of the group in pursuit. With enough money and manpower, they would quickly correct any mistake and be very hard to shake. Mick wished in vain that he had a motorcycle around, but pushing a machine that hard with a precious passenger was out of the question. Besides, there was no motorcycle.

While on the train, Mick called Peter and left a message for assistance. The recording assured the caller that the matter would be handled quickly and efficiently. The train reached the Muhlhausen stop, and Mick and April quickly got off at the small station. They were far north of Triska's apartment and would have to have transportation of some sort to return. Mick didn't want to consider leading anyone back to Triska, if he could help it. This was going to be settled today, right now. He was starting to look for places that he could kill out of the public view, an enclosed space with no witnesses. It was the sort of place their pursuit team would also like to catch them in. A place that events would occur explosively and have a certain outcome. One side would win, and the other would lose. Mick didn't intend on being on the losing side.

Their pursuers couldn't be sure that Mick was fleeing, couldn't even be sure that Mick and April were aware that they were being followed. Mick still had surprise working for him, that and the other side would not expect him to revert to lethal force, only attempt to flee. U.S. Army Special Forces training is intense and directed at killing the enemy as rapidly as possible. Soldiers practice taking headshots with their handguns over and over until it is second nature. Unexpectedly encountering a combatant with this training usually proves quickly and certainly fatal, and that would be the fate awaiting those chasing them.

The train station was nothing more than an open platform

with a large highway on one side and the tracks on the other. Across the tracks was a familiar sign, "Kentucky Fried Chicken," and just down the small street squatted a small shopping center. After the train left, they walked purposely across the tracks, heading toward the larger building. Mick was alert, and every passing car was observed carefully. Just before they entered the building, two identical black cars pulled in to the small lot. One glance told him the bad news. The faces of the men inside the car were stern, threatening and looking right at them. Seven, by his quick count. Mick felt better about it after seeing their number. It was going to be relatively easy once he maneuvered them into position. He led April into a large grocery store, and he instructed her to pick a cart and shop normally, ignoring anyone approaching her. The store had few shoppers and many aisles. The perfect spot for an ambush. Mick walked ahead and disappeared into the tall aisles, the snake coiling to strike.

The automatic glass doors lurched open, and four men in dark clothing stood looking inside, scanning the interior methodically before continuing inside where they could sense a hint of danger floating in the air.

"One moment!" a man said from outside the store, and the men turned to look, irritated at the interruption. "I desire to speak to you," the man said loudly. He was short but thick and wore a heavy topcoat, and there was an accent, heavy, yet familiar. There was no doubt that the man was Slavic, not only because of his pronunciation but his wide face and the worn sturdy teeth that he showed in his artificial grin. He motioned for them to come outside. They hesitated, looking back and forth, unsure of what to do. Just then, two more men appeared suddenly, as if out of nowhere, and stood back a few meters as if ready for something to happen. The four pursuers quickly and silently conferred. They decided to confront the men outside before entering. After all, three of their fellows guarded the rear exit. Grundy and Chauncy were not going to be able to leave.

"What do you want," one of them asked the short man.

"I am here only to save your lives. You should talk to me before it's too late." The four looked at each other again.

The one in charge looked around before speaking. Two more rough men were standing beside a nearby car, looking on with interest. All of them wore overcoats which could conceal almost any kind of lethal weapon. The interlopers were obviously experienced and had elected positions which would create a crossfire impossible to protect against. The pursuers hesitated. They were likely outgunned and, without a doubt, were caught by surprise.

"Just how are our lives in danger? From you?" the leader asked the short man.

"Yes, from us. We will not allow you to take this couple. They are protected by Russian security forces. You only see a small sample here. Besides, your training is inadequate to deal with this man. I feel certain that he wanted you to enter, and believe us, he would have shown you no mercy. This way you have a chance, a small chance, to live to see another day. But it is still your choice."

The four started to look apprehensive, and all of them looked toward the road, evidently expecting some other group to arrive shortly. The short man laughed. "They will not come as you expect. Their car has met with an unfortunate accident not far from here. Your men in the rear are also having problems at this moment. Now, follow my instructions carefully. You will slowly put your weapons on the ground, also your identification. Remove your shoes and your jackets. If I find any weapons remaining on you, you will regret it. Is that understood?" As he spoke, he loosened his coat and slowly brought a formidable automatic weapon up to point at the men. Without discussion, they complied and were searched by one of the other Russians. He picked up the identification folders and brought them to the short man.

"Impressive!" he said after looking at the documents. "Department of State," he read, tossing the folders back to the pavement. "It would have been easier for me to let your prey kill you, but I was instructed otherwise…this time. Pass the word to your superiors. Any attempt to capture or even talk with Mick Grundy will prove fatal, and repercussions will be extensive. Grundy is off-limits for you forever. If this is not clear, then I would be happy to shoot one or more of you right now to make my point."

"No, we have the idea. You made your point. May we leave?"

"Not until you have enjoyed a swim in the nice green river behind the building. Move!" he commanded as his men displayed their automatic weapons. The four men were herded behind the building where the others were standing with hands in the air. As directed, all seven of them jumped into the water as the Russians laughed from the bank. From somewhere in the parking lot could be heard two bursts of automatic fire as their cars were destroyed. As quickly as they appeared, the Russians vanished. The seven Americans slowly drifted with the current looking for a place to climb out of the cold water.

At the sound of gunfire, Mick came out of the glass door, gun in hand, and was met by the short man who was smiling and motioning for Mick to come toward him.

"Greetings from Comrade Dvorkin. I am told that he is a good friend!" He extended his hand for a shake.

Mick took his hand, asking, "What happened to the seven men chasing us?" He looked around for them unsuccessfully.

"They are playing games in the river just now. I don't think they will bother you again, and if they do, just let us know. May I offer you a ride somewhere? Perhaps back to your grandmother's?"

"And who are you?" Mick asked. He inspected the man closely and saw a thick, stocky body over a sagging, brooding face, complete with a thick head of dark hair and a Stalinesque mustache. A Russian or Ukrainian.

"Jaska Kozlov, Colonel Kozlov, GRU." One of the cars started vigorously burning, thick black smoke curling high into the air.

"We better leave soon. I'll get my companion and be right back," Mick said and ran back into the store.

Before they left the area, Mick counted at least ten Russians, some of whom waved at him when he caught their eyes. They settled into the rear seat, as Kozlov occupied the passenger seat while his underling drove.

"We have seen you before, April Chauncy. You just weren't aware we were looking you over. You'd be amazed what my Russian colleagues write about how you look!" Kozlov said, grinning at her over the back seat. "I want to extend my congratulations on your wedding plans, by the way. General Dvorkin instructs me to remind you that he wants to attend and that you are not to disappoint him." Kozlov laughed and slapped the seat for emphasis.

"I assure you that I have not forgotten," April said. "He will get the first invitation. Where, exactly, do I send it?"

"Just give it to any of my men watching over you, or you could just send it to the Russian Embassy in Berlin."

Chapter 35

Chapter 36

A Game In Play

Triska's Apartment, Stuttgart

Mick put down his coffee cup and picked up the phone. "*Guten Morgen*, Peter. I presume you are responding to my call, quickly and efficiently as your recording says."

"I have to apologize to you, *mein Bruder*. Was it important? I hope that it wasn't."

"Only at the moment. The problem has been solved. How does this morning find you?"

"Troubled. There is big news from abroad. May I come over and discuss this with you in person?" His tone indicated that there was still suspicion that their phones were tapped. The Americans back in Washington might be listening.

"Surely. Anytime, but perhaps at our favorite coffee cafe?" Mick suggested.

"About two hours. *Bis bald*," Peter said, clicking off.

"Something going on?" April asked.

"I think so. We'll find out soon."

Cafe Moulu Senefelderstraße

Peter had the usual sparkle in his eyes and made a show of assisting April with her chair, bowing at the waist and clicking his heels as he did so. He was out of uniform and casually dressed to avoid calling attention to their little gathering. Mick had selected a small out of the way table and ordered the coffee and *schnecken*.

"My, you look marvelous this morning, April," Peter said, smiling broadly. "The long trip across town was worth it just to see you!"

"Enough, Peter, but thank you just the same," April said.

"Mick, I want you to know that after your call, two teams were dispatched to your location, but all we found were several Americans swimming in the Neckar river and two burning cars."

"What did you do with them?" Mick asked.

"We fined them for illegal swimming and for leaving their cars burning while they did so. Very irresponsible for representatives of the U.S. State Department."

"They were very lucky to be able to go for a swim. It was a fine day for it," Mick said.

"And what's the news that brings you here, Peter," April asked and patted him on his arm.

"You recall that several stinger missiles were captured by radical Sunni elements recently in Iraq?" Peter asked conspiratorially, his eyes crazily going between their faces.

"Yes, what about it?" Mick asked.

"Your intelligence services are going wild looking for them. The speculation is that they have been shipped back to the U.S. through your porous border."

"That was always the danger from giving high tech missile gear to unstable countries in the Arab world. I'm not surprised."

"Your country is not in a good place right now. We hear that there is a lot of dissent about the present leadership. Europeans always envied your stability and your fidelity to your Constitution…but now we are concerned that the whole government is a stack of cards about to come down. All you need to set things off is an attack by terrorists, or worse, more than one."

"I hear your concerns, but April and I are no longer part of what goes on over there. We are going to live and work in Germany and try to be honest hardworking citizens. At the moment, I am at peace with the world."

"Well, let me poise a theoretical question for either of you," Peter said. "Your military people don't seem to like your President very much. He had no military experience previously and has not done much for them since starting his term. Do you think they would turn on him, or even protect him if trouble starts?"

"Ours is a professional military. The men and women who serve are there by choice and are the finest troops in the world. They will absolutely do their sworn duty and that includes protecting and obeying the President. Yes they will, you can count on it." Mick said.

"But, vigorously, enthusiastically?" Peter persisted.

"Of course. The ones I knew and served with would," Mick answered.

April leaned forward. "My opinion is based on my experience with professionals in law enforcement, you understand. There is more politics mixed into that group. Same with the legal profession and the judicial branch. Party affiliation is a strong determinant of attitude and will play a role with those groups."

"And that would include the intelligence services. Support for this President may not be as strong there," Mick observed.

"Heard from Zeskie recently?" Peter asked quietly. Mick and April shook their heads. There had been no contact. The scandals had stopped and things were quiet…too quiet. Mick understood the implication and where Peter's mind was going.

"To answer your first question about the military. Let me make it clear that they will obey their legal leader. Change leaders and they will follow also," Mick explained, also to himself. He became lost in thought for a moment. This far away, he knew nothing. Everything was speculation from here, though there were some out there who might treat terrorists like a pet viper. Dangerous, but when placed in the right spot…useful also. After the viper has bitten your enemy, he can be eliminated, because he was expendable all along. You can always go capture another, and since everyone knows a snake cannot be trained, you cannot be blamed for whom it might strike next.

"Are you still here?" April teased and kissed Mick on the cheek.

"Just thinking. Sorry."

"My people tell me that there are several Russians who have been seen in the vicinity of Triska's apartment," Peter said, changing the subject. "Have either one of you seen them?"

"Of course, Peter," April said. "We wave to them at times. They are very friendly."

"It takes a load off of my mind to hear you say that, and now I understand a lot that I didn't previously. Dvorkin has changed things, as he said he would."

Montgomery County Airpark, Gaithersburg, MD, USA

A blue sedan pulled up in front of the fence and stopped, motor idling as the two men inside inspected the landing strip and the surroundings. The airport boasted a four thousand foot runway and three aircraft service facilities as well as two separate aircraft sales offices. Perfect, just as they were told. As they were watching, a small executive jet moved into position, ready for takeoff. There was a brief whine, and suddenly the plane jolted forward and was airborne in four seconds.

"That means they sell jet fuel," the older man observed.

"Of course," the younger man answered. He had done the legwork to find this place and was trying not to be boastful about discovering the perfect location, just as he was commanded to do.

Still, it was hard to be silent when he was second-guessed on every issue.

"Where is the hanger you rented?" The younger man pointed to a group of buildings on the other side of what substituted as a terminal building. The older man nodded, still assessing the location. "What was the agent's name again?" he asked. The younger man sighed and pulled out the paper contract he had picked up earlier.

"His name is Neil Drasing. I don't know what he looks like, but he sounds older over the phone. Knows his stuff though. We talked a couple of times, and I know that he is in his office today."

"When and how are the supplies suppose to arrive?" the older man asked, still looking around, watching the arriving planes.

"They are arriving in Newport News tonight in a ship full of clothing…on route from Bangladesh. It will be two more days before we can get at the container. I'll send a man over there in the morning."

Details. They are important, Gahiji knew. In his days in the Egyptian Air Force, he had survived by paying attention where it mattered. It was a long time ago, it seemed, and he hadn't been in the air at all in ten years. Such a waste. He was still superior to the young bucks who strutted around, more proud of their attractiveness to females because of their uniforms than how many encounters with the Israelis they had experienced. He was glad to part with all of them. The next live shooting war would wake them up…that is if they survived the first mission.

Gahiji looked over the hood and past the fence and tried to visualize a Mig 21 landing here. Thankfully, there would be no need to deploy the drag chute to do it because that would attract a lot of attention. Night time would be the best. His very own Mig! It was hard not to be excited. Such a privilege to be chosen. It was all his friends in the Brotherhood talked about, that and revenge. Only he was the one that actually was in position to do something other than talk. He glanced at Moazzam, if that was his real name. Gahjji remembered that Moazzam meant respectable. A poorly chosen alias, because this Moazzam was anything but.

"I'm ready," Gahjji said. "You remembered the folder, I hope."

"I have it right here," Moazzam said holding it up and shaking it, causing the papers to rattle. He was angry, and Gahjji didn't understand why. Preparations this complex are bound to have oversights, if everything wasn't double-checked. He opened the car door, a signal that the work was to begin.

Neil Drasing was behind his desk and hard at work typing in an online bid for a customer. It was the usual back and forth trying to establish a price that both parties would accept. He enjoyed the face-to-face encounters of bargaining, but that was quickly becoming a way of the past. There was a rap on the door, and Neil turned on his swivel chair to see who was calling so early. Betsy wasn't even at work as yet. "Enter," he shouted toward the door. Two men entered, one older, who looked very serious and finely dressed in a dark suit, the other more scruffy but wearing an engaging smile.

"Greetings," the younger man said, giving a little wave. "I am Josh Gammal…we spoke earlier?"

"Oh, yes," Neil said, raising slightly from his seat. "That conversation I remember. You are the one who inquired about finding an old Soviet fighter plane?" They shook hands as Neil looked them over more closely.

"Yes! That's me. Actually I found the one we want, so I saved you a lot of work." Josh had no accent, unless a New Jersey one qualifies. Neil looked questioningly at the older man who still wasn't smiling. Josh noticed immediately and laughed.

"This is Captain Fakhoury. He is an expert on the Mig 21 we

wish to purchase." The Captain gave a short smile and brief nod of his head, but his piercing dark eyes never blinked.

"I see. Could I ask what you want this aircraft for?" Neil asked and leaned back in his chair, studying the two men in front of him.

"Oh my!" Josh exclaimed. "They are a favorite at air shows, and people are paying big for rides. We figure to make a lot of dough on this plane."

"That is, if you can maintain it. Expensive, I hear," Neil said. Neither man in front of him flinched. Oh well, he shrugged, it was their money. "Which one have you picked out?" he asked, turning toward his computer keyboard.

"A MiG-21bis, currently at the Reno airfield," Josh said.

"I'm no Mig expert, but that was one of the later ones, wasn't it?" Neil asked as he continued to type. "Ah, this must be the one…" he trailed off studying the page full of data. "Yes, this model is what Nato dubbed the Fishbed-L," he continued to read as he spoke. "This one still has the Bulgarian markings, and they say that it is flyable just as it sits."

"Yes, you have the right one. Want to place a bid for us?" Josh asked.

"Well, there is no auction here. You have to make an offer…in cash…and have approval from the FAA. Do you have those things?" Neil asked, turning to face them again.

"We even have a hanger at this same airport!" Josh said, handing him the papers. Neil studied them closely and shrugged again.

"The asking price is one hundred eighty thousand and some change," Neil remarked, studying the pair for any reaction. "I'd say that was a really cheap price for a functioning fighter plane that many countries still use," he added.

"An out-of-date one. We have seen them go for sixty-five, also in flying order. Few people are qualified to fly it or have the money to buy one. A small market of buyers," Josh observed. "We are prepared to go to ninety. Willing to make an offer for us?"

"Before I do, you have to tell me if you are going to pick it up in Reno or have them deliver it for you. You can expect a charge of a few thousand for the service, and, by the way, they will never accept ninety. Can we consider that a starting bid?" He studied the so-called Captain Fakhoury, who had not uttered a word. "Will you be the one flying that bird?" he asked, looking at the Captain.

"I will, sir. I assure you that I have adequate training and experience," Fakhoury responded with crisp British-accented English. His voice was deep and authoritative, a man accustomed to commanding men.

"Yes, but are you current?" Neil asked.

"I was checked out in Florida, just two weeks ago. I am current."

And so the back and forth haggling for the Mig began and was to take most of the next two days. When it was over, Fakhoury and Gammal agreed to pay one hundred fifteen thousand dollars and after a money transfer was authorized, the deal was concluded. The seller agreed to transport the plane to Dayton and Fakhoury…Captain Fakhoury was to fly it from there in two days.

Neil Drasing was nobody's fool. He had been around planes most of his life and also served in Viet Nam flying an F4 while looking over his shoulder for a Mig 21 to appear like a lethal gnat on the horizon. He didn't like Mig's and didn't like anyone who liked them. Especially this shifty Captain Fakhoury. Neil decided that after his fee was safely in his account, he would call the FBI. Something was fishy about the entire thing. A Mig 21 is a very capable and lethal weapon and is as fast as any modern F16. With missiles attached and with a competent pilot, it would become a terrorist's dream. He picked up the telephone, his paperwork spread out before him. Just as he was about to key in the number of the FBI, he heard a 'click' and felt a gun muzzle pressing into his neck.

After scheduling with local flight services regarding the inbound fighter, a move necessitated because of the unusual nature of the aircraft coming in, they began preparation of the hanger and started moving in special equipment. The Mig would arrive well after dark at 0200 hours and would be moved quickly into the hanger following landing. Everything was going according to plans…so far.

Chapter 36

Chapter 37

From Out Of Nowhere

Montgomery County Airpark, Gaithersburg, MD

The plane was nearly finished and the tools and men gone. It sat on the smooth concrete gleaming like a new toy, an 18,000 pound one. All unnecessary hardware had been stripped, and the markings removed and repainted. A transponder, a stolen one, was installed that would generate a Mode S signal indicating that the plane was a Learjet owned by a Canadian Lumber concern. The turbine had been adjusted and tweaked by a master mechanic and his assistant and was now capable of producing power meeting new engine specifications. A larger drag chute had been installed which would permit landing on a very short runway of just under three thousand feet. Using a runway that short would require an expert pilot to accomplish, since it was far below minimums for this plane. In addition, the intended landing was to be at night on an unlighted strip approaching from low altitude. The plan was both masterful and bold but also complicated, dependent on many unknown and unknowable sequence of events. In the end, the mission would come down to luck, either good or bad.

The hanger door slid open just wide enough to admit visitors, one at a time. Two shadows came in and stood before the Mig 21, admiring their completed fighter.

"Fueled yet?" Gahjji asked.

"Completely topped off. Estimated range using afterburner would be five hundred kilometers…no more, but easily enough," Moazzam responded.

"Have you calculated the distance to the secondary site?"

"Straight line, fifty kilometers. One pass around to the south will add ten more. Once you takeoff from the secondary site, and if we are given a timely signal, flight time to target will only be thirty seconds."

"Will he have fighter escort?"

"No reason to. No, we feel that there will be no fighters aloft. However, there will be an alert at some point, and fighters will be vectored from several locations, but too late to stop you."

"Electronic countermeasures?" Gahjji inquired, his forehead furrowed.

"Short of being hit with a missile or mechanical failure, nothing can stop you. Allah will ride with you, your goodness will prevail, because it is His wish and your destiny."

"One more question, Moazzam. Are you ready at the secondary site?"

"We have ten men, two trucks standing by. They will arrive as soon as you leave here. Do not worry, Moazzam has every detail attended to. We will not fail."

Gahjji did have to worry, nevertheless. It was to be he and he alone who would determine the success of the mission. And he was having second thoughts about the entire matter.

Tuesday, 2200 hours

The signal came. It was time for the final phase of his mission to start, and Gahjii breathed deeply, trying to steel himself against the stress of the coming hours. He looked around at the night sky, taking in the stars and the slowly moving shadow clouds, listening to the night sounds. Life was pleasant to the living, to those who understood that it was all temporary, intensifying the joy of it. He had to do his part as a soldier of Allah and leave these things behind. More good will come to him in the afterlife by killing the enemies of Islam, he had been told. Was it true or was he just wasting his life in a futile effort? Gahjii sighed again. He couldn't know the answers to those questions right now. He would find out the truth soon enough. Behind him, he heard a clanking sound as the large hanger doors started to open and the nose of the jet stood stark and bloodless in the moonlight. The weapon which had no feelings, no sympathy and was designed to kill rapidly and effectively, the arm of Allah, of Mohammed and of all the Imams of the ancient world. It was to be their day of joy at the defeat and humiliation of the West. The tractor motor started noisily, and the plane was drawn out of its nest, shimmering under the blue light of the full moon. There were no other planes moving about, because of the late hour and the light activity of the small airport. He would have the runway to himself.

"Ready?" Moazzam asked from behind.

"Yes. You?"

"I am in happiness. Everything is perfect. Your flight plan has been filed listing Richmond as your destination, just as you specified. The route will vector your path around Washington. Your call number is 'C-ERS,' and in case you are contacted, your plane is a Learjet 60."

There were no more words to be said. It was the appointed time. Gahjii climbed up the ladder and entered the familiar cockpit and immediately started flipping the toggle switches. With a last look down at Moazzam, he pulled the canopy closed as the whine of the jet engine started underneath him.

The muscular Mig 21 leaped down the runway, not even close to needing its afterburner. According to rules, Gahjii was required to contact Washington Approach Control after gaining altitude, that is if he were to gain altitude. The plan called for keeping the jet at the treetops, under radar, so that the plane could not be seen at all. In case he was spotted, and questioned, he would claim a malfunction needing an emergency landing. The distance of fifty kilometers would be covered in under ten minutes. All he had to do is make one turn and find the flares that Moazzam promised would be lit.

His altitude was 250 meters and speed just under 300 knots, when to the left, a bright green flare sprung to life, catching his eye. He started a slow turn, careful to not drop altitude and then the second flare, a red one, blinked on at the end of the small runway. Gahjii raised the nose of his Mig to thirty degrees and let the speed fall to 130 knots, sinking into the runway instead of flying. He held his breath as the black runway approached, because he could not see it, and no longer even see the red flare at the far end, only the nose of the jet. Just before the altimeter registered 20 meters, he fully dropped the flaps and the drag chute. The big plane nestled onto the pavement, giving little chips from the tires as its speed dropped dramatically. A flag man was standing near the red flare frantically waving his arms, and Gahjii did stop…with ten feet to spare. He quickly shut down the turbine and soon felt the plane being pulled around by a ground tractor, dim shapes of several men moving around in darkness. He had arrived to wait again as the coming dawn and another liftoff approached. It was to be the last takeoff of his career or his life.

Traffic Control Command, Andrews AFB, 2207 Hours

"Sir?" Sergeant Jones called from his radar station. He heard the Duty Officer walking his way, and he kept his eyes on the big display in front of him.

"What's the prob, Jones?" he asked, also looking at the screen over Jones' shoulder.

"Well, nothing right now, but just a moment ago, I saw a small blip right here," Jones said, pointing to a location just at the outer ring of the Washington Class B Control space.

"Too bad JLENS isn't up yet," the officer said, still looking at the screen. "Any transponder data with the sighting?"

"No, sir, just a quick ten second blip."

"Well, how big was it? The size of an airliner or what?"

"No, sir. Small, as if a plane was just below radar height and part of it showed for a moment."

The officer looked around thinking for a moment. "I'll have someone check flight plans from that area. We might have a disaster on our hands, and it's bad timing. There is an alert just posted for a POTUS flight in that direction soon."

Lieutenant Murphy knocked on the door before entering, "Sir, I might have a problem." Captain Rodgers held his hand over the phone receiver and grimaced, holding up a finger toward Murphy. He murmured into the phone something personal and soft then hung up, irritated at the interruption. He sat back and waited.

"A flight control technician saw something on radar ten minutes ago, and I wanted you to know about it." Murphy said.

"I'm listening," Captain Rodgers said.

"The sighting was brief, and we've even replayed it. Undetermined what it was at this time. I checked the list of flight plans and found one from Gaithersburg which has not been activated yet. There are no reports of crashes, and the state police haven't heard anything."

"So?"

"So, what do you want me to do next, sir?"

"What is the nearest airport to the sighting?" Captain Rodgers asked.

"There is an old general aviation airport near there called College Park. Short runway."

"Yes, I remember that one," Captain Rodgers said. "College Park goes back to the Wright Brothers. Call them."

"There's nothing but an answering machine. I tried that."

"Then call the county cops or send a couple of MPs over there, and make it fast." The Captain glanced at the clock. POTUS would be leaving the White House just now. There would be hell to pay if his flight was interrupted.

College Park Airport, 0300 hours

The patrol car crept cautiously forward down Corporal Frank Scott Drive toward the airfield. The two patrolmen had been asked to look for a possible crash, and they were looking for smoke or flames, but the area was dead quiet. They entered the parking lot and directed the spotlight around before entering the tie-down lot at the east end. Driving between the silent planes, they could tell that nothing was moving and wouldn't move until dawn. On the other side of the parked planes, the runway area was dark.

"Call it in. See what they want us to do," Frankin said.

"Car 430," Smith said into the small mike. "Ask the desk sergeant what he wants us to do."

A smooth female voice came back over, "He said to look on the runway and be sure that no planes are down."

"Roger that. Better drive out onto the runway," Smith said, pointing to the asphalt lying sleeping in the darkness. Their spotlight shown into the recess of the takeoff and landing area, but no planes were in sight. "That's enough for me. Let's get out of here," Smith said. The car pulled around and slowly cruised out of sight. If they had looked closer, they might have seen a Mig 21 positioned at the far end of the runway, covered by a black sheet of non-reflective fabric. The plane was pointed down the strip, ready to make a noisy, maximum power run down a runway of asphalt too short for successful takeoff of an aging but still potent Russian warplane.

College Park Airport, 0530 hours

The eastern sky lightened, rapidly brightening with a rim of pink showing at the interface of the night sky and the sleeping land. Gahjii wiped his sweaty hands on his coveralls. There would soon be planes trying to use the runway. Time was running out. At least one of their trucks was still nearby. He could still try to get away. The Mig would have to be abandoned just where it was, but it would only be hours before the authorities would connect Gahjii to the plane. Questions would be asked and the chance, the one chance, to act would be lost. He willed the phone to ring, and it did, making him jump at the noise. Men suddenly leapt out of the back of the truck and frantically started pulling off the camouflage covering the Mig.

This was it. There was no turning back. Gahjii sprinted for the plane, just as someone provided the ladder. He flung himself into the tight cockpit and fastened his belts, immediately feeling his plane being moved into position at the farthest reaches of the pavement. The whine of the motor started as he continued to flip the switches setting up the preflight check and parameters. There was no need for radios. There would be no communication. He knew the course of his target by memory and knew the exact time the enemy aircraft would lift off from Andrews. There could be no mistakes now, and the first hurdle was to get off the short runway. He would need all the power possible to accomplish it. The terrain was flat past the end of the runway, and if he cleared the dual lane Kenilworth Avenue, he would begin the rapid, near vertical ascent into the sky as he veered to the north. Gahjii calmed himself as the RPM of the motors started to cause a shriek which could be heard for blocks, if not miles. He flipped a switch, lighting the afterburner, and disengaged the brakes as the jet launched, pressing him firmly into the seat. The runway disappeared under him as the jet passed within inches of the treetops, while a thick tongue of flame extended from the rear of the plane. Clear! Gahjii pulled back on the stick, and the plane jerked its nose toward space and pushed its way into the heavens.

Chapter 38

Angel In a White Gown

Matthäuskirche, Stuttgart

"Quit worrying," Peter said, brushing Mick's tuxedo from the rear. "You look very impressive, very handsome. Any woman would marry you, I guarantee it! Don't you agree, Kurt?" There was a quick wink exchanged. Kurt took in the message without a response.

"My own brother wearing a monkey suit! It teaches you to never say never, doesn't it. I would have expected you to attend your wedding in a leather racing suit. Though…it suits you, so to speak, as long as you quickly take it off after the ceremony," Kurt said, trying in vain to keep from laughing. Mick reached around and cuffed him playfully on his ear and returned to study himself in the mirror. He fussed with his bow tie, twisting it right and left, but it kept returning to being slightly down on one side as if it had a mind of its own. He sighed deeply and looked around the small room, with its high ceiling and single narrow gothic window occupying a wall. The woodwork was thick and dark and gave the room an historic feel. Organ music drifted on the air as if it echoed out of some other century, and the floor creaked in unison each time Mick shifted his weight.

"Did either of you look to see how many guests have arrived?" Mick asked, hoping the number was small.

"Oh, don't worry about that either, Brother," Peter said. "The church is going to be filled with people standing in the aisles! We are going to have a full house!" Mick groaned out loud causing his two brothers to laugh again. "Did you ever discover who will give the bride away?" Peter asked. His mischievous eyes indicated that he knew the answer and was delighted to bedevil his brother with the question.

"No. Do either of you know?" Kurt and Peter shook their heads in an exaggerated manner, expressing that they didn't know but really did but weren't telling.

"I guess you will have to wait and see," Kurt suggested.

There was a soft knock at the door, and after a polite pause, it opened. Ron Zeskie entered, wearing a black tux and a big smile.

"Ron Zeskie!" Mick shouted and rushed to give him a big hug. "I thought you were in the States running for your life!"

"Not at all, my boy. You are looking at the newly appointed CIA Director of European Operations."

"Wow, so fast!" Peter said, shaking his hand in congratulations.

"Back in Washington, we have a lot of catching up to do, and there is no time for fussy deliberation."

"We heard about the President's plane going down but not a lot of detail. How about a summary of the real events?" Mick asked.

"As you probably heard, there was a midair collision between Air Force One and a smaller jet. There were no survivors, of course. After the pieces were assembled, it was apparent that the smaller plane was a Mig 21, recently purchased legally within the U.S. The speculation is that it was a suicide mission."

"We knew about the Stinger missiles being smuggled in. Why weren't they used?" Mick asked.

"They were, in a way. The Vice President correctly assumed that he was next and resigned before the terrorists could shoot at him," Zeskie said smiling. It was the outcome they all wanted, and the country needed.

Peter shook his head, still perplexed by events. "I don't understand, Zeskie. How could the terrorists know exactly where the President's plane would be and when it would get there? Isn't that highly classified knowledge?"

Zeskie shrugged. "There is a lot which will never be known, but the calamity will cause writers and reporters to speculate on one plot after another for years and years. To me, it doesn't matter who may have been involved as much as my concerns about the security and integrity of the United States. We have that back again and can finally do what we need to do to help stabilize the world." He caught Mick's eye briefly, but it was enough communication between old friends to tell Mick what he already knew.

The organ music changed, becoming louder and more persistent. Wagner's Wedding March started drifting in gentle waves through the air. The four men looked around at each other as if for the last time together, unmarried and free. It was a universal moment of empathy among men before an interloping woman steals a man's heart and occupies his time and thoughts for the rest of eternity. Mick took a deep breath and sagged slightly, more apprehensive about the ceremony than marrying the woman he loved and wanted to join. A small voice on other side of the big oak door came through as a whisper, "It's time."

"One last thing," Zeskie said and stood before Mick. He took the carnation from his lapel and inserted it into Mick's and patted his cheek affectionately. "You should know that no one hunts for you any longer. It will be a life of freedom and happiness for you and April." He hesitated for a moment looking at Mick in a funny way. "But, if you miss the action, I can always use your knowledge and skills again. You remember that."

"Thanks, Zeskie. And thanks for all you have done for me in the past. As for going back into the field again...I have too much to lose now, so don't expect me to ever return to that again. My pistol has been put away in a safe place." Zeskie nodded that he understood and took Mick's arm for the trip toward the alter, Mick's brothers following in a solemn parade.

The men entered the vast gothic nave of the main church, vaulted with pointed arches, extending far toward the heavens, the walls and floor bathed in colored holy light streaming from leaded glass windows. It was a clerestory designed to humble men with the presence of God, something so impressive, so grand that a mere mortal would shrink to insignificance. The alter was stationed just beyond the crossing, and the minister was already in position, his hands folded.

Mick was escorted to the place marked for the groom and stood with Peter by his side, watching the doorway at the end of the long aisle, waiting for his bride to appear. The church was filled, as Peter said, and Mick had time to look at the happy faces of those assembled, most of whom he didn't recognize. On the left front row, reserved for the bride's family, was Stella sitting beside her son, Kurt. Triska sat on the right front row, beside her, smiling and exquisitely dressed, was Dorff. The two exchanged glances furtively like two schoolchildren with a crush. Behind them, a big bushy head caught Mick's eye, and Dvorkin gave him a little wave and smile, then clasped his hands together and held them over his head.

The organ started in earnest, filling the chamber with waves of sound that could be felt as well as heard. Every head turned toward the rear to see the bride as she made her way slowly forward, her flowing white gown in stark contrast with the somber church. Holding her arm and beaming broadly was Alfred Michner, at this moment, proud father of the bride.

The End

Elapid *by Alexander Francis*

A Note of Appreciation

The worst and the best writers seek one thing above all others. A reader who not only reads their book, a work of astounding personal effort, but who shares his/her experiences with the world. We want to know what you think about our work. Truly we do. Of course, we want you to like it, and us, and will be so grateful if you take the time to give us even the smallest amount of praise. I really entreat you to do so.

If you have constructive criticism you want us to hear, please, out with it! Writing is such an isolating experience. I begin to live in my books and come to nearly feel that my characters are real. When someone criticizes one of them, I feel their pain. And some of my own.

But if you enjoyed this novel, I beg you on scuffed knee to give a positive review for me. I assure you that is the best way to see more of my work in the future.

Thanks again for reading this far.

Alexander Francis

Other Novels by

Alexander Francis

Are We A Band Yet?
Mick Grundy...Spy Hunt
Mick Grundy...The Russian Connection
Mick Grundy...Elapid
Geminknot
The Green Scarf
Revenge of Jesus
Beware the Exit
An Anthology of Childhood
Schemers and Dreamers
Memory Gap

www.ingramcontent.com/pod-product-compliance
Lightning Source LLC
Chambersburg PA
CBHW051253210726
48287CB00002B/478